The Churchill Commando

Ted Willis was born in London in 1918. After leaving school at the age of fifteen, he found himself moving through a succession of odd jobs, and his experience during this period attracted him to journalism. During the war he served with the Royal Fusiliers, latterly working as a writer of War Office films and Ministry of Information documentaries. His first play, *Buster*, was produced at the Unity Theatre in 1944. Since that time he has written numerous plays for stage and television, including *Woman in a Dressing Gown*, as well as several television series, the most famous of which is *Dixon of Dock Green*.

In 1963 he received a peerage as Lord Willis of Chislehurst and takes it as a great compliment that he is widely known as 'Lord Ted'. He is married to Audrey Hale, the actress, and they have two children. His novels *Death May Surprise Us*, *The Left-Handed Sleeper* and *Man-Eater* are also published in Pan.

Ted Willis

The Churchill Commando

Pan Books in association with
Macmillan London

First published 1977 by Macmillan London Ltd
This edition published 1978 by Pan Books Ltd,
Cavaye Place, London SW10 9PG
in association with Macmillan London Ltd
© Ted Willis Limited 1977
ISBN 0 330 25338 7
Printed and bound in Great Britain by
Hunt Barnard Printing Ltd, Aylesbury, Bucks

For Joy and Jon Cleary
in friendship

The author and publishers wish to thank the Society of Authors as the literary representative of the Estate of A. E. Housman; and Jonathan Cape Limited, publishers of A. E. Housman's *Collected Poems*, for permission to use 'Epitaph of an Army of Mercenaries' by A. E. Housman.

Chapter One

1

'LISTEN,' said the man at the other end of the line, 'listen carefully. I shall tell you this once and once only.'

'Who is that?' The Reverend Clifford Bond was sitting at his desk and until the telephone interrupted him he had been preparing a sermon for the coming Sabbath service. He did not like to be interrupted on these occasions and he was conscious that he had spoken with some irritation.

'Never mind that. I'm calling about the Clark girl – Joy Clark. If you want to help her, you'd better get this down.'

'Clark! Look, if you know anything you should call the police!'

'I'm calling you, man. Right. Are you ready? Tell the pigs to take the A245 road out of Cobham, towards Leatherhead. Just past a bridge over the river there's a house with green shutters. Five hundred yards beyond this, a track on the left, leading to a stone cottage. There's a field at the back – '

'You're going too fast!' The scrap of paper was sliding under the minister's pencil and he was trying to control it and write with one hand while holding the telephone in the other. He felt a spasm of fear and panic and fought to control himself, sensing that every word was important, that he dare not miss one detail.

The soft, almost sing-song voice continued almost without pause. 'At the back of the cottage there's a field. The girl is buried in the middle of a clump of bushes on the left of the path.'

'Buried!' Horror tightened the minister's voice. 'You mean – she's dead? The girl is dead?'

'She wasn't the last time I saw her. But you'd better tell the pigs to hurry. The battery won't last forever.'

The man laughed, there was a sharp click and the black receiver in the minister's hand purred harshly, extending the moment of mockery.

The minister stared at the instrument for a moment and then dropped it back on to the cradle, closing his eyes as though to wipe out a vision of evil.

2

The kidnapping of Joy Clark, the 17-year-old daughter of a millionaire industrialist, had been front-page news for two days. She had disappeared after playing tennis at a club near her home at Gerrard's Cross in Buckinghamshire. It was a Wednesday afternoon and she had last been seen at 4.30 p.m. Her red MG sports car was found in the lane outside the tennis club where she had parked it on arrival, and later, when the police searched the car, they found a long typewritten note under the front seat demanding a payment of £250,000 for the girl's safe return.

The note bore no signature but it did give an indication of the motives of the kidnappers. The final paragraph stated: 'This action has not been taken for personal gain. Every penny will be devoted to the struggle to overthrow the rotten and corrupt capitalist system. Thus the money will go to help the working masses from whom it was stolen.'

This much information was released to the press and was reflected in massive front-page headlines; but there were other features of the ransom note which the police and the Clark family, for obvious reasons, kept to themselves.

For example, Raymond Clark, the girl's father was instructed to place an advertisement in the personal columns of *The Times* and *The Daily Telegraph* within 48 hours, indicating that he accepted the kidnapper's terms and that the money would be paid over in old notes of small denomination. Even the phrasing of the advertisement was spelled out. It was to read: 'J darling – I am longing to see you again. All the problems have been resolved. Contact me soon and I will meet you any time, anywhere. All my love – R.'

The most chilling part of the note was the section which described the circumstances in which Joy Clark was being held. In this, and in some other respects, the kidnapping was a replica of one which had taken place in Atlanta, Georgia in the United States some years before. It was obvious that the criminals had studied the American case closely and modelled part of their own operation upon it.

Joy Clark had been buried alive.

She was imprisoned below ground in a specially constructed and reinforced box, only slightly larger than an average adult coffin. The kidnappers appeared to take a bizarre pride in this construction for they described it in some detail. It was eight-foot long by three-foot square, it contained a supply of drinking water, chocolate, biscuits, fruit and aspirins, and was furnished with a cushion, a blanket and a flashlight. It was obvious from the dimensions of the box that the girl would be forced to lie at full length with her head on the cushion and her hands within reach of the water and the food; she would not be able to sit up or raise herself more than a few inches.

Behind the cushion the kidnappers had built a plywood partition with a circular airvent to which they had connected a hose with an outlet above ground. This section of the box was also equipped with a water-pump and a small ventilator fan operated by switches which were within reach of the prisoner. The pump and the fan were connected to a battery. 'With reasonable care,' said the note drily, 'the battery should last between five to seven days. We have warned your daughter that excessive use of the pump and the fan could reduce the life expectancy of the battery to much less than this, perhaps as little as three days. Either way, you will realise that speed is of the essence, and that it is important that you accept our demands without delay. We shall contact you with instructions as soon as your advertisement appears. Do not allow the police to interfere. If they do so, we shall simply abandon the operation. We shall have lost the money, but at least we shall be free to try again on another occasion, whereas your daughter will die – and not very pleasantly at that. Remember – when the battery runs down she will have no more time.'

Strangely, the girl's father, a man noted for his energy and stamina and for his ability to take command in a crisis, wilted under the stress of these events. He seemed unable to think coherently, to escape from the vision of his daughter stretched out helplessly in her underground coffin; he began to panic, to issue a stream of incoherent and even contradictory orders and then, quite suddenly, he cracked under the strain and suffered a severe heart attack. He was rushed to the Intensive Care Unit at Guy's Hospital and his wife Margaret with their son, Robin, took over. The newspapers were not informed of Raymond Clark's collapse, so that the news would not reach the criminals and perhaps complicate the negotiations.

Margaret Clark, who had seldom had to take a decision of any consequence in her entire life, revealed unexpected powers of authority. She arranged with her bank for the money to be collected and made available to her and for the advertisement to be placed in the newspapers. She made it plain to the police that she intended to fulfil the kidnapper's instructions to the letter; she was prepared to help the authorities, but would do nothing which might reduce her daughter's chances of survival. The police understood and accepted her decision, while at the same time they set up a Special Operations Room and began their own intensive investigation.

The advertisement appeared in both newspapers on Friday morning and Mrs. Clark took turns with her son to wait by the telephone for the kidnappers to ring. The police were installed in an adjoining room ready to monitor any call, and to attempt to trace its origin – although they knew that this would only be possible within certain limits. The day passed, hour after hour of mounting anxiety and tension, but the telephone remained silent.

And then, at 4.50 p.m. the manager of the Berkeley Arms

Hotel at Cranford, near London's Heathrow Airport called the local police in a state of some agitation. He had received a letter marked PERSONAL – VERY URGENT, and delivered by hand. It had been put on the counter of the reception desk during an exceptionally busy period and the two girls on duty could not recall seeing anyone actually leave it there. The manager did not get the letter until 4.40 p.m. when he returned from a business visit to London.

When he opened it he found a brief note, typed in block letters: IF YOU WISH TO HELP JOY CLARK YOU WILL SEE THAT THIS GETS TO HER FATHER IMMEDIATELY. HER LIFE IS IN YOUR HANDS. The message was attached to a second, sealed envelope which was addressed, with odd formality, to RAYMOND CLARK, ESQ. The manager had no idea why he should have been chosen as an intermediary, but he had been following the accounts of the kidnapping in the newspapers and recognised the name of the victim immediately. He rang the local police, and within a few minutes the letter was on its way to the Clark home.

It contained detailed instructions about the delivery of the ransom money and a further stern warning about any interference from the police. 'No tricks! We shall be watching closely. If there are any police within a mile of the pick-up point we shall know. If you use any bugging or other devices in an attempt to trace or follow us, we shall know this too. Play it our way, and within four hours of the receipt of the money we will inform you where your daughter may be found. Otherwise you must take the consequences. Let us remind you that by this evening the battery on which she depends will have been in operation for 48 hours. You can work out for yourself how much time there is left.'

After some discussion, the senior officer in charge of the investigation, agreed that the Clarks should follow the instructions to the letter, and that the police would keep clear of the pick-up scene. What they did not tell Margaret Clark or her son was that they were pursuing certain leads, and already had a reasonable idea of the identity of the criminals though not of their whereabouts. However, at this stage, it was vital not to make any move which might panic these suspects and drive them to cover. The primary concern was to find the girl and bring her out safely.

Later that night Robin Clark eased his father's blue Mercedes into a lay-by on the northbound carriageway of the A1, just beyond Hitchin in Hertfordshire and braked to a halt. With the help of the police he had taken elaborate precautions to avoid the press reporters and he was sure that he had not been followed. He checked his watch with the clock on the facia; both confirmed that it was 10.25 p.m. He was five minutes early, but the important thing was that he had made it on time.

Three years before he had given up smoking, but the pressures of the last two days had driven him back to it, and now he lit a cigarette and inhaled deeply, with a sense of relief: then he switched off the engine and the main headlights but left the parking lights on, as instructed by the kidnappers. It was part of the arrangement that the money should be carried in the Mercedes with its distinctive number plate RAC 100. At 10.30 p.m. exactly he got out of the car, opened the rear door and stood beside it. The suitcase containing the money lay on the back seat, within easy reach. It was late April but the evening was chill and damp, like something left over from November, and Robin shivered, regretting that in his anxiety he had forgotten to bring a top-coat: then, with a surge of guilt he remembered his sister . . .

He waited ten minutes and by this time his mind was seething with doubt. Had he come to the right spot? Was it a trick, simply a way of testing him? Had the police broken their promise and staked out the area, thus frightening off the kidnappers? At this time the traffic was intermittent, odd busy patches in which the cars and trucks flowed past as though in convoy, and then brief, dark silences in which the road was empty.

It began to drizzle and as he turned up the collar of his

12

jacket his thoughts turned again to his sister. He had read the account of the previous kidnapping in Atlanta, and the one hopeful feature of the present situation was that the girl in that case, Barbara Jane Mackle, had been rescued alive after 83 hours in her underground coffin. Barbara Jane Mackle had behaved with exemplary courage and appeared to suffer no ill effects. He knew that his sister would be no less brave, but he also knew that Joy suffered from slight claustrophobia; she hated to be confined in small, enclosed spaces, to be hemmed in.

He shivered again, his whole body quivering, as he imagined her terror. He was a pleasant, easy-going, good-natured young man who found it difficult to arouse any strong feelings of animosity towards other human beings, but at this moment he felt a fierce murderous hatred towards the kidnappers. It was a monstrous injustice that there was no punishment which would fit their crime, no retribution which could match what they were doing to his sister. He had never thought deeply about capital punishment; a week ago he would probably have counted himself on the side of those who opposed it. But not now, certainly not now. If and when the kidnappers were caught, he wanted to see them die, to see them kicking and choking at the end of a rope.

A car came out of the darkness, heading towards him, and some sixth sense told him that this was it, that the waiting was over. He tightened expectantly, his heart racing, as the big, black Ford Granada slowed down, moved on to the lay-by, and stopped alongside the Mercedes. The driver, a young woman, had pulled a scarf up over her face, revealing only her eyes: she kept her head to the front and did not look at Robin or speak.

Her companion, a stocky man in a dark blue donkey-jacket, was wearing a nylon stocking which both hid and distorted his features. He spoke through the open window.

'Who are you?'

'Robin Clark. I'm Joy's brother.'

'We were expecting the old man.'

'I've got the money.'

'Surprise, surprise,' said the man drily. He got out of the car and opened the back door of the Ford. 'Shove it in there,' he said. 'And make it quick.' He watched the other man, his hands linked behind his back.

Robin took the heavy case from the Mercedes, but paused as he held it in the space between the two cars. 'My sister – ' he began, his voice cracking with nervousness.

'You'll get the instructions!' said the man sharply.

'Is she all right?'

'That's up to you. If you've played it like we said, she'll be O.K. If not, it'll take you a million years to find her. Now – put that in the back! Quick!'

Robin lowered his head and heaved the case into the Ford; as he did so the man reached down inside his jacket, pulled out a cosh and, measuring his aim with care, struck him heavily on the neck. He staggered under the blow, looked round as though in surprise, and the man hit him once more. Robin groaned and fell to the ground, his hands clutching the open door of the kidnapper's car. The man kicked him clear, slammed the door shut and got back into the front seat as the woman urged the car forward. A moment later it had disappeared into the darkness, heading north.

The pick-up had taken just under two minutes. A half-hour later the police, concerned because Robin had not contacted them, arrived at the scene and found him, still unconscious, lying by the open door of the Mercedes.

3

A night passed and most of Saturday morning. Robin Clark was in hospital recovering from his injuries and his mother sat by the telephone in their home, putting aside all suggestions that she should rest. As the hours passed and no word came from the kidnappers she could feel the despair growing within her, the hope draining away. At intervals she prayed silently, asking God for help, to intervene, to be merciful; and later, when the police came to her with the news that the kidnappers had made contact through a Church of England minister, she saw this as a sign that He had heard her prayers and responded to them.

Margaret Clark insisted, against all advice, on going to her daughter. The police argued that their men were already on the way to the field near Cobham, that it would be better for her to wait at home for news of Joy, but she was adamant. In full command of herself again, she asked a friend to tell her husband and Robin of this new development, and to arrange for a private room in Leatherhead Hospital to be prepared for Joy. She left in a police car with a motor-cycle escort, taking with her the case she had packed the night before, in which there were clothes, nightwear, and toilet articles for herself and Joy. It was her intention to stay at the hospital with her daughter until she had recovered from her ordeal and was considered fit to go home.

On the long, awkward cross-country journey from Gerrard's Cross to Surrey, a radio message came through from a senior officer at New Scotland Yard, informing her that the three kidnappers, two men and a girl, had been arrested at a house in Luton and the money recovered. She showed little interest in this news, it gave her no satisfaction; her thoughts were all on her daughter.

When they arrived at the stone cottage, nosing their way along the narrow track past an ambulance, a file of police cars, and a growing crowd of newspapermen, she felt a sudden icy surge of fear. It was the faces that frightened her. They were stern, shocked, angry, and when a young woman police constable helped her from the car she saw, with astonishment, that tears were glistening in her eyes. The girl turned her head away quickly as though she could not trust herself to meet the older woman's look.

A senior C.I.D. man, whom she recognised as one of the men in charge of the case, touched her elbow gently, his face grave, his voice low. 'Perhaps you'd come into the cottage for a moment, Mrs. Clark?'

'Oh, God!' she said. 'It's gone wrong! You haven't found her!' She trembled violently and he tightened his hold on her arm.

'Come inside, please,' he said.

She pulled away from him in anger, her voice rising. 'Tell me! Tell me, for God's sake!'

'We found her,' he said gently. 'But I'm afraid we were too late.'

She stared at him for a moment, as though she hadn't understood, the words roaring and echoing in her head, then she nodded and he saw that she was making a conscious effort to gather herself.

'I want to see her,' she said slowly. 'Where is she? I want to see her.'

'I don't really think – ' he began, shaking his head.

'I want to see my daughter!'

He took her round the side of the cottage to the field beyond. The area around a clump of bushes had been roped off and within this circle detectives and photographers were at work. They moved back when they saw Margaret, watching her with pity and embarrassment and then looking away, as though they felt that their presence was an intrusion on a personal and private grief.

The girl lay in the box where they had found her, three feet beneath the surface, looking frail and waif-like in her short tennis dress and grubby white cardigan. She was lying in six inches of brown water and her flesh had a mottled, bluish tinge. The knuckles of both hands were bruised, her fingernails torn and broken, evidence of her efforts to make herself heard, to claw her way out of her hideous prison. Her eyes were open, staring at the sky she had longed to see again.

'She couldn't breathe,' said the C.I.D. man awkwardly. 'The rain. Washed the earth into the hose and blocked it up, so no air could get through. That's what happened, we think.'

'Don't leave her there,' said Margaret.

'No, no, of course not. As soon as we've finished – '

'I want her moved. Now. I want her moved!' Her voice rose to a trembling shout.

He signalled to the waiting policemen and she watched as they raised the box to the surface. The girl was lifted out and placed on a stretcher, but as one of the policemen took up a blanket to cover the body, Margaret moved forward.

'Not yet!' she said.

She knelt on the wet ground beside her daughter, touching the icy hands and the face with her fingers. She straightened the sodden dress, and brushed the dank hair back from the girl's forehead. She thought of the young woman police constable, recalling the tears glistening in her eyes, and wondered why her own tears were so slow to come.

She drew the blanket over her daughter and stood up. The C.I.D. man took her arm and she looked at him, shaking her head, beyond speech. Her strength was gone and as he led her back to the cottage she leaned on him, head down and back stooped, like an old woman.

4

Hugh Wilcox rose at 7 a.m. every day, whatever the season or the weather, and spent one hour on the programme of exercises which he had drawn up on the first day of his retirement. He was 56 years of age, although he neither looked nor felt it, but he was very conscious of the passing years, he had a fear of falling into decrepitude. He had seen men whose shrunken, enfeebled bodies were unable to respond to the demands of minds which were still sharp and alert, and he was determined that this should never happen to him.

On this Sunday morning he allowed twenty minutes as usual for a series of Swedish exercises, and then went down to the covered Fives court behind the stables, where he spent a further twenty minutes throwing the ball, competing strenuously against himself, making the play as difficult as possible. He drove himself until his heart was thudding in his breast, until breathing was almost a pain, until the sweat flowed down his forehead and stung into his eyes. Then the sharp shock of a cold shower and a final plunge into the pool, where he swam fifteen fast, punishing lengths, before turning over to float lazily on his back.

These were the moments he looked forward to, when he could relax the tension, and his mind and body glowed with a sense of achievement, of well-being. The pool was heated, the water kept at a pleasing, comfortable temperature for this very purpose, so that he could linger floating gently, and turn his thoughts to the day ahead. But relaxation did not come easily this morning, although the weather had turned and a bright sun was climbing happily into a clear, blue sky.

He did not know Joy Clark, he had never met her, and he was not a sentimental man, but he felt outraged by the manner of her dying. He had sat grim-faced the previous evening, listening to the news bulletins, anger, disgust and a sense of despair churning inside him. All right, so the police had been efficient, the criminals had been caught. And the commentators, the professional pundits, were already raising their voices in horror, discussing in soapy tones the morality of bringing back the death penalty. But within a day or so, he knew the clamour would die down, Joy Clark would be forgotten and the Great British Public, numbed and bewildered and weary, would turn to face yet another crisis, yet another assault on its peace and liberty.

Now, as so often happened, the gentle motion of the water seemed to clarify his thoughts, and the idea, which had occupied his mind for so many months, took on shape and form. He felt a sense of excitement and exhilaration as he climbed out of the pool, put on a towelled robe, and went into the house, to the study, his feet making damp indentations in the dark-blue carpet. He checked a telephone number in a small, black book, and then dialled. A drowsy voice, rising out of sleep, answered him.

'Hello? Who's that?'

'Hugh Wilcox.'

'Sir!' The voice was sharper, more alert, now. 'What can I do for you?'

'I want you to come down, Mac. At once.'

'Is anything wrong?'

'I'm bringing forward the plan. I intend to begin operations in three days.'

'We're not ready, sir.'

'We will be. I shall expect you here by noon.'

Wilcox put the telephone down and as he did so, his eye fell on a book he had been dipping into some days before, a collection of essays and speeches by Edmund Burke, the eighteenth century M.P. He remembered that he had marked a phrase which seemed to have particular relevance to his current mood, and he took up the book and read the words again.

The only thing necessary for the triumph of evil is for good men to do nothing.

Chapter Two

1

IT had been a great day, one of the best that Rick Simmonds could remember. A pity, he thought, with a sigh of regret, a bloody pity, that it was the last month of the season. The summer months were slow and boring, there was no excitement at the weekends, and so very little to do in the long, light evenings. True, there was cricket, but that was never the same, it lacked the tension, the fierceness, the instant conflict of football, it did not arouse the same tingling, swaying passions.

Perhaps, he thought, perhaps I'll get myself a motor-bike, a Yamaha 350, or one of those new Hondas, the GL1000 Gold Wing. Expensive, too bleeding expensive and Christ knows where I'd get the cash, but it would take the curse off the summer. I'd be mobile, I wouldn't be tied down to that handful of rotten streets, that stinking city centre back home. Home! That was a laugh! It was a nothing, a load of old crump, a right slag of a place. Home was a flat, wedged in on all sides by other flats, block after block after block, all concrete, all the same: and walls so thin that you could hear the crackle of nylon when the girl next door undressed for bed.

Rick lifted the metal can to his mouth, tipped it up to catch the last drops of light ale, and tossed the empty out through the open window on to the railway line. He grinned happily at his mate, Ginger, who was sitting opposite and leaned forward in the semi-darkness to peer into his face.

'How's the eye then, Ginge?'

Ginger touched the purple bruise surrounding his half-closed left eye carefully, but with a hint of pride. After all, the wound was an honourable one, received in the punch-up after the match; it was proof that he had been in the thick of the action.

'You should have seen the other bloke!' he said, grinning back. 'I got him right in the goolies. And as he doubled up I caught him in the mush with the old knee. Whoosh! Christ, you should've seen the blood – came spurting out of his mouth like tomato sauce!'

'Great!' said Rick. 'Great!' Ginger had told him the story at least three times, but what did that matter? It had been a great afternoon; a great day, and he'd seen enough of the action himself to feel properly satisfied. They'd got pretty well tanked-up on the journey down that morning and then they'd had a couple more beers at King's Cross station before catching the Underground to the match, so that by the time of the kick-off they were just about ready to take on anyone or anything. They all knew that this was the last outing of the season, they were determined to make it something special, a day to remember. And that meant aggro, of course. What was the point of going all that way, spending all that money on fares, if there wasn't a bit of aggro at the end of it?

There'd been one or two skirmishes outside the ground before the match, but nothing much, nothing to write home about. The police were out in strength, they had it all organised; the fights were broken up quickly, efficiently and the rival mobs of teenagers were marshalled in chanting groups at separate ends of the stadium.

It had been good at first, as it always was for Rick. He could imagine nothing more exciting than those minutes before a game when you stood shoulder to shoulder with your own crowd, chanting and singing and swaying. That's what it is all about, he thought, that's really living. Some force seemed to take possession of him at such moments; he felt as though he was a different person, stronger, taller, a man not a boy, someone to be reckoned with. But later, as the afternoon progressed, the mood changed to one of irritation and then of anger. It wasn't enough to stand and watch like all the others, to be part of the anonymous crowd, or even to hurl abuse at the opposing team and the referee; he wanted to explode into action himself, to vent his frustration on a more positive target.

The opportunity came after the match. The word was passed along and they slipped past the watchful police in twos and threes, hiding their coloured scarves and favours under their coats, and reassembled, as arranged, in a side-street nearby. There were about a hundred of them in all, and they spent a useful half-hour waylaying small groups of home supporters and putting the boot in. This was interesting but hardly satisfying, so they turned their attention to some of the little stores nearby. A small greengrocery was robbed and vandalised, they smashed the plate-glass window of a neighbouring butcher's, and then looted a confectionery and tobacco shop, terrorising the elderly couple who owned it. Two girls, returning home from a shopping expedition to Oxford Street, were waylaid by some of the mob, and chased down an alley, where they were cornered. Rick had been in the forefront of this foray and in the dim light of the railway compartment he grinned to himself, remembering the terrified look on the face of the younger of the two girls as he pulled up her skirt and thrust his hand, palm uppermost, between her thighs. Her mouth was open and she tried to scream, but no sound came out.

'That's nice, darling,' Rick had said, 'that's really beautiful.'

He'd been forced to leave the girl as shouts of warning and the sound of approaching police-sirens sent the mob scurrying off again and eventually, in small groups, they made their way back to King's Cross. It was not possible to make an accurate count, but Rick reckoned that about twenty lads were missing, probably arrested. The police were out in force at the station; they packed Rick and his friends into the last two carriages, locked the doors, and waited in a line along the platform until the train drew away.

The gang had taken the precaution of stocking up with more beer, and as they drank this they set about the systematic destruction of the carriages. Light-fittings and luggage racks were torn out and thrown through the windows on to the track; they ripped up the upholstery, carved crude messages in the woodwork, lit a fire in one of the lavatories, and took it in turns to extinguish it by urinating on the flames. The orgy continued for an hour. Nothing that could be cut or wrenched from its moorings was left in place, no surface remained unscarred.

And now it was more or less over. The chanting, the singing, the laughter, the excitement – all this was over. Exhausted, drowsy, but satisfied they sat back on the ravished seats or squatted in the corridor, reliving the afternoon's adventures. Rick yawned, took a packet of the looted cigarettes from his pocket and lit up. He thought of the girl again, and recalling the smoothness of her legs under the dark tights, he moistened his lips with the tip of his tongue and stirred uneasily.

It was a minute or two before he noticed that the train had stopped.

2

They were in a station, but there were no lights and it wasn't possible to see any platform signs. Rick thrust his head out of the window and thought he could see some men moving on the track at the front of the train but he couldn't be sure.

'Where are we?' asked Ginger.

'Don't know. Some crummy station. Can't see a bleeding thing,' said Rick.

A moment later they heard a loud grating sound, the clang of metal on metal, and the carriage gave a slight lurch. And now Rick could clearly see the shadowy figure of a man standing only a few feet away. He appeared to be signalling the engine with a flashlight: there was a pause, Rick saw an answering flash from further up the line, and then to his astonishment he saw and heard the front portion of the train begin to pull away.

'Hey!' he shouted, 'they're leaving us behind! They've uncoupled our carriages!'

'What?' said Ginger.

'The bastards! It's the cops, it must be the bloody cops!'

Suddenly two searchlights snapped on, cutting through the rising clamour as though with a knife. The beams seemed like long white fingers poking out of the darkness towards the train, dazzling its silent, wondering passengers. Coming from right and left, the lights moved slowly along the carriages until they were playing on the doors, and as the movement stopped a voice called from the darkness beyond, a man's voice, crisp and full of authority. He was speaking through a loud-hailer and his words came back as a faint, hollow echo from the station walls.

'You people on the train. Listen! You will stay where you are and stay quiet until you are ordered to leave your compartments. Stay where you are, and stay quiet.'

A moment of heavy silence followed and then an answering voice came from the train. 'Bugger you, mate, whoever you are. I'm getting out and I'd like to see you stop me. Here, lads, give us a hand.'

A chorus of defiant shouts and catcalls rose from the train as one of the older lads was hoisted up to the window and began to wriggle his way through. But he had scarcely got halfway when out of the darkness there came a flash, a booming explosion, and a bullet crashed into the wood-work at the top of the door, a foot or so away from the heads of the escaping youth and those who were crowding behind him. He hung in the window space for a moment, as though petrified, then scrambled back inside, thrashing his arms in panic. Once again there was silence: then, after a while, like the stirring and rustling of fallen leaves, a murmur of voices rose from the train, low, frightened, urgent voices.

'What was it?' whispered Ginger. 'What was that?'

'It was a gun!' said Rick. 'Someone fired a gun.' His voice trembled slightly. 'They're shooting at the train!'

'Christ!'

Two men stepped out of the shadows. Both were masked, both wore berets, dark overalls and masks and one of them carried a rifle. The unarmed man moved forward, unlocked the doors of the two carriages, swung them open and stepped back.

'Attention! Attention!' The loud-hailer boomed out again. 'You will now leave the train, one by one. Do as you are told and no-one will get hurt. Right. Move!'

There was no movement from the compartments and after a moment or so of waiting the second man raised his rifle and went towards the open doors. The group nearest the platform fell back, shielding their eyes from the glare of the searchlights, but they were shoved forward again by the crowd behind, who were pushing towards the doors in an effort to see what was going on. The masked man thrust the muzzle of his rifle towards one of the youths, inserted it under the rim of the brightly-coloured woollen hat he was wearing and flicked it off. The man raised the rifle so that the hat hung from it like a trophy.

'Right, sonnie,' he said tersely. 'You lead the way. Come on!'

The boy looked up at the gun in disbelief and then his frightened eyes went to the masked face. 'Bloody hell!' he murmured. 'Bloody hell!' The man dropped the gun, allowing the hat to fall, and drove the barrel into the other's stomach; the boy screamed, doubled-up in pain and staggered out on to the platform.

The others began to follow him, chastened and quiet now, torn between bewilderment and fear. Two more armed men stepped out of the shadows and directed them in single file through a narrow gate into the forecourt of the station and towards a wall at the far end. The gravel crushed under their tread, but otherwise they moved in silence. Two more searchlights played on their pallid faces as they reached the wall and turned; then, as the first shock passed away, some of the bolder spirits began once again to murmur among themselves.

'Quiet! No talking!' commanded the unseen man with the loud-hailer.

As the last of them came through the gate into the yard, a thin youth in patched jeans who was ahead of Rick stopped suddenly, looking in terror towards the wall where the others stood in huddled silence, pinned down by the fierce white beam of the searchlights. One of the armed men pushed him forward roughly, ordering him to keep moving, but the thin youth suddenly broke free and began to run in the opposite direction. Two masked men appeared out of the shadows to block his path, and as he checked a third came up from behind and brought the butt of a rifle down on his back, between the shoulder blades. The thin youth gave a shrill scream and crashed to the ground, where he lay sobbing with pain, his face pressed into the gravel. The third man looked down at him for a moment as though considering the next move, and then, with a deliberation which bordered on contempt, kicked him in the ribs. The youth rolled over, and looked up at his tormentor; his eyes were filled with tears and he was blubbering incoherently.

'Up!' the man said. 'On your feet! Up!'

The youth made an effort to rise, but his knees buckled under him and he fell forward, his head lowered, as though in prayer. The man motioned to Rick and his friend Ginger.

'You – and you! Take him over to the wall! Come on, move yourselves!' The voice, though slightly muffled by the mask was unmistakably cockney in tone, and the command was delivered with a sharp, military ring.

Rick and Ginger lifted the whimpering boy to his feet and half carried, half lifted him to the wall where the others, shocked and silent, made space for him. Blood was beginning to bubble up from the heavy graze made by his fall on the gravel, and as he leaned against the wall he pulled out a grubby handkerchief and held it to the wound. He was trembling as though with fever, his teeth chattering noisily.

3

'Attention! Attention!' The man with the loud-hailer materialised out of the darkness, a tall, athletic figure, dressed like the others in dark overalls and a mask. He handed the hailer to one of the armed men, moved slowly forward between the searchlights to within a few paces of the crowd at the wall, and stood, hands on hips, looking deliberately along the rows of bewildered faces, as though he was challenging them to stare him down. The other men fell back respectfully, leaving no doubt that this was their commander.

He stood thus for a long time, dominating them, his dark eyes almost luminous in the semi-darkness; the night, the station yard, seemed to be filled with the force of his personality, as though the air was charged with an electric current. When he spoke at last, the breaking of the silence came to them almost as a physical shock. He said only a few words, in a scornful, half-jesting tone, but behind them there was the unmistakable ring of steel.

'Well, lads,' he said, 'you've had a good day, have you? Put the boot in here and there, frightened a few old ladies, looted a few shops, smashed up a bit of railway property, eh? And I daresay you were looking forward to a little more of the same when you got home. Nothing like shoving an old woman off the pavement, is there? And there's always a few around. They just won't lie down and die, will they? They won't get out of your way – so if you kick 'em in the guts it's their own fault, isn't that so? Mind you, the odds must be right. Like this afternoon, for instance. You see, I know what you've been up to. I know a great deal about you. What were the odds in that shop you smashed up and looted? There were two of them and what? – twenty or thirty of you. Odds of ten or fifteen to one in your favour. Oh, you're a lot of brave lads, we have to grant you that. Bonnie fighters one and all.'

He moved a step or two nearer, and he seemed to hurl his words at them like daggers.

'Louts! Every one of you! Gutless, spineless, chicken-livered louts!' He shook his head as though lost for words, and muttered, half to himself. 'God help us! God in heaven help us!' He moved his right hand in what seemed to be a signal, and the masked man with the cockney voice took over.

He was squat and heavy, and he stood before them like a bull, lifting his massive head towards them in an aggressive manner.

'Right, my lucky lads,' he bawled. 'Hear me! I shan't say it twice. Start stripping off. The lot – right down to your underpants. We'll let you keep them on – don't want you to catch a cold in your vitals, do we? If you haven't got underpants, that's your bad luck. Right – get cracking. Throw the stuff in front here. I'll give you two minutes. Anyone who takes longer than that will get the sharp edge of a rifle in his guts!'

There was a pause and then a murmur of protest rose from the crowd, ascending in volume, and some of the boys at the rear, well-screened from view, began to shout abuse, but the revolt was crushed before its infection could take hold. Four masked men with sub-machine guns, closed in, menacing the group, and the protest fell away into silence. One by one the youths began to pull off their clothes, prompted by the armed men who moved along the flanks of the group prodding viciously at those who were slow or seemed reluctant to start.

The pile of clothing grew rapidly, forming a long, low mound in front of the Cockney, who stood with one eye on his watch and one on the crowd of youths. From time to time the masked men poked among the clothing and re-moved the odd weapon, which they tossed to one side. There were a dozen lengths of bicycle chain, several knives, even a piece of brick in a sock and a couple of knuckle-dusters.

'Time! Stand still there! Stand still!'

The Cockney moved forward and ran his eye along the rows of white, shivering bodies. Most of them were wearing underpants of one sort or another, but there were several who were completely naked and most of these were making pathetic efforts to shelter behind their friends, as though they felt ashamed or vulnerable.

'Right, my lads,' said the Cockney. 'When I give the signal – and not before – you can start heading for home.' He pointed to a gate in another part of the wall. 'You go thataway. Turn left outside and keep going. If I was you I'd run, to keep warm. Now, wait for it.'

He turned towards the man who seemed to be the commander. The man nodded and moved forward.

'Remember this day,' he said. 'Remember it well. The party's over. From now on neither you nor anyone else will be allowed to get away unscathed with what you did today. If the law won't punish you properly, we shall. Pass the word. And remember we shall be watching. We shall know. And one way or another we shall make you pay.' He stepped back. 'Right. Clean them up!'

There was a momentary pause and then, from out of the darkness two great jets of water began to play on the crowd by the wall. There was a kind of collective yell of shock, and they pressed together more tightly as if this would give them shelter.

'Right!' shouted the Cockney, 'run for it!'

Shouting and cursing the youths began to break, holding their heads down as they ran for the gate, pursued all the way by the relentless icy, arching columns of water.

A short path led from the gate to form a T-junction with a narrow lane, but the right-hand turn into the lane was blocked by a truck, and four more armed men. Gasping, breathless, the youths turned to the left and fled into the darkness.

Rick was one of the last to go and as he turned away from the truck to follow the others, he was sure he heard the sound of men laughing. The laughter seemed to pursue him for quite a long way.

4

Later that evening a taxi-driver handed an envelope to the commissionaire on duty at the *Daily Express* building in Fleet Street, after which he returned to his cab and drove away. The envelope was addressed to the editor of the *Sunday Express* and marked VERY URGENT. In due course it was delivered to the editor who put it to one side; at that moment he, with senior members of his staff, was pre-occupied with a series of reports which had been trickling in for the past half-hour and which looked to have the makings of an extraordinary, not to say, sensational story.

The first of these reports was in the editor's hand at this moment. It came from a journalist named Hemmings who worked for a local newspaper in Bedford and occasionally earned a few pounds on the side by acting as a stringer for the *Express* group. Hemmings was a good and experienced newspaperman with a plain, impersonal, muscled style in which scarcely a word was wasted, but on this occasion he had been unable entirely to suppress his own feelings; there was, the editor noted, a hint of mocking satisfaction in his report, as though he approved of the events with which he was dealing.

He lived in the village of Little Warling, a few miles south of Bedford and earlier that evening, on his way to a dinner engagement he had chanced upon the youths from the train. Tired, cold and dispirited, they were strung out in melancholy procession along a half-mile stretch of narrow country lane. Most of them were now sheltering in the local church hall, in the care of the police, but Hemmings had taken three of them to his own home, where after being fed and roughly kitted out with some of his old clothes, they revived sufficiently to tell him their strange story. Hemmings had set all this down and added, in conclusion, that he was on his way to the disused railway station at Warling, where the attack on the youths had taken place, and that he would ring back within the hour with further news.

The other reports were centred on the same area. A signal box on the main line had been invaded by two armed men, both wearing masks, and the signalman had been forced at gun point to stop the 6.45 football special from King's Cross. The train was halted for about two minutes, after which the signals were re-set and it continued its journey. The armed men warned the signalman to make no attempt to raise the alarm, and instructed him to continue with his normal duties. They stayed in the box for thirty minutes and only when they left was he able to warn his superiors.

The final report, less detailed and more nebulous, referred to rumours that a train had been hi-jacked in the same area. It seemed to fit with the other stories and the editor ordered that this should be checked out immediately. Only after he had made other dispositions did he turn his attention to the envelope lying on his desk. It took him thirty seconds to read the typed message it contained and when he had done so he sat back in the chair, fingering his thin hair in amazement and disbelief. Then he read it through once again, more slowly this time, weighing each sentence as though to test its truth.

In the right-hand corner at the top of the single sheet of white paper there was a sign, made by a rubber stamp. It consisted of a red triangle, similar to that used in road signs to represent DANGER, and within this there was the letter C. The message was set out in neat, numbered paragraphs:

1. At 18.35 hrs. on Saturday, April 30, at Warling Station, one of our units took punitive action against a large group of hooligans and vandals. The operation was successful, and should be taken as a demonstration of our purpose.

2. That purpose is to alert the British people to the dangers which threaten our way of life. The signs of corruption and degeneracy are all round us and need no emphasis. In the name of freedom the law is mocked and defied, violence, terror and perversion have become the common currency of our cities, the simple decencies of courtesy, good manners, consideration and respect for others have been replaced by vulgarity, boorishness and ignorance.

3. A journey of a thousand miles begins with a short step. Today, at Warling, we took that first step. There will be others. We shall continue to harass and punish the guilty until this nation finds its way back to sanity.

4. We pose no threat to any decent citizen, whatever his age, race, colour or religion. We are neither racialist nor fascist, we do not seek to destroy democratic institutions. But we believe that there can be no democracy without discipline, no peace without strong laws and the will to enforce them, no liberty without order and virtue.

5. We make only one specific demand. In accordance with the wish of the vast majority, as indicated by the public opinion polls, we call upon Parliament to restore the death penalty immediately and to extend it to cover acts of terrorism, kidnapping, and other serious crimes of violence.

6. We have adopted, as a symbol of our purpose, the name of one of our greatest leaders. We call upon the people of Britain, in his name and inspired by his indomitable spirit, to make a supreme effort. Let us make a new beginning – let us make the coming months a season of national revival and regeneration! Restore order, courtesy and discipline in the home, in the schools, in the factories and offices, on the streets! Let each be responsible for his own.

(signed) THE CHURCHILL COMMANDO.

Inevitably, the remarkable events at Warling were featured prominently in all the Sunday newspapers and became the main lead story in the radio news-bulletins. The *Sunday Express* took pride of place with its exclusive publication of the communique from the so-called Churchill Commando, and this became the subject of much comment from the professional pundits from all corners of the political arena.

The radio stations seized the opportunity to conduct an exercise in *vox pop* sending their reporters out on to the streets to sample the reaction of the public. Almost ninety per cent of those interviewed expressed approval of the action of the self-styled Churchill Commando, their comments ranging from the cautious to the outright enthusiastic. The general feeling was summed up by one housewife, a Mrs. Plumrose from Chelsea, who was questioned on her way home from church.

'Well, you have to fight fire with fire, don't you? These hooligans have had things their own way for far too long. Half the time, it isn't safe to walk the streets. Now they've been given a taste of their own medicine, that's the way I look at it. It's a bit of a laugh really, isn't it? I mean, you have to laugh – the idea of those hooligans getting washed down. I'd have given my right arm to have seen it. I say good luck to these men, these commandos, whoever they are. If this country had more like them, if we had another Churchill running things, we shouldn't be in such a mess.'

No senior ministers had been persuaded to comment, but on the BBC lunchtime programme *The World This Weekend*, both an Under-Secretary at the Home Office and a high-ranking police officer at Scotland Yard sternly condemned the instigators of the incident at Warling, and warned of the dangers inherent in such vigilante-style activity. An M.P. for a West Country constituency, appearing on the same programme, agreed with them in principle, but tempered his condemnation with a sort of postscript.

'I'm bound to say,' he said, 'that there is very real concern among the ordinary citizens of this country about the inability of the responsible authorities to deal with these hooligans and vandals and with the rising level of violent crime generally. I'm not blaming the police – they're under-manned and over-worked and they do a fine job – and I don't think they get sufficient support from Parliament. There are far too many do-gooders in this country – woolly-minded permissive liberals who seems to have more sympathy for the criminals than for the victims. We need to strengthen the police and bring in tougher punishments for law-breakers – unless we do that, and do it quickly, there will be more outbreaks such as the one last night. As I say, I don't approve of this Churchill Commando, but on the other hand, I must add that, in my view, we have allowed violence and permissiveness to go too far. Sooner or later a backlash of this sort was bound to come. We ought to heed the warning.'

Another M.P. from Yorkshire issued a statement in which he announced that he would be putting down a motion asking Parliament to restore the death penalty and extend its operation to other serious crimes.

Later that evening the television news programmes reported at some length on an extraordinary new development. All over Britain, people were bringing out photographs of Winston Churchill. Most of them were old war-time pictures showing Churchill in his most pugnacious mood and they were going up in their thousands in the front windows of houses, in the rear windows of motor-cars, in public houses and clubs.

It was as though the incident at Warling had touched off some spring in the British people, releasing a long pent-up frustration. The general mood was one of amused satisfaction; strangers talked to each other in trains and pubs just as they had done in war-time, commenting with smiles on the humiliation of the hooligans as they or their parents had once spoken of the victory of the 8th Army at El Alamein as a turning-point in the war.

Neither the Prime Minister nor the Home Secretary shared this mood. After watching the television news they spent ten minutes on the telephone discussing the situation, following which the Home Secretary summoned the Commissioner for the Metropolitan Police and other senior officials to an emergency meeting to be held at the Home Office at 9 a.m. the following morning. The Home Secretary told his Private Secretary to inform the Press that he would be making a full statement to the House of Commons on Monday afternoon and that until then he had no comment to make.

An hour later, as the Minister was relaxing at his home with a few special guests, a man named Tom Barr went into the Queen's Head, a public house in Camden Town and ordered a large whisky.

Chapter Three

1

FEW people noticed Tom Barr sitting quietly at the far corner of the public bar of the Queen's Head. There was always a nucleus of strangers in the pub, especially at weekends and so long as they did not usurp the tables and interfere with the unwritten rights of the regulars, they were tolerated. At intervals Barr caught the barman's eye and ordered another Scotch which he tempered with water and ice, and occasionally he turned his head to glance round the room, but for the most part he sat there quite happily, his chin resting up on clenched fists, as though content with his own company.

He had been there for just over an hour, and was on his fourth whisky when the Brothers came in. There were four of them, ranging in age from about 30 to 45 and the conversation fell away to a whisper as they jostled their way to the bar. They brought with them the smell of sweat and stale beer, and in face of their swaggering arrogance the warmth of the crowded room seemed suddenly to fade, the atmosphere to become chill and uneasy. The change was so marked that even Barr looked up from his thoughts. He glanced at the four men for a moment and then returned to his drink, as though they held no interest for him.

The eldest of the four, a heavy, ox-shouldered man with a Zapata-type moustache, whom the others addressed as Frankie, banged loudly on the counter and ordered four pints of special. The barman acknowledged the order with an ingratiating smile and out of the side of his mouth muttered to the young Irish girl who was helping him.

'Find the guv'nor,' he said. 'Tell him the Brothers are in the public bar.'

A space had opened up around the four newcomers and there was a stir of activity among the other customers as some of them began to finish their drinks and move out. Clutching his beer, Frankie turned to face them, propping his back against the bar, and one by one his three brothers followed suit, grinning broadly. The youngest one, his face flushed, staggered slightly as he did so and put a hand on a nearby stool to steady himself.

Frankie looked around with a kind of benign deliberation, clearly enjoying the effect his arrival had made on the company. No-one was allowed to avoid his eye: each in turn looked up and smiled respectfully or nodded, silently according him the submission he demanded. Only Barr kept his head down, as though he was unaware of what was going on or unconcerned. Frankie frowned, and made as though to move towards him, but at that moment he was interrupted by a middle-aged couple who got up and began to move towards the door.

'Where you going then, Dad?' he asked.

The couple stopped and the woman touched her husband's arm nervously, looking up into his face. He turned back to Frankie, twisting a cloth cap in his hands, and cleared his throat.

'Home, mate. We're just going home, like,' he said uneasily.

'Just going home,' echoed his wife.

'You don't like our company, eh?'

'No. It ain't that, Mr. Dill.'

'Then stay!' said Frankie sharply. 'The party's just beginning.'

He straightened up and pointed a finger at the man with the cloth cap as if an idea had suddenly occurred to him. 'As a matter of fact, you're just the sort of bloke I'm looking for. I want to ask you a question.'

'We've got to go,' said the woman. 'He's got to be up in the morning for his work.'

'When I'm talking to the organ-grinder, missus,' said Frankie, with deceptive mildness, 'I don't want his bloody monkey to stick its nose in.' He moved towards them. 'You,' he continued, tapping the man's shoulder, 'I'm asking you, Dad. What do you reckon to this Commando caper last night, eh? What do you reckon?'

'He don't know nothing about that,' began the woman. 'We mind our own –'

'I warned you, missus!' snarled Frankie. 'Keep your trap shut!'

'I don't know enough about it,' said the man carefully, backing off slightly.

'I know your sort, mate!' said Frankie, and his brothers murmured their agreement. 'I bet you been laughing your head off all bloody day about it! You think those bastards done the right thing – that's it, annit? All your lot think that. I seen the pictures going up in the windows. Well now, Dad, where's your gun? Bring out your little gun and do the same to us, eh?' He looked round once more. 'Come on, you lucky people! Anyone fancy his luck?'

There was a long silence. No-one moved. Frankie grinned and shook his head. 'Wouldn't you know?' he said. He spat out his contempt. 'Shit! Soft as shit, the lot of 'em! The Churchill bleeding Commandos – look at 'em! Shit!'

He swung round towards Barr, glaring at him malevolently. 'You! What do you reckon, eh? You're keeping bleeding quiet. Let's hear from you!'

Barr did not answer or turn. He raised his head very slowly, then lifted his glass and drained it. 'Same again, barman,' he said quietly.

Frankie hesitated, puzzled by the man's indifference but aware also that it constituted a kind of challenge and that the others were watching, wondering how he would respond. He moved towards Barr and as he did so the middle-aged couple scuttled out of the bar in relief. Their example started a small stampede, until only a handful of customers remained, pressing back against the walls, watching as though hypnotised.

'I'm talking to you, mate!' said Frankie.

Barr gave an audible sigh and put down his glass. He

still did not turn his head, or raise his voice, and he addressed himself to the barman, ignoring Frankie and his heavy breathing.

'You know the trouble, don't you?' he said. 'All those Westerns on television. It goes to their tiny minds. Tell him this is Camden Town, not bloody Texas!'

The barman gave him a nervous, neutral smile but made no comment. Frankie was puzzled and a shade apprehensive but he was in no position to retreat.

'Funny!' he sneered. 'Very humorous!'

'Piss off, cowboy,' said Barr mildly.

A woman at one of the tables giggled nervously and Frankie whirled round at her. She put a hand to her mouth, and the sound gurgled away in her throat until there was silence. As Frankie turned back he was dimly surprised to find that the man in the corner was no longer sitting down. He was on his feet and moreover, he looked big, chunky, and very confident.

Frankie swung a large fist at nothing, for the man slipped the blow with exasperating ease. Those watching saw a kind of blur as Barr seized Frankie's wrist with both hands, turning and lowering himself in almost the same movement; the astonished Frankie executed a clumsy arc, and as he did so Barr's knee came up with painful sharpness and sank into the folds of bulging beer-fat in the region of his stomach. Frankie crashed into a stool and rolled into the corner, his face puce, his lungs pumping desperately, tears of pain and humiliation watering his eyes. He scrambled towards his opponent, gasping for breath, but with the precision of a ballet-dancer Barr took aim and kicked him on the body, just behind the right hip. Frankie screamed like a child in terror as his right leg tightened up, the calf folding against the thigh like the two levers of a nutcracker.

With a roar, one of the other brothers charged forward, an empty beer-bottle in his hand; and again there was that strange blur of action. When it cleared the second brother was lying beside the whimpering Frankie.

As the other two brothers hesitated, the landlord pushed

his way forward, a huge man with red hair, a fiery red beard and light blue eyes: built like a gladiator, he seemed to fill the narrow space behind the bar. Two hands that looked as hard and as big as housebricks shot forward with astonishing speed, grasped the remaining brothers and swung them round until their sweating faces were only inches from the beard.

'Out!' said the landlord softly mouthing the word. 'Out! And don't come back! Out!' To emphasise the point, he jerked them together sharply, and their heads collided with a crack which made the watching customers wince.

Barr moved aside as they shuffled across and helped the other two to their feet. Frankie, his face drained of blood, groaned as he put weight on the injured leg; he tried to pull himself erect, holding on to his brothers, and his lips moved several times before any sound emerged.

'I'll cut you for this!' he croaked. 'I'll cut you!' He looked at Barr and at the landlord, including them both in the threat. The landlord took two steps towards him, thrust a hand across the bar and seized him by the collar of his coat.

'You're Frankie Dill, right?' He shook Frankie like a rattle until he nodded in response. 'Right. I've been waiting for you to pay us a visit. My name's Noonan. I'm running this place now. And I don't allow pisspot rubbish like you in here. Understand?' He shook Frankie again until he received the required acknowledgement, and then pulled him closer. 'Now, my son, what was that about cutting? What did you say just now?'

'Nothing,' muttered Frankie.

'Mr. Noonan,' said the landlord.

'Nothing, Mr. Noonan,' said Frankie.

'Good boy. Because if you try any tricks, my old son, I'll deal with you in person. I'll work on you, bit by bit. Understand?' He tightened his grip and Frankie closed his eyes in pain. 'And if I hear that you've so much as touched one of my customers I'll come looking. Now – on your way, the lot of you!'

Noonan waited until the swing doors closed behind the four men, until the excited babble of comment that followed had died down, and then he poured out two large Scotches and placed one before the man in the corner.

'On the house, Tommy,' he said, smiling. 'And thanks.'

'No problem,' said Barr. 'Who are they?'

'Local tearaways. Been terrorising this place – and others – for years. Last landlord had a nervous breakdown. I think the brewery gave me the pub out of sheer desperation.' He paused and leaned forward. 'How long have you been back in town?'

'Since yesterday.'

'How did you know where to find me?'

Barr smiled. 'I heard you were in the pub business. So I just asked around for a big red-headed bloke named Noonan. I soon got the answer.'

'Well, you must admit, I laid on a nice welcome for you,' said Noonan. 'Took me back a bit, seeing you get stuck into them fellers. Beautiful. Just like the good old days.'

Barr grinned and shook his head reflectively. The murmur of voices in the bar, the laughter, seemed to recede; silence surrounded the two men like a frame as the warmth of memories flowed between them. They had first met each other twelve years before in Salisbury, Rhodesia, in a bar which had been tarted up to make it look like an English pub, and both agreed that the decor was as unconvincing as the beer. They had fortified their comradeship in a fight with a group of drunken, white Rhodesians who – like the brothers Dill – had swaggered into the bar and tried to take possession of it. The damage on that occasion was considerable, and the owner of the bar did not appreciate their intervention. The exploit had cost them a night in jail and a fine which relieved them of most of their cash resources.

They discovered much in common during those hours in the cell, including the coincidence that each had been born on the same day of the same year, 1940. Noonan took some pride in being senior to Barr by about five hours. Each had travelled a different route to Salisbury, but there was much in their backgrounds which was similar. Neither had shown much interest in school, and had left, without credits or regrets, at the earliest possible moment. Barr's home was a small farm in the West Country, about twenty miles out of Plymouth, which his father, with the aid of a small legacy and a large mortgage, had bought in 1938. It had been hard going at first, for the property was in a near-derelict condition, but his father's combination of ambition, drive, and efficiency had turned the shabby acres into a neat and prosperous farm. Barr had worked with him for a while after leaving school, but he had no real taste for farming and at eighteen he joined the Army on a five-year engagement.

Noonan came from Belfast, and all he knew about his father was that he had been a sergeant in the Irish Guards with hair that was a conspicuous red. By the time his mother discovered that she was pregnant, the sergeant had moved on with his regiment and she did not bother to trace him. Instead, she bought a brass ring in Woolworth's for sixpence, put this on the third finger of her left hand, and changed her name from Miss Duffy to Mrs. Noonan. Her family and the neighbours approved, for they understood that this was as much a concession to their own sense of propriety as to her own. Later, when his mother met and married another man, exchanging the brass ring for the genuine article, Noonan continued to live with and to be brought up by his grandparents. The arrangement suited him for his feelings for his mother had never run very deep, and he actively disliked her choice of husband. When his grandmother died in 1958, he too enlisted in the Army. Within three years he reached the rank of sergeant, a circumstance which yielded him a certain amount of private amusement: he had the feeling that his unknown father would have approved.

After their army service both men had been drawn to

Africa. Barr spent some time in Nigeria with a transport firm; growing bored with this, he had accepted an offer to join the President's elite guard as an auxiliary, with special responsibility for training. The President was becoming paranoic about his personal safety and at this time he believed that Europeans, who had no political ambitions or tribal affiliations, might provide the loyalty he needed. Barr enjoyed himself for a few months, although he found the Presidential megalomania difficult to take, and when a friendly Ibo officer warned him that the President had now decided that no white man could be trusted, he packed his kit and moved on to Rhodesia.

By chance, Noonan arrived at the same place at the same time and in similar circumstances. In the past year he had been pursuing an unsuccessful career as an arms dealer in Mozambique with an ambitious Portuguese gentleman as partner. Essentially, Noonan was a simple, reasonable man, who lacked the cunning and application for such a complicated occupation and when he found that his partner had double-crossed him for the second time he decided that this was once too often, and after a short, acrimonious meeting which the partner found rather painful, he cut his losses and went north to Salisbury.

During their night in jail, the two men discussed the past and debated the future. The next morning they paid their fines and, wasting no time, sought out a Belgian named Molenkamp, a storekeeper who was rumoured to have some connection with the recruitment of mercenaries for the Congo. Molenkamp turned out to be a cautious man; he stoutly denied any knowledge of the mercenaries, and even managed a fairly convincing show of indignation at the suggestion that he was involved. Nevertheless, within 24 hours, Barr and Noonan were approached by another man, an American named Laird (who, in his turn, denied any link with Molenkamp), and two days later they were in Stanleyville.

The story of their lives for the next seven years was the story of Africa. They marched and fought in one war after another, pausing at intervals to spend what money they had earned on women, and in drinking bouts which were almost as savage and dangerous as the battles. For the most part they did what they were paid to do, no more, no less, serving their paymasters faithfully but rejecting any ideological or political involvement. The only departure from this traditional mercenary standpoint came when, in response to an appeal from his old friend the Ibo officer, Barr accepted a command in the Biafran forces and persuaded Noonan – who was back in Salisbury recovering from a leg wound and disporting himself with a nubile Irish nurse – to join him.

Both men found themselves falling under the spell of the Biafran leader, Colonel Ojukwu. They admired him as a soldier, respected him as a man, and some of his passionate dedication to the cause of his people rubbed off on Barr in particular. In the moment of final defeat, when he clasped Ojukwu's hand in farewell, he had to call upon all his self-control to stop his grief and frustration from showing.

The Biafran experience changed Barr, although he was not fully aware of this himself. He went back to Salisbury with Noonan and after a brief, drunken holiday they enlisted in an elite unit of the Rhodesian Army known as the Selous Scouts, whose main function was to put down the small guerilla groups which had begun to operate along the borders. Barr soon learned, however, that the Selous Scouts put a very wide interpretation on this brief; he had seen ruthlessness in his time, had been ruthless himself, but much of what he now saw sickened him.

Matters came to a head when his section was ordered to cross the Zambesi on a search-and-destroy mission. At that time the guerillas were few in number and badly organised and apart from one minor haul of antiquated weapons Barr's unit found nothing. The section commander, a Dutchman named Lutz, decided however that he would leave his mark and ordered the destruction of every village on the route. When the natives at one village showed signs of resistance he shot the headman himself and marched the other adult male inhabitants into the bush to receive similar treatment. The young boys of the village were subjected to a simple test. Lutz lined them up and measured them against the height of a rifle: if they stood taller than the upright rifle by as little as a fraction of an inch they were classified as adults and sent to the bush to share the fate of their fathers.

When Barr refused to participate in this massacre, he was placed under close arrest. That night Noonan strangled the guard, released Barr, and they made their escape together. Two months later they reached Mozambique. Noonan, being of a superstitious turn of mind, felt that he ought not to press his luck too far, and decided to return to England. That was in September, 1970. The reunion in the Queen's Head was their first meeting since that time.

3

'Well,' said Noonan, 'what's the word with you? What have you been doing with your life?'

'This and that,' said Barr. 'Singapore. Australia. Tangier. Europe for a while. This and that.'

'Doing what?'

'Looking,' said Barr.

Their eyes met and Noonan nodded, apologising mutely for the question. In the circles they moved in, you did not ask a man, even a friend, about his personal affairs, you waited until he volunteered the information. The glass, almost hidden in his hand, went to his mouth and he tossed the whisky into it. He ran a huge finger around the inside of the empty glass and sucked it thoughtfully, looking at Barr.

'I saw one of Whitaker's boys about a week ago,' he said. 'He asked me if I'd be interested in a job. I told him I'd retired.'

'Whitaker!' Barr smiled and shook his head. 'Is he still at it?'

'Stronger than ever.'

'Where's the war this time?'

'He wouldn't say. He was just sounding me out, like. When he saw I wasn't bothered, he dried up. Would you be interested?'

'I don't know. I don't think so.'

'That's what I thought. It's all right for bloody Whitaker. I doubt he's ever heard a shot fired in anger. It's the poor buggers he recruits who have to lay it on the line.'

'They get bloody paid for it. They don't have to go,' Barr said tersely.

'All the same,' said Noonan, shaking his head, 'I mean – what about that time they sent them fellers to Angola? Most of them didn't know their arse from their elbow. Holy God, what a hillaballo that one turned out to be!'

'That doesn't sound like Whitaker,' said Barr. 'He doesn't usually deal in amateurs. Anyway, I'm out of it now. I've decided to live to be a hundred.' He drained his glass. 'See you, Mike, see you around.'

'Wait!' said Noonan. 'For Christ's sake! Look, we've got to get together over a few jars – it's been years, bloody years.'

'I'll see you. I said that.' Barr touched the other man's arm briefly and smiled. 'You ginger-headed Irish bastard!' he said.

'You toffee-nosed English git!' said Noonan.

Barr decided to walk back to his hotel in the King's Cross Road. He had been away a long time and he was enjoying the mildness of the evening, the gentle touch of the southern breeze on his face; he wanted to soak himself in the Englishness of it all. He had been told that the country had grown shabby in his absence, and he supposed it to be true, but tonight he did not wish to think of that. Shabby or not, he was glad to be home, he had not realised until this moment how much he had missed England. Tomorrow, he thought, tomorrow I'll go to Devon, to see the old couple and the farm, and a moment later he grinned wryly, wondering about this strange attack of sentiment.

He had thought about his parents often enough, and with affection, but he had written only twice in all the years he'd been away, and until this evening had felt no desperate urge to see them. Now he had a picture in his mind, clear as a film, of the red earth smoothly turning aside from the plough, of neat fields made rich by sweat and husbandry, of his father's kindly, quizzical, brown face, and he realised with a kind of shock that he was homesick. Christ, Barr, he told himself, Christ Almighty, you're getting old!

He stopped at a stall near Mornington Crescent and bought a dish of jellied eels. It was pure impulse, for he had never before tasted this cockney delicacy, and he approached it with some caution. The fat woman in the white coat who served Barr, watched with amusement from behind the bowls of cockles, eels, whelks, shrimps and winkles.

'It won't bite you, guv'nor,' she said.

He grinned, took a generous mouthful, and found himself enjoying the soft fish with its subtle chicken-like flavour. 'Good!' he gulped.

'Set you up for the night that will,' she said. 'You won't be able to leave your old woman alone.'

'Is that what it does?' he asked, smiling.

'I had a woman here last night begging me on her bended knees not to sell her husband any more eels. She didn't have time to do her housework, she reckoned. He was at her morning, noon and night. She said her drawers were going up and down like Tower Bridge.'

'What did you say?'

'I told her – you should be so lucky, I said.'

It was then that Barr became aware of two men standing in the shadows, just beyond the pool of light.

'Mr. Barr?'

One of the men stepped forward. His broad, young face, yellowed by the street lights, was adorned by a bushy moustache which curled upwards at the ends, and he was smiling in the affable manner of a doorstep salesman. Barr recognised him at once. Twenty minutes before, during his conversation with Noonan, he had caught a glimpse of this same face in the bar mirror. The man had entered the public bar from the saloon, as though looking for a friend, and then moved through to the street.

'Lovely evening,' said the man. 'Marvellous.' He turned the smile on to the fat lady.

'We'll have to pay for it later,' she said, shaking her head.

'Pardon?'

'We'll have to pay for this weather.'

'Well, we have to pay for everything in this world, isn't that so?'

He included Barr in this profound observation, but drew no comment.

'What can I get you?' said the fat lady. 'Jellied eels?'

'No, thanks,' said the man. 'I'm trying to give them up.' He put a hand inside his tired fawn raincoat and Barr tensed warily.

'It's all right, old son,' said the man. 'It's harmless.' With the air of a conjurer he withdrew his hand and held it out long enough for Barr to register that he was looking at a police warrant card. 'Chandler. Detective Sergeant,' the man continued, replacing the card. 'A friend of yours would like a word.'

Barr put the empty dish on the stall-counter before replying. 'You're quite a joker,' he said slowly. 'You should be in pantomime. I've only got two friends. I've just seen one, and to my certain knowledge, the other is in New Guinea.'

'Benedict,' said Chandler. 'Harry Benedict. Does that ring any bells?'

'A tiny one,' said Barr. 'Very faint.'

'We've got a car across the road,' said Chandler. 'Shall we go?'

Barr took a deep, slow breath and spread his hands. 'Why not?' he said.

4

At about this time a Buckinghamshire farmer telephoned the police at Aylesbury to report a fire. He reported that, when looking out from an upper window, he had seen smoke and flames coming from the direction of the Old Lodge, an isolated house about a mile from his property.

The police knew the house well. Eighteen months before it had been purchased by a young dramatist named Purcell, though not, as it turned out, for his personal use but as a country headquarters for the small left-wing party of which he was an active member.

Since then the Marxist Workers Revolutionary Front had used the old house regularly for summer schools, seminars, and conferences, and the locals, after an initial bout of indignation, had grown accustomed to the comings and goings of these strange people. All the dire warnings about what would happen to the neighbourhood proved to be groundless; the revolutionaries kept themselves to themselves behind the high, red-brick walls of the Old Lodge and troubled no-one.

When the police and the fire-brigade arrived to investigate the farmer's report, they discovered a huge bonfire burning in the grounds, and, on closer investigation, that it was composed of hundreds of books and pamphlets. The house, which was some distance from the fire was untouched.

What puzzled the police was that the place seemed to be deserted. There were clothes and suitcases in the bedrooms, a half-eaten meal was set out on the large kitchen table, and a half-dozen cars were parked in the drive or in the out-houses. It was known that a meeting of the political leadership of the MWRF had been going on over the weekend. That involved at least eight people, and in addition there were four others, permanent residents, whose task was to act as guards and caretakers. There was no sign of these twelve people. They had disappeared.

However, it seemed that those responsible had left their calling-card. It was pinned to the front door of the house and it consisted of a postcard on which was stamped the letter C enclosed in a red triangle.

Chapter Four

1

THE journey from Camden Town took about ten minutes and during that time Barr closed his eyes and slept. This ability to cat-nap was one he had cultivated over the years, and he used it now partly because he was tired and partly as protection against Chandler's crushing affability. After a couple of minutes the detective took the hint and cut off the rattle of words, replacing it with a low, almost tuneless whistling. He seemed to be a man who looked upon silence as a personal challenge.

Barr did not stir, even when the car was halted by traffic lights, but when it drew up at a building in Westminster he woke immediately, as though he knew instinctively that they had reached their destination. He was taken in through a rear entrance, past empty offices and along corridors wrapped in a Sunday evening hush, to a small, barely-furnished room which had the appearance of a slightly superior cell.

'Won't keep you long, old son,' said Chandler, grinning as he closed and locked the door.

Left alone, Barr briefly explored his new surroundings: a bed, a small table and two wooden chairs standing on a square of dark green haircord carpet, and a Lowry print hanging in the centre of an otherwise bare, cream-coloured wall. The picture looked a little out of place, as though it had been put there as an afterthought, a concession to the maxim that man does not live by bread – or policework – alone. A door by the bed was half-open and beyond this Barr found a lavatory, a wash-basin, and shower cubicle, equipped with towels and soap. He went back to the room, stretched himself on the bed, and resumed his sleep.

Fifteen minutes later the door was unlocked and two

men entered. Barr opened his eyes and turned his head towards them but he did not get up. One of the men moved across and looked down at him, the hint of a smile on his face.

'Harry Benedict!' said Barr. 'You're a bit off your beat, aren't you?'

'How are you, Tom?' Benedict was a tall, thin man and he lowered himself carefully, as if from a great height, until he reached a sitting position on the bed. His face was long and austere, with dark, deep-set eyes which seemed to emphasise the unhealthy, yellow pallor of his skin.

'I'm surviving,' said Barr. 'You?'

'O.K. Had a bout of jaundice. I'm back in London for a while.'

'You look bloody terrible!' said Barr.

'Thanks.'

'I'll give you two weeks, three at the most. Don't forget – you promised to leave me your bicycle.'

'I'll see you off, don't worry,' said Benedict. The third man coughed impatiently and he turned towards him. 'Tom. This is George Lydd. He'd like to talk to you.'

'One of your mob, is he?'

'Not quite. I'm only here as a middle man. Because I know you.'

'You don't know me,' said Barr.

'No,' said Benedict. 'I don't suppose I do.'

'I would like to ask you a few questions, Mr. Barr,' said Lydd rather formally, as though he disapproved of the relaxed, familiar manner of his colleague and intended to redress the balance. He was a man of middle height, healthy-looking, with quick, bright, bird-like eyes: he gave the impression of being neat, compact, self-confident. His suit was standard bank-manager issue, and he wore a Junior Carlton Club tie.

'Help yourself,' said Barr. 'Anything to pass the time.'

'It would help if you would sit up. If you don't mind, that is. I like to see who I'm talking to.'

Barr glanced at Benedict and their eyes exchanged a

smile. He swung his legs round and sat up facing Lydd. 'That better?' he said.

'It's an improvement,' said Lydd drily. His voice gathered pace. 'Where were you last night, Mr. Barr?'

'In bed. Sleeping.'

'I mean, yesterday evening.'

'Ditto. In bed. Sleeping.'

'In the evening?'

'Listen. I was tired. I got in from Singapore yesterday morning. So I slept. Alone, unfortunately.'

'Where are you staying.'

'The Mount Pleasant Hotel in King's Cross Road.'

'Why have you come back to this country?'

'I'm a citizen, I have a right.'

'Have you got a job?'

'No.'

'What do you intend to do?'

'Survive.'

'Have you a job in mind? Has anyone made an offer for your services?'

'They're not forming a queue, not as yet. But it's early days. If you've anything to offer, I must warn you that I'm rather on the expensive side.'

'You were employed as a mercenary, I believe. For several years. Is that true?'

'You know bloody well I was. Don't tell me that Harry hasn't given you a run-down on my career. He's got a dossier.'

'You were a mercenary. Did you return to England because you heard that someone over here was in the market for experienced mercenaries?'

'Which someone? Tell me, I could be interested.'

There was a tiny pause before Lydd replied and when he did so, his tone was almost off-hand. 'Well, like for instance, a man named Joss Whitaker? Also a former mercenary. You know him, of course?'

'Know him? That's a deep question. Let's compromise and say I've met him.'

'Did you meet him last night?'

'I told you, I was in bed. And as far as I know I don't walk in my sleep.'

'Today? Did you meet him today?'

'No.'

'Why did you go to the Queen's Head? Was it in the hope of meeting Whitaker?'

'I went there for a drink.'

'And to meet your friend, Mr. Noonan?'

'And to meet my friend, Mr. Noonan.' Barr looked at Lydd wearily. 'Look, would it be too much to ask you to cut the cackle and get to the point?'

'You served with Noonan in Biafra, I believe?'

'And in other places.'

'Including Rhodesia – the Selous Scouts, for instance?'

'You have read the dossier.'

'Dossiers are never complete, Mr. Barr. Dates, places, and so forth. They mean little until you actually meet the man concerned.'

'Well, you've met me now. Now let me ask a question. What the hell is this all about?'

Lydd took a pipe from his pocket, examined the bowl carefully, tapped it gently on the palm of his left hand, then put it in his mouth and applied a match. As the smoke billowed out, he smiled for the first time.

'Mr. Benedict tells me that you were very helpful to him and to his organisation in Berlin and in one or two other areas, Mr. Barr.'

'I'll do almost anything for money,' said Barr. 'Almost.'

'What about Biafra – and Colonel Ojukwu? What did you serve him for? Money or love?'

'He paid,' said Barr tersely, 'he paid on the nail. He was funny like that – he kept his promises. Now, leave him out of this, will you? You're not fit to lick his bloody boots, let alone talk about him.'

'You are a man full of surprises, Mr. Barr,' said Lydd.

'I'm also a man who needs his sleep,' said Barr. He stood up and put a hand to his mouth, holding back a yawn. As he lowered the hand he said: 'Sorry. Jet-lag. If you've finished, I'll be on my way.'

'I'd rather you spent the night here, Mr. Barr.'

'No, I don't fancy it, thanks all the same. The Mount Pleasant isn't exactly the Dorchester but it's clean and comfortable, and I've come to think of it as home.'

'Sorry, I must insist.'

'I see,' said Barr slowly. 'Like that is it?'

'It isn't like anything,' said Lydd. 'As you say, you're tired. I'd like to continue our talk in the morning, when you've caught up on some sleep, that's all.'

'Hobson's choice,' said Barr. 'No bloody choice at all!'

'You'll find an electric razor, toothbrush, and so forth in the little washroom,' said Lydd. He paused with a hand on the door-handle. 'Would you like me to have some food sent in for you now?'

'Champagne, caviare, steak-and-kidney pudding and a bit of Stilton cheese,' said Barr. 'I can't sleep on an empty stomach.'

2

As Barr settled down on his unfamiliar bed, a certain Carl Heslop arrived back at his Knightsbridge apartment.

Mr. Heslop was a man who went to extraordinary pains to appear respectable and it must be said that he almost succeeded. For instance, he never allowed himself to be seen in public with scrubbers; his women were always elegant, cultivated, and he behaved towards them with scrupulous courtesy. His acquaintances (he had no friends) were people of substance and position, his London apartment and his two country houses were furnished and decorated in quiet, good taste with no hint of vulgarity. Moreover, he was always soberly dressed in expensively tailored suits which made the best of his rather flabby figure, and with his well-groomed silver hair, gold-rimmed spectacles and urbane, polite manner he might easily have been taken for a wealthy, conservative banker.

It was unfortunate for Mr. Heslop that he could do nothing to disguise his eyes. They were like dark stones, hard and lifeless, reflecting no feeling even when he smiled; they seemed somehow to be disconnected from the rest of the man, they stared out from behind the pose of respectability and contradicted it. Over the years, there were many who, on meeting Heslop for the first time, had looked into those eyes and felt a chill of apprehension, a cold prickling of the scalp, as though they had just touched the skin of a dead man.

His passport described him as a company director, for he was indeed the chairman of several prosperous companies, all of them legitimate. There was, however, a file on Mr. Heslop at Scotland Yard which went into his activities in considerably more detail. He was, to use the police vernacular, a big-time villain. He controlled something like seventy per cent of the market in hard pornography, and it was estimated that over five hundred call-girls were on his books operating in London and seven other major cities.

In the past few years, moving with the times, he had extended his services to an ever eager public by recruiting a large number of high-class male prostitutes, and for those customers with inclinations towards paedophilia the organisation was also able to supply young children, though these tended to be expensive and, in consequence, were available only to rich and trusted customers. On occasion, some of his underlings had been prosecuted, and a few had gone to prison, but Heslop himself had never been arrested or charged. It seemed to be impossible to gather sufficient positive evidence against him, although there were some cynical people who held the view that he had purchased influence and protection in very high places.

He arrived back at the garage below the apartment at about 11 p.m. having enjoyed a pleasant dinner in the Grill Room at the Savoy. Apart from the chauffeur he was alone, for after the meal he had courteously dismissed his companion; she was one of the most exclusive and expensive girls on his list and, never a man to put personal pleasure before business, he had seen her into a taxi and sent her back to work. In any event, he preferred his own company, he tolerated other people in public but tended to avoid them in private, and his own sexual needs were minimal, almost non-existent. On the rare occasions when they intruded he satisfied them ruthlessly and efficiently, with a minimum waste of time.

Heslop was a careful man, who understood the dangers inherent in his trade, and he had taken elaborate measures to ensure his own safety, even to the extent of having his chauffeur, a former middleweight boxer, trained in the art of unarmed combat. The entrance to his penthouse was under the constant if unobtrusive surveillance of a number of neatly-dressed young men working in relays in eight-hour watches. He had the utmost confidence in these arrangements which had so far worked to perfection.

As he left the car and began to walk towards the private, high-speed elevator which would take him to the penthouse without interruption he was surprised but not unduly perturbed to hear a scuffle behind him. Turning without undue haste, he was in time to see the chauffeur crash face down on to the oil-stained floor of the garage, and to find himself faced by three men, two of whom were pointing revolvers at him. He was alarmed now and moved as though to make a dash for the elevator.

'Don't try it, Mr. Heslop!' said one of the men. 'Don't try it!'

'What is this? What is this all about?' he demanded angrily.

'Shut up!'

Two of the men moved in on him. He tried to struggle, to shout, but as they spun him round he felt something chop at the base of his neck, his spine arched in agony, and he fell unconscious.

He woke some time later, as though to a nightmare. Lights were exploding in his face like fireworks and he could hear the low murmur of voices. He shivered violently, and suddenly became aware that his clothes had gone, that he was completely naked. Naked! He found it impossible to comprehend, he shook his head violently as though this would bring some order to his thoughts. How long had he been lying in this place, what had happened? The cold was intense, it seemed to have penetrated through to his bones, yet there was an odd smell of fetid heat in the air which quickened his stomach.

He tried to scramble to his feet, but as he did so he felt a sharp tug at his ankle and looking down he saw that one of his legs was chained to a thick post. He pulled at the chain in panic but it would not yield and, exhausted by the effort, he fell forward. The soft earth squelched beneath him, smothering his face and body in dark, foul-smelling mud; he could taste it in his mouth, feel it clinging to his hair. He lay there, retching and heaving, until he was roused again by the sounds of movement nearby and wiping the stinking mess from his eyes he saw a low yellow shape edging towards him. Behind this shape, in the darkness, there were others, grunting angrily, threateningly. He felt the sudden pressure of rough skin against his own, the lights flashed and popped again momentarily blinding him, and, overwhelmed with terror, he lost consciousness again.

He was discovered at about 1 a.m. that morning by a farmer whose wife had been lying awake for the past hour wondering why the dogs were so noisy and restless; with some reluctance for he was inclined to be an irritable man, she had prodded her husband awake. He hurried down to the pig-sty which was some distance from the house, alarmed by the excited grunting and squealing of his normally placid pigs, by the shrill barking of his two dogs and by other sounds which he could not identify.

He saw Heslop crouched in one corner, his body blackened and stinking with mud. He was gabbling a string of incoherent words, as he thrust desperately at the jostling, curious pigs with a piece of wood torn from the side of the pen. The farmer kicked the pigs aside and forced a way through to this strange prisoner. The long gabble of words changed to a whimper and then to great, gulping sobs of relief as Heslop seized the farmer, clinging to him as if he were his only hope.

'Help me, help me!' he croaked. 'Please – please, please. Help me!'

There was life in his eyes now, they were dead no longer. They glowed in the darkness like the eyes of a child who has woken from a fearful dream.

3

Early on Monday morning all the principal national and provincial newspapers received a communique from the so-called Churchill Commando. They had been handed in at the London office of an express delivery service at 9 a.m. by a young woman who paid the fee in cash and within the hour they had been delivered. Each of the brown manilla envelopes contained an 8″ × 10″ print of a photograph, attached to which there was a brief caption, bearing the now familiar stamp of the Commando.

> *This is Carl Henry Heslop, a specialist merchant in the corruption of children, in perversion and in pornography. Let others of his kind be warned. We offer our profound apologies to the pigs.*

With each photograph there was a list giving details of Heslop's activities, together with the names and addresses of his chief associates and the various premises at which they operated. The newspapers knew most of this already but for legal reasons they had been unable to use the information. The same restrictions applied now, but the photograph presented them with an opportunity too good to miss. It appeared in the early midday editions of the evening papers together with factual accounts of the hijacking of Heslop. In later editions, they also published hastily prepared features about the scandal of the vice empires and editorials which demanded to know why the police were dragging their feet in this urgent matter.

The photographs had clearly been taken by an expert and showed the naked Heslop on all fours, wallowing in the mud, looking up in fear and astonishment towards the camera, with two large pigs muzzling at his legs. The caption had to be modified, but the Churchill Commando was quoted as the responsible source and most newspapers printed the apology in the last sentence of their message.

Most people who read the story drew the correct inference; there was little sympathy for Heslop, although some were concerned at the implications behind the act. The vast majority, however, saw it as a huge joke, just the sort of thing to liven up a dull Monday.

4

At 9 a.m. Sir Maurice Jennings and George Lydd, representing MI5, attended a meeting in Whitehall at which the Home Secretary was briefed on the latest developments and given a run-down of the steps the police were taking. Besides these two, three other men had been called in: the Commissioner for the Metropolitan Police, the Chief Constable for Bedfordshire, and the Minister's Private Secretary.

Lydd was flattered to be present; his immediate boss was convalescing after an operation, the Head of Operations was abroad, and it had fallen to him to take over the job of holding Sir Maurice's hand at this crucial meeting.

The picture that emerged was largely negative. Every possible witness had been or was being interviewed, but the results so far were not encouraging. There was no clue whatsoever as to the whereabouts of the dozen or so members of the Marxist Workers Revolutionary Front: it was clear that they had been kidnapped but the motive behind it was less obvious.

In the course of his career as Deputy-Director of Administration, Lydd had met two former ministers and he had not been impressed. In his view, this man was the worst so far, a vain, woolly-minded do-gooder who was far too soft in his attitudes. Lydd had now come to the conclusion that all politicians were impossible; they were too easily swayed by outside pressures, they advanced policies which were impractical, and nine out of ten of them had no conception of administration, of the need for efficiency. The only virtue this one had was that he was lazy; he was quite prepared to leave the bulk of the decision-making to the Civil Servants and that was some help at least.

To be fair, there was no hint of what Lydd called 'politician's panic' in the Home Secretary's attitude this morning. He listened calmly to the various reports, occasionally making a note or asking a question, and afterwards led a brief discussion. At the end of this, he nodded his approval and said: 'Thank you, gentlemen. I don't think there is anything useful I can add. I needn't stress the urgency of this matter, I'm sure. I'm worried by the amount of public sympathy for these terrorists – because that is what they are. The danger as I see it is that other people will follow their example and take the law into their own hands. Mob rule. So they must be rounded up quickly, before the contagion spreads. Thank you again.'

As they rose to leave he added almost apologetically: 'There is one small point that occurred to me. The first communique from these people – ' He picked up a copy of the document. 'There is a phrase in it which caught my attention – where it says that there can be no liberty without order and virtue. It struck me as being not only curious but familiar. I spent some time last night trying to recall where I might have seen those words before. They are, in fact, an indirect quotation from Edmund Burke.' He picked up another sheet of paper and continued: 'This is what Burke wrote. *The only liberty I mean is a liberty connected with order, that not only exists along with order and virtue but cannot exist without them.*'

He paused again, and smiled. 'It probably means very little. But taken together with the tone and style of the document as a whole, it does suggest to me that the man we're looking for is someone with a military background and a pretty good library!'

'And money, sir,' said the Commissioner. 'It takes money to buy guns, transport, searchlights and so on.'

'Yes,' said the Home Secretary, 'a wealthy, well-read, ex-military man.' He smiled again. 'You see, gentlemen, I've made it easy for you.'

Chapter Five

1

IT was after 10 a.m. when George Lydd and Harry Benedict went back to see Barr. The eager spring sun was shining through the small, barred window, and the shadow of the bars, greatly magnified, lay across the tiny figures in the Lowry print on the opposite wall. Barr seemed unperturbed by the delay or by his enforced stay; they found him lying on the bed calmly reading the morning paper. A tray holding the remains of a cooked breakfast was on the table.

'I see they've been looking after you,' said Benedict.

'Very well,' said Barr. 'They do an excellent bacon and egg. I can recommend it.' He pushed himself up into a sitting position. 'Right. What's the proposition? Do you want to tell me – or would you rather I said no straight out and saved time?'

It wasn't easy to tell if Lydd was smiling, but Barr gave him credit for trying. The cheeks expanded, the eyes glinted, and then it was back to business again. But there was a discernible change in his manner, and his tone was less hostile. 'I'm sorry for ramming the questions at you last night,' he said. 'Harry knows you, I don't. I was just trying to probe – find out a bit about you. As I said, a dossier doesn't tell everything.'

'Did I pass?' asked Barr drily.

'I can't think of anyone better suited to the job we have in mind.'

'What are you by the way, MI5 or Special Branch?' asked Barr. He jerked a thumb towards Benedict. 'I know what he is – but what are you?'

Lydd ignored the question. 'I have to warn you first.

This meeting – everything that is said here – is covered by the Official Secrets Act. Whether you accept the proposal I shall make to you or not.'

'Oh, Christ,' muttered Barr. 'Not that rigmarole again!' He sighed. 'All right. I'm still listening.'

'Good.' Lydd pulled up a chair and straddled it, leaning his arms on the back as he faced Barr. 'Last night I asked you about this man Whitaker, Joss Whitaker. Information has come our way that he has been trying to recruit experienced mercenaries – on a very selective basis.'

'What does that mean – selective?'

'Well – how can I put it? You know about Angola, they recruited all the odds and sods they could find. A shambles.'

'I heard Whitaker was in on that.'

'He was. But he operated on a different basis. He recruited only the best, not more than fifty or sixty trained men, all of them with experience of African conditions.'

'Yes.' Barr nodded. 'That sounds more like him. He's a shrewd bastard.'

'Tell me,' said Lydd, 'tell me about him.'

'Whitaker? That's it. He's a shrewd bastard. He's made a business out of war, and within limits he plays it straight. His customers need arms or men or both – and they're not looking for rubbish. They want quality and reliability and that's what Whitaker gives them. He never lets them down and he never fiddles the contracts – mainly because it would be too dangerous. He's in a high-risk business – he doesn't believe in shortening the odds. That's why he's survived.'

'And prospered.'

'Oh, yes. He's a winner, one of nature's winners.'

Benedict made a sudden interjection. 'What are his politics, Tom?'

'Politics! Harry, you have to be joking – he wouldn't recognise the word if you put it up in six-feet neon lights.'

'O.K. What I should have said – what I meant was – what are his prejudices?'

Barr frowned, as though he hadn't caught the drift of the question. He stood up, moved over to the breakfast tray and wrapped his hands round the teapot, testing its heat. Finding it cold he picked up a small china mug and drank what little milk it contained. A smear of white appeared on his bottom lip and he rubbed it off with the back of his hand.

'Eighty per cent of the mercenaries I've met are against the Reds,' he said slowly. 'They haven't thought it out – most of them couldn't anyway – they just hate the commies. And even that is just a label. It covers trade unions, socialists, liberals, Jews, what-have you. They even hate the blacks, though they don't mind taking their money. With some of them it doesn't run too deep. Basically they're in it for the loot but they like to pretend they're defending the world against the dreaded Bolsheviks. With others – yes – it's in the blood stream. They're the toughest. If they had lived under Hitler they'd have been SS men, Gestapo.'

'And Whitaker?'

'He'd supply the arms, the uniforms, the men – and throw in the barbed wire for the concentration camps.'

'You don't like him,' said Lydd. It was a statement, not a question.

'That doesn't put him into a minority,' said Barr. 'I don't like people in general. It's a habit of mind I've developed over the years.'

'Where do you stand, Tom?' said Benedict, slowly.

'Nowhere,' said Barr mockingly. 'My kitbag is full of iron rations and other essentials. I've no room for politics and that sort of rubbish.'

It seemed for a moment as though Lydd and Benedict had run out of questions. Lydd sat in silence, stroking the side of his nose with his index finger and staring at Barr thoughtfully.

'We want to know,' he said at last, 'we want to know why Whitaker is recruiting mercenaries, where he is sending them, who is paying the bills.'

'He's in the country,' said Barr. 'Why don't you pick him up and ask him? He can have this room, I've more or less finished with it.'

'We've got nothing we can lay on him. And in any case, we don't want to frighten him off. Look, all we know is this. In the past five or six weeks at least a dozen former mercenaries have disappeared. Maybe more. They've simply vanished. We don't know that Whitaker had anything to do with it – but it began to happen soon after he returned from a trip to South Africa.'

'Coincidence,' said Barr, 'it could be just coincidence.'

'I doubt it,' said Lydd. 'Either way, we'd like to know what happened to those men.'

'If Whitaker did recruit them they're out of the country by now. He'd see to that. Give me some names.'

'Names?' Lydd hesitated.

'Come on!' said Barr. 'I'm covered by the Official Secrets Act, remember?'

'Barnes. Colleano. Meysell. Piotrowski,' said Lydd. 'There's four to be going on with.'

Barr nodded, clearly impressed. 'I don't know Barnes, but I've heard of him. A bloody good soldier, by all accounts. I was with Pete Piotrowski and Joe Colleano in the Congo, at Stanleyville and Paulis. Pete was also with my outfit in Biafra. And that's where I met Meysell.' He nodded again. 'You're right. If Whitaker has recruited people like that, he's being very selective. Those four alone could take a battalion of raw recruits and turn it into a disciplined fighting unit in six weeks.'

'Where would they have gone? Who is buying them?' asked Benedict.

'Jesus,' said Barr, 'look in an atlas! Any one of a dozen places.'

'We want you to find out,' said Lydd. 'For obvious reasons we can't put one of our regular men on to this job. Whitaker would simply close up. We need someone clean, someone he knows and trusts, and who has the qualifications he seems to be looking for. That's why Harry recommended your name. If you hadn't come back yesterday, we were coming out to get you. Let me make it clear. We want you to do a little more than simply find out the background. We want you to go in, sign up with Whitaker, and take it from there.'

'Take what from where?' asked Barr.

'I don't know, frankly,' said Lydd. 'We'll have to play it by ear, see how things develop. When we know a little more about the people behind Whitaker and what they are up to, we shall be better able to judge what our next moves should be.'

Barr looked up at the Lowry print, held out a hand and clicked the finger and thumb together several times, as though he was responding to some inner beat or rhythm; then he turned and his eyes moved from Lydd to Benedict and back again. 'Now,' he said, lowering his hand, 'tell me the rest.'

'The rest?' said Lydd.

'Ah, come on. You've told me just so much. I'd like to know it all.'

'There isn't any more,' said Lydd. 'The rest is speculation, it comes under the heading of hunches. It could be wrong to hell. It certainly wouldn't help you.' He smiled. 'That's the truth.'

'I believe you, as they say,' said Barr mockingly.

'Will you take the job?' asked Lydd impatiently.

'I'm retired. Harry knows that. I told him six months ago in Berlin.'

'What are you going to do?'

'Something peaceful for a change. Away from the sound of gunfire. A bit of fishing for a start.'

'Put it off for a while, Tom,' said Benedict. 'Put it off. The fish will wait. This won't.'

'Christ, Harry,' said Barr, 'there must be a hundred men you can call on. I'm just an amateur, a freelance.'

'We've been through the list. You're one of the few people Whitaker will accept without question.'

'I don't get it,' said Barr, 'I don't get it. A few mercenaries have taken to the hills. So what? Why should you be so concerned? If they want to get their heads blown off in someone else's war, that's their affair. I should think you'd be glad to see the back of them.'

'It is not quite so simple as that, Mr. Barr,' said Lydd. 'I wish it were. The question is – are you willing to help us?'

Barr took a spoon from the tray and began to tap it against the cup. He stood looking down at the table and for a long time the only sound in the room was the tinkle of the metal against the china. When he spoke at last it was to Benedict.

'No,' he said. 'I'm sorry, Harry. This isn't my scene. What I did for you before – well, that was different. I could give you a half-dozen reasons, but what would be the point? Let's just say – I'm not open for hire any more.'

'If it's money – ' Lydd began, but Barr interrupted him angrily.

'No – it isn't bloody money! If you want to know, I don't want to play games – not yours, not anybody's. I'm out, and I'm staying out!' He looked down at the spoon in his hand, saw that it was bent double, and relaxed suddenly, smiling. He dropped the spoon on to the tray. 'Sorry about that,' he said.

Lydd moved to the door. As he went out he said: 'I'm sorry too. I shan't keep you a moment.' His tone was flat, without expression.

Benedict took out a card and wrote a number on the back. He held it out to Barr. 'Take this,' he said, 'put it somewhere safe. Or better still, memorise it.'

'What's it for?' asked Barr.

'If ever you want to contact me – '

'I shan't,' said Barr.

'Take it anyway,' said Benedict.

Barr shrugged and put the strip of card in his pocket. As he did so, Lydd returned with Chandler.

'Right, Mr. Barr,' he said. 'Detective Sergeant Chandler will see you safely off the premises. And of course you will remember that what has passed between us – '

'I've forgotten it already,' said Barr.

When he had gone Lydd closed the door and turned to

Benedict with a sigh. 'Well, that was a monumental bloody waste of time.'

'Not entirely,' said Benedict.

'It was from my point of view. Will he keep his mouth shut?'

'If he said so, he will.'

'You put a lot of faith in him.' There was a touch of sarcasm in Lydd's voice, but Benedict appeared not to notice it.

'I think we lost him when you mentioned those names. Piotrowski – Colleano – the others,' he said.

'Why?'

'For Christ's sake! He told you, he was with them in the Congo, Biafra. That means something – at anyrate, it does to a man like Barr.'

'I rather gathered that he didn't have much time for people – for anyone.'

'That doesn't mean that he is prepared to sell them out.'

'Honour among mercenaries!' Lydd smiled. 'Do you think he knows what Whitaker is up to?'

'It's possible.'

'It seems strange that he should come back just at this moment, after all those years abroad. I think I'll have someone keep an eye on your Mr. Barr.'

'He isn't mine. Not any longer. As a matter of fact, I don't think he belongs to anybody except himself.'

Lydd paused at the door. 'What exactly did he do for you? The file doesn't give the details.'

'A couple of hit jobs. One in Stockholm, one in Beirut. Very important at the time. The last assignment was East Berlin. He went in and brought out two of our people. A man and his wife. We got word that they'd been blown, and we had to move damn fast. None of the regulars was available so I got Barr.'

'He did a good job?'

'What do you think? The best.'

'For which you paid him. And paid him bloody well, if I'm any judge.'

'Of course.' Benedict looked at Lydd in surprise. 'Men like Barr don't come cheap. He's a professional. We work for money too, don't we?'

'Not enough,' said Lydd drily. 'And I like to think that we have other motivations as well.'

'You mean like we're serving the old country?'

'That's a concept that you find dreary and old-fashioned, is it?'

'I don't know,' said Benedict. 'It's simply that I haven't felt that way for years. I suppose I'm like Barr in that respect. I've seen too much of the play. I gave up trying to justify the job a long time ago.'

'Then it's time you got out!' said Lydd stiffly.

'Now, that's something I have been thinking about,' said Benedict. 'I'm working on it.' He spoke half-jocularly but Lydd did not respond.

'Shall we go? I've a lot to do,' he said pointedly, coldly, and held the door open for Benedict.

2

Cheryl Layton woke up in some distress and it took her a moment or two to realise that the cord around her wrists seemed to have tightened, cutting into the flesh. Her hands were tingling with the sort of sensation she would have once described as pins-and-needles, except that it was more painful than anything she had ever known. She had slumped forward whilst asleep and this had put increased pressure on the cord; by pushing herself up into a sitting position once more she managed to ease the tension and relieve the pain, but this only made her more aware of the acute throbbing in her head. The man who had tied the blindfold had been none too gentle and the strip of dark cloth, smelling faintly of oil, felt like an iron band around her temples, the knots which held it fast were biting into her neck.

It astonished her that she had been able to sleep at all. She had no way of telling how long they had been travelling, but she knew that some hours must have passed since she had been pushed into the truck and tied, with her hands behind, to some kind of wooden rail along the side. She could not see her companions but she knew that Adrian and some, if not all of the others, were in the truck with her. At the beginning of the journey Adrian had attempted to sing, to start up the *Internationale*, in an obvious attempt to bolster their spirits but she had heard the sound of a blow and a groan of pain from Adrian, and the song had died in his throat.

'Anyone of you who opens his mouth will get the same – or worse! I want silence, complete and utter silence!' She remembered how the voice had echoed with menace in the darkness, and the taut, fearful silence that had followed.

Who were these men? Certainly not the police; even the pigs would not go to such lengths, she was sure of that. Or was this just another bourgeois aberration on her part, was she being betrayed yet again by her old upper middle-class upbringing? Adrian had scolded her many times for her tendency to underestimate the class enemy. Perhaps, after all, they were in the hands of the police, of some special secret branch which was allowed deliberately to operate outside the law?

No. She shook her head as if to clear her thoughts. It was much more likely that they had been attacked and abducted by an extreme right-wing group: the armed men who had burst into the Old Lodge with such speed and ruthlessness had looked terrifying in their nylon masks and dark, military-style overalls, exactly like fascists. And when she had been slow to move, one of them had whacked her across the bottom with the back of his hand, a hard stinging blow which brought tears to her eyes, and shouted:

'Move, you red cow, move!'

She felt another tension now, a pressure in her bladder which after a few minutes became almost unbearable. 'Is anyone there?' she asked timidly.

'Shut up!' The voice came from the rear of the truck, from the same man she had heard shouting at Adrian.

'Please,' she said, 'I need a loo. I want to pee.' She was hot with shame at her own weakness.

'Do it in your knickers!'

'If she's wearing any!' This was a different voice, coming from the same direction.

'Why don't you go and look?' said the first man, and they both laughed.

At that moment, to Cheryl's intense relief, the truck slowed down. She felt it turn to the right, and heard the springs complain as it edged forward over some rough ground. Then it jerked to a halt.

'Well,' said the first man cheerfully. 'We're here. This is the end of the line for you lot.'

And then, cutting through the silence like a knife, she heard a sharp, metallic click. It was not a sound with which she was familiar; she had heard it only once before in her entire life, a few hours before, when the men had confronted them over supper in the kitchen of the Old Lodge, but she recognised it now with a small, quivering shock of terror.

It was the sound made by the magazine as it connects with an automatic pistol.

3

Barr left the building in Westminster in an anonymous blue Ford delivery van, accompanied by Chandler and a driver, and he was set down, at his own request, in the Mall on the edge of St. James's Park. He stood on the pavement, waiting deliberately until the van drove off, and watched it disappear into the surge of traffic; then he crossed the road and entered the park. It was a sweet, mild morning and he found himself a seat in the sunshine by the lake. There were things he had to think about.

In the course of his career Barr had learned that curiosity can be fatal, he had seen good men die of it. But the meeting with Lydd and Benedict had both puzzled and intrigued him. Why should two men of their high rank concern themselves with the activities of a handful of former mercenaries and adventurers? There were many areas of conflict in the world but none where the addition of a dozen or so men, no matter how expert, would make any significant difference – at least, not that he could see. Why had they been so anxious to involve him? It was obvious that Lydd knew a good deal more than he had been prepared to tell; he had slipped Barr's direct question by talk of speculation and hunches but the evasion had been clumsy and unconvincing.

In the normal way, none of this would have bothered Barr, he would have put it behind him and gone his own way; what he could not forget were two of the names Lydd had mentioned – Pete Piotrowski and Joe Colleano. He and Noonan had marched and fought with these two men in a half-dozen African countries, and he knew them to be superb professionals. If they were together again and lined up with men like Barnes and Meysell, there could only be one explanation. They must be on to something good. And good, thought Barr with a tinge of envy, not only in terms of pay; these men charged premium rates for their services, but the consideration which weighed most heavily with Piotrowski, Colleano and Meysell (he did not know Barnes) was the nature of the assignment. They were, at heart, adventurers who sought challenge, danger and excitement; they were drawn to these things as metal to a magnet.

And suddenly he felt the need to be with them again, the old longings stirring in his blood. For the past six months he had been working as manager of a small and respectable restaurant and club in Singapore, operating it on behalf of a Belgian he had known in the Congo; it had been his first, half-hearted attempt to escape the past, to achieve a sort of normality, but it had failed dismally. As the months wore on he had found himself drowning in boredom. His life had always been governed by impulse, and it was impulse that had made him quit the job three days ago, and driven him back to the Britain he had not seen for ten years.

He clicked his fingers suddenly and stood up, smiling broadly, as though he had come to terms with himself, resolved his uncertainty. A woman sitting on the bench beside him, looked up at Barr in surprise at his abrupt movement.

'It's a lovely morning!' he said cheerfully.

She responded with a little nervous nod and turned her head away, as though afraid of further contact. Barr shrugged and walked away. A sober-suited man was feeding the ducks at the water's edge, taking pieces of bread from an official-looking briefcase and tossing it to the eager fowl. Barr watched him for a moment and then, taking a deep breath, moved off again, his arms swinging. Benedict was right, he thought happily, dead right! The fish can wait!

He left the park, crossed Trafalgar Square, and walked up Charing Cross Road. He found a post office on the corner of Chandos Place, near St. Martin's-in-the-Fields, from where he made two telephone calls. The first was to Noonan, to ask where he could contact Whitaker, the second was to Whitaker himself.

Ten minutes later he caught a District Line train from Charing Cross Underground Station to Barking, where Whitaker had an office and a warehouse.

4

At about the same time, a sealed envelope, marked PRIVATE AND CONFIDENTIAL and addressed to the General Secretary of the Labour Party, was handed in at Transport House, the party's headquarters in Smith Square, Westminster. It contained photostat copies of documents emanating from the Marxist Workers Revolutionary Front, attached to which was a slip of paper stamped with the now familiar emblem of the Churchill Commando and bearing the words: WITH COMPLIMENTS.

The documents revealed a long-term plan to infiltrate the Labour and Trade Union movement in Britain. Considerable progress had been made. There was a list of local branches in which members of the MWRF and their sympathisers had managed to secure key posts, and a further list showing those areas where the MWRF leadership considered that a successful take-over might be possible. There were other papers setting out tactics and strategy. The General Secretary knew a good deal about all this already, but the extent of the penetration by the MWRF surprised him, as did the names of some of the individuals who featured on the lists.

He locked the documents in the safe, and then telephoned the Chairman of the party – who happened also to be a Cabinet minister – requesting an urgent meeting.

5

They had not been shot, after all, at least, not as yet. After the man had spoken those ominous words about the end of the line and clicked the magazine into his pistol, there had followed a long, terrifying silence. In those moments, Cheryl Layton sat hunched in fear, her head down, waiting for the bullets to explode, to tear into her body. She was very young, she was not prepared for death, although she had often thought about it in a romantic, revolutionary way, imagining that if ever she should face torture or execution at the hands of the class enemy she would do so with dignity and defiance. But somehow she had not seen it like this, sitting in the darkness, her hands bound, her legs made sore and uncomfortable by the urine which, despite her effort to control, had soaked her pants and jeans.

The gun did not fire. She heard sounds, the door of the van opening, a faint murmur of voices, the door slamming back into place, and after that the silence settled on them again.

The fear passed to be replaced by a sense of shame. She had let her comrades down, she had allowed herself to be humiliated by these fascist bastards; this was the first test, the first real test, and she had failed! And with this thought, anger came flooding in, anger prompted as much by her own feeling of failure as by hatred of these unknown men.

She tugged frantically at her bonds and to her surprise, she felt them give. She tried again, pulling with increased desperation and her hands were suddenly free, the broken cord dangling from her wrists. She tore the blindfold from her eyes, and was disappointed to find that she was still in darkness; but it was not the utter blackness of a moment before and gradually her eyes grew accustomed to the dim light. She was able to make out the pale faces of her comrades, lying around the sides of the van; she tried to get to her feet but her legs were weak, so she scrambled towards them on her hands and knees, tearing frantically at their blindfolds. Adrian was lying unconscious and she shivered as her fingers touched the sticky, half-congealed blood on the side of his face.

At this moment, she heard a sound from outside the van; the doors rattled, and suddenly they opened, flooding the interior with light. Cheryl shielded her eyes, blinking painfully, as a voice shouted: 'There they are!' Through the curtain of her fingers she saw faces peering up into the van, curious, friendly faces. Then they came scrambling towards her, lights flashed, and she fainted.

6

It was all in the late editions, and there was film of the scene in the television news-bulletins. At noon, the news-editor of STV, the Scottish commercial television channel, had received an anonymous telephone message from a spokesman for the Churchill Commando. He was given an automobile registration number and told that he would find the vehicle parked on the outskirts of a small town in Ayrshire, a few miles N.E. of Kilmarnock. The contents of the van, said the caller, might prove to be of some interest.

Barr heard about it that evening at his hotel when he rang room-service and ordered a drink. When it came, the waiter said affably: 'Did you hear the news, sir?'

'No,' said Barr.

'Those Commandos. Been at it again. You got to hand it to them. They've got the cheek of the devil.'

'What have they done this time?'

'What haven't they done, you mean! You know they kidnapped a bunch of them what-do-you-call 'ems – communists, marxists – well, do you know where they dumped them?'

'Tell me,' said Barr, without too much enthusiasm.

'Moscow!' said the waiter.

'Moscow?' Barr was curious now.

'Yeh. Moscow. They sent 'em to Moscow.' He paused for effect. 'Not the one in Russia, worse luck. There's a place called Moscow in Scotland. They dumped them there. Still, a nod's as good as a wink, right? You can see what they're driving at.'

The waiter was so full of it that he forgot to wait for a tip. At the door he turned to Barr and shook his head.

'Moscow!' he chuckled. 'Moscow! You've got to hand it to them Churchill blokes – cheek of the devil!'

Barr heard him chuckling as he went down the corridor. He closed the door, locked it, and settled down with his drink. He had been busy all day with his own affairs and had given little thought to this business of the Churchill Commando and their exploits. Now he began to wonder about them. The word Commando had a military ring to it and that in itself was intriguing. The paper he had read that morning had referred to the incident with the train and the football hooligans as a 'military-type operation', and one of the boys, when interviewed had said that the men involved had behaved 'like soldiers'.

He was just beginning to put it all together in his mind when the telephone rang. It was the call he had been waiting for since his return from what had proved to be a brief and somewhat unsatisfactory interview with Whitaker.

The man on the other end of the line was his old comrade-in-arms, Pete Piotrowski.

Chapter Six

1

BARR left the hotel and walked along King's Cross Road until he found a telephone box; but when he tried to use it he discovered that it had been vandalised. The next one he went to was in a similar state of disorder and eventually, cursing to himself, he ended up at the railway station where some of the telephones, at least, seemed to be in working order. He went into a booth and dialled the number Piotrowski had given him.

'Yes?' He recognised Piotrowski's careful voice.

He pushed in the coin. 'Barr,' he said.

'Ah, Tommy. Good, good. Listen, where are you speaking from?'

'King's Cross. I'm in a call-box.'

'Were you followed?'

'I don't think so.'

'Make sure. Are you listening?'

'Of course I'm bloody listening!'

'All right, all right!' Piotrowski laughed, the deep throaty laugh which Barr had heard so often. 'I'll meet you at 7.00 p.m. sharp. Go to White City Underground Station. When you come out of the station, cross the road and walk down towards the BBC Television Centre. Keep walking in the same direction, towards Shepherds Bush. Don't stop. Look out for a maroon Jaguar XJ6, which will be coming towards you. I'll be driving. Have you got that?'

'Yes. Except that I don't know London very well. I wouldn't recognise Shepherds Bush if I saw it.'

'Never mind that. You can find the White City Station — and you can't miss the BBC building opposite. Right?'

'Right.'

'Better check out of that hotel too, bring your gear with you.'

'That could be a bit premature,' said Barr.

'Well, you won't be able to get back there tonight – you'll only be wasting money if you keep on the room.'

'If you say so.'

'Good. Check that you're not being tailed. It's important. See you.' Piotrowski hung up abruptly.

It took Barr a few minutes to pack the old canvas hold-all which he had lived with and out of for ten years and which was the nearest thing to a home he'd known in all that time. It took him considerably longer to get to the White City Underground station, for he changed trains three times, doubling back and forth, to elude any possible pursuer. The exercise irritated him, as did the condition of the trains and the stations. On his first visit to London he had marvelled at the Underground system and to see it thus, in such an evident state of neglect and even decay, was something of a shock.

At one point he emerged into Leicester Square and walked along Coventry Street to Piccadilly Circus but the littered streets, the tawdry buildings, reinforced his sense of depression. And he found no comfort in the people. They seemed to be less cheerful and easy-going than he remembered, and certainly more aggressive.

He tried to break this chain of thought, telling himself that his reactions were simply those of a traveller who returns after a long absence to find that the nostalgic pictures he has carried in his mind have little to do with reality. All the same, he could not escape the feeling that things were worse, that some quality to which he could not put a name – something to do with spirit or pride – had gone. A tiny whiff as of decay prickled his nostrils; it was, as yet, no more than a hint, but he found it ominous.

By the time he reached the White City station he was fairly sure that he was not being followed; but he was no expert at this sort of game and he could not be absolutely certain. At any rate, there was little more he could do about

79

it. Congratulating himself on his timing, he walked out into Wood Lane at one minute before 7.00 and followed the directions Piotrowski had given. At two minutes past the hour the red Jaguar appeared. It pulled up beside him, he climbed into the front passenger seat, and a few moments later they were speeding westward along the Westway section of the A40 motor road. Piotrowski checked the rear-view mirror two or three times and then relaxed.

'You weren't followed?'

'I don't think so.'

'Good. We've quite a way to go, so sit back and relax.'

Barr glanced at the other man. He was much as he re-membered, except that he was now beardless; the same gaunt face, the prominent nose slightly askew, the dark eyes almost feverish in their brightness, the thin, wiry body, the hands with their long, beautifully shaped fingers. Once, in the Congo, one of the mercenaries had unwisely taken it upon himself to mock Piotrowski's name and Barr recalled how those fingers had locked round the offender's throat, how it had taken three men to prise open their iron grip.

Piotrowski was smiling, but he seemed indisposed to talk, and Barr put his head back, content to wait. The man was an odd mixture, he thought, with his Polish name and broad Scottish accent. The memory of another evening in the jungle surfaced in his thoughts, an evening when a fresh stock of liquor had just arrived from Stanleyville, and Piotrowski, bottle of vodka in his hand, had talked, with passion, about his background.

2

This man, who lived by the profession of war, owed his existence, in a sense, to an accident of war. After the col-lapse of Poland in 1939, his father, Feric, a fighter-pilot with the Polish Air Force, found his way to Britain via Rumania and France. He rose to the rank of squadron-leader with the Polish 303 Squadron of the RAF, and while stationed at Leconfield, near Hull, he met and married Jean

Colson, a Scots girl serving in the Women's Auxiliary Air Force. Feric Piotrowski died early in 1944, in a bizarre but typical fashion, in the course of an argument with one of the early German flying-bombs. The RAF had discovered that by flying alongside a V1 and flipping it over with a wing-tip, it was possible to put the rocket off course and send it down in the Channel. This was rather more dangerous, but more exciting than the conventional method of shooting it down from a range of two hundred yards, and Feric took up the sport with some relish. Unfortunately the Germans decided to counter this manoeuvre by fitting explosive charges to the wings of the rockets. Feric was one of the first RAF pilots to come up against a V1 equipped in this unsporting fashion, and he was blown to pieces. His son, Peter, was three months old at the time.

After the war his mother took Peter back to Scotland, to Dundee, where she eventually remarried. The boy was brought up with her new husband's name, as Peter Campbell, but at the age of fourteen, against all protests, he reverted to Piotrowski and would answer to nothing else. He forced his mother, his step-father, his school and his friends to accept it.

He had, in effect, awarded himself the status of a Pole-in-exile. His father had been born in Kovel, on the river Turgya, a town that was now part of the USSR; Piotrowski had never seen it, but he thought of it as his home. He carried with him a half-dozen faded photographs, showing his father as a youth, with his family outside the spacious white house at Kovel. There were servants in the pictures, and a gleaming Mercedes limousine, and a view from an upper window, looking out over the estate. And in his heart he carried the story, told by his father to his mother and passed on by her, of how his grandparents and their two daughters had been killed for resisting the Russian troops who invaded Poland in 1940.

He hated the Russians, he hated the regime in Poland and this hatred had, in time, extended itself to any country or any person showing the slightest sympathy for communism.

This hatred had become the motive force of his life, it burned in him like a furnace; for him, communism was another name for evil, something beyond argument or debate, and he would only discuss it in these terms.

On that night in the Congolese jungle, Barr had learned to avoid the subject. The intensity of Piotrowski's feelings embarrassed him, he found it difficult to understand how a man could so relentlessly tie himself to the past, allow himself to be driven by a single negative passion.

It was Barr's nature to be self-contained, self-sufficient, to keep a cool distance between himself and other people. He had been speaking the truth when he told Detective Sergeant Chandler that he had two friends only. There was Noonan and an Australian girl named Iris whom he had last seen eighteen months before, in Papua–New Guinea. Beyond these, there was a circle of a dozen or so people, mostly men he had campaigned with, for whom he had developed a certain admiration and respect.

Colonel Ojukwu, the former Biafran leader, headed the list. And, in a different category, there was Piotrowski. The two elements in his make-up had somehow combined to make him a superb soldier. He possessed all the qualities of dourness, tenacity, courage and fierce fighting ability which are notable in the Scots, while from his Polish father he had inherited a flair for leadership and something of that quixotic unconcern for danger which is the mark of the Pole.

He was a good man to have at your side, or at your back, and beyond that Barr was not concerned.

3

They drove along the A40 for almost an hour in silence, and then, a few miles east of Oxford, Piotrowski turned right into a minor road. He continued along this route for a mile or so until they came to a small, comfortable-looking inn, The Three Jolly Drovers. Piotrowski drove into the car-park at the side, reversed, and parked with the nose of the car facing the exit. He switched off the engine, checked his watch, and turned to Barr.

'Would you care to see something interesting?'

'Like, for instance, a large Scotch?' said Barr.

'I can show you something even better.'

'I doubt it,' Barr said, 'but try me.'

Piotrowski grinned, reached backwards and took a newspaper from the rear seat. He clicked on the interior light, opened the paper, and folded it back neatly. 'First,' he said, 'you must read this. I want you to get the full flavour.'

'Bloody hell!' said Barr. He took the paper, and held it so that the light fell on the page.

'That's the story,' said Piotrowski, tapping it with his finger. When Barr frowned and glanced at him in some bewilderment, he added: 'Read it, go on, read it.'

'I could have read a bloody newspaper in London,' growled Barr, but all the same, he settled back and began to read.

M.P. ATTACKS POP PARTY

The £100,000 Costume Ball, which is being planned by Jig Sutton, lead singer and founder of Britain's top group, *The Pineapple Truck*, came under fire last night from Mr. Patric Bierce the M.P. for East Devon. Speaking at a meeting in his constituency, Mr. Bierce said that he had no objection to people enjoying themselves, but it was irresponsible in the extreme for people to flaunt their money in this ostentatious fashion with the country in dire economic straits and well over a million and a half people unemployed. 'How can we expect people to moderate their wage-claims when they read of this sort of vulgar junketing by overpaid pop stars,' he demanded.

The Ball is to be held at Grantleigh Hall, the famous 17th century mansion in Oxfordshire. Jig Sutton bought the Hall with its 18 bedrooms and 32 acres of grounds only last month at a reported cost of £300,000. Over 1,000 guests have been invited.

A jumbo jet has been chartered to bring guests from

Europe, and they will be ferried from Heathrow in a fleet of chauffeur-driven limousines to join their fellow-guests from Britain. They have been asked to come dressed in the styles of ladies and gentlemen of the court of Louis XIV of France. Estimates of the cost of the Ball vary but one expert has put it in the region of £10,000.

Last night, Jig Sutton, 27-year-old son of a Tottenham bus-driver, who is reputed to be one of the wealthiest people on the pop scene, shrugged off the attack, and said the Ball would go ahead as planned. 'Who is Bierce?' he asked.

And the cost?

'Listen,' he said, 'I'm like the squire of the manor now, O.K.? That's why I called this gig a Ball, see. Like it's got to have dignity, O.K.? As for the money, that's nothing. No problem.'

Barr folded the paper and tossed it on to the back seat. 'So what?' he said.

'You've heard of Jig Sutton?'

'I've seen the name.'

'He's rough. A little monster. Too much money too soon.'

'I can see how that might be a problem.'

'The sort who believes his own publicity. An arrogant creep. And most of his friends are the same – long-haired, jet-setting, degenerate layabouts. The General thinks they should be taught a little modesty.'

'The General?'

'You'll meet him later. Well, would you like to drop in on the party? It's tonight.'

'I don't think I'm dressed for it,' said Barr.

'No-one will notice,' said Piotrowski.

Barr shrugged and settled back as the car moved forward. He was a stranger to the area, he had no idea where they were, but his companion drove as though he knew every twist and turn of the narrow roads. After about fifteen minutes of steady driving, they reached a turn-off where an AA sign marked GRANTLEIGH HALL pointed in the direction of a shadowy lane. A man in a uniform which Barr could not identify but which he thought might be that of a security guard, was directing a large car towards the lane. Piotrowski pulled to a halt at the side of the road, waited until the car, edging forward cautiously, had disappeared and flashed his headlamps three times. The man came towards them; he was of average height, but broadshouldered and heavy, and he walked with a kind of rolling gait which made Barr quicken with recognition.

'How is it?' asked Piotrowski.

'A doddle,' said the man. 'No problem, no problem at all.' He looked through the open window, past Piotrowski, towards Barr. 'Evening, Major,' he said.

'Colleano!' said Barr. 'Joe Colleano. Christ, don't tell me you've come down to directing the bloody traffic!'

'I heard you were coming, sir,' said Colleano. 'With you around, it'll be like old times.'

'I'm not sure that I will be around,' Barr said. 'I don't know anything about the set-up yet.'

'No problem, no problem at all,' said Colleano, cheerfully. 'It's the best caper I've ever been in, no kidding. I haven't enjoyed myself so much since my old woman fell down a manhole.' He turned back to Piotrowski. 'They're thinning out now. Just the odd car.'

'Yes. Time to pull out. Jump in.'

With Colleano in the back, Piotrowski drove past the lane and continued on for about a mile. Barr noticed that there were AA signs, similar to the one at the turn-off, fastened to trees at the side of the road, all of them pointing back in the direction from which they had come. Along the route they had to pull in to the side on two occasions to allow cars to pass them; in each of these cars Barr saw people dressed in elaborate costumes, guests on their way to the Ball.

They came, at length, to a junction where three roads met. Two of them were blocked by poles resting on trestles, with red warning lights at each end. From each road-block there hung a large NO ENTRY sign; a bigger notice bearing the inscription GRANTLEIGH HALL and an arrow, was positioned to one side, directing traffic along the third road. A small blue truck was parked at the verge of the lane.

A man, dressed in the same sort of uniform as Colleano, approached the Jaguar. 'All okay,' he said.

'Right,' said Piotrowski. 'That'll do. Pack up and get out.' He pointed to one of the road-blocks. 'Push that aside. I want to get through. I've got to pick up Purcell – and I've got a friend here who wants to see the fun.'

The man glanced at Barr curiously and shrugged. He signalled to a second man who was standing in the shadows by the truck, and together they picked up the pole on one of the blocks and hurled it to one side. Piotrowski acknowledged this with a wave of the hand and drove on.

The sky was heavy and overcast and swirling wraiths of mist forced Piotrowski to slow down from time to time. Beads of moisture gathering on the windows, mingled with each other and trickled in streams down the glass. Peering ahead, Piotrowski chuckled.

'Couldn't have picked a better night for it, Joe!' he said.

The road dipped for a few yards and then began to climb. At the summit Piotrowski slowed and pulled up alongside a barred gate. 'Now,' he said, 'let's take a look.'

The night air was damp and chill after the warmth of the car and Barr shivered as he joined the other two men at the gate. The open ground beyond sloped downwards and below, in the distance, he could see a big, irregular area of bright yellow light; but then, as his eyes became adjusted to the scene, he saw that this effect was caused by what seemed to be hundreds of different lights cutting their individual swathes in all directions through the enveloping darkness, as though someone had massed an army of spotlights down there in the valley. As some lights went out, others came on, like so many will-o'-the-wisps flickering over the ground. To the right, on high ground overlooking the valley, he could see more lights and the outline of a great country house. And then, faintly at first, his ears captured a low, intermittent blare, like the sound of a distant traffic jam.

Swirls of mist began to eddy across the field, blotting out their vision, and Piotrowski cursed expressively. He took a flashlight from the car, climbed the gate, and began to find his way around the edge of the field, followed by the others. The ground, even on the higher slope, was soft and squelchy, and here and there little pools of water gleamed in the rutted earth. Barr could feel the mud sucking over the tops of his light shoes, the damp soaking into his feet, and he marvelled at his own stupidity in allowing Piotrowski to lead him such a devil's dance. Yet at the same time, he was intrigued, for with every step, the angry blaring of car-horns grew louder and in among that chorus he began to make out the sound of people shouting and calling. At one point, imposing itself on the general noise, he heard a woman's voice raised in a shrill scream.

They were very close now and Piotrowski, switching off the flashlight, moved more cautiously. As they emerged from a screen of low trees, the mist cleared suddenly, like a curtain lifting on a play, and Barr looked with astonishment on a scene of unbelievable chaos. The field beyond the trees was thick with cars, jammed together so tightly that it was almost impossible for any one of them to move. Those in the front had clearly tried to reverse and break out but they had been hemmed in by later arrivals and now they were all stuck in the marshy ground, car facing car, their headlights blazing at each other like angry beasts. A Rolls-Royce, with a small pennant hanging limply from the bonnet, its engine roaring, sent up a stream of mud as its wheels churned in the soft earth, desperately trying to take hold.

Beyond all this, at what seemed to be the entrance to the field, other cars were arriving to add to the confusion, and a steady stream of people, almost all of them in costume, was moving towards one end of the field. Barr saw a woman, her elaborately piled hair beginning to fall about her ears, her long, ornate gown held up to the knees, picking her way carefully through the massed cars. A man in a powdered wig and silken hose, his costume glittering in the light, was holding the woman's arm in one hand and a pair of buckled shoes in the other. Another man, in the scarlet robes of a Cardinal was screaming obscenities at a uniformed chauffeur, while a girl dressed as a pageboy clung to his arm and wailed hysterically.

Piotrowski made a signal and they went on, skirting the chaos of cars, and moving parallel to the line of people, until they reached the limits of the field. There was a stile here, and beyond it a steep, narrow track which appeared to lead upwards to the house on the hill. A man in uniform stood by the stile, a flashlight in his hand, directing people towards the track. He was affable and apologetic at the same time as he helped the angry women over the obstacle and turned aside the abuse hurled at him by the men.

'Sorry about this, sir. Not my fault. You're nearly there now, though. Up that track and you'll find the house. Sorry.' He repeated the same phrases over and over again.

If anything, the ground was in worse condition here than in the field below, and hampered by their costumes, they slipped and slithered up the track, desperately trying to maintain their balance. One stoutly-built man in the uniform of a Swiss Guard tripped and fell face downwards in the mud; he clutched at the legs of the man in front in an effort to pull himself up, but only succeeded in bringing him down also. They slithered back down the track, struggling wildly together, bringing others down with them. The air quivered with the sound of weeping and cursing, and the wild shouts of those who had been separated from their companions.

'I told you it would be better than a large Scotch,' whispered Piotrowski. 'What a bloody sight! Did you ever see or hear anything like it!'

'It's the best yet, the best yet!' said Colleano.

'Hold it!' said Piotrowski urgently.

He stood listening, his head cocked. Above the noise from the crowded field and the track, it was possible to hear the wail of a police siren; and then, as if it were an echo, another siren sounded from the opposite direction.

'Get Purcell,' said Piotrowski, 'we'd best be moving.'

Colleano broke cover, moved over to the man at the stile, and whispered to him. The man nodded, and as soon as a gap appeared in the line of people, he slipped away to join Piotrowski and the others. The four men began the ascent back up the field to the car.

As they drew near the gate, Piotrowski checked suddenly, clicking off the flashlight and holding up a hand in warning. He waited a moment, moved forward a few more paces, and stopped again. Barr was close behind. He could see the gate now and the shadowy figures of two uniformed men, hear them talking together.

'Road-blocks. They put up road-blocks a mile from the Hall and directed all the cars down the lower road, along Platt's Lane, into Long Meadow. Look at the bloody mess down there – you can see it from here.'

'Who the hell would want to do that?' said another, younger voice.

'I reckon myself it's them Churchill chaps. I mean, who else would have the nerve?'

'Bloody right too, if you ask me,' said the younger man. 'All that money on a party. 'Tisn't right. Take me, forty years to earn what they're spending in one night.'

'Maybe. All the same, they've broke the law and that's where we come in.'

'Reckon this car belongs to them, do you?'

'We'll see, won't we? When they come back, we'll be waiting.'

Piotrowski signalled to Colleano and Purcell, indicating that they should try to get on to the road lower down and approach the Jaguar from behind. He whispered briefly to Colleano, who nodded in response, and then the two men slipped away into the darkness, disappearing like wraiths.

'What the hell have you got me into!' hissed Barr, and it was a challenge rather than a question. Piotrowski dropped a hand on his arm, and grinned.

'Not to worry, not to worry,' he murmured soothingly. He shaded his watch with his hand, and studied the luminous dial, while Barr watched in growing irritation.

'Right!' Piotrowski said, and straightened up. 'Wait here till I give the all clear.' He switched on the flashlight and began to move towards the gate, whistling cheerfully.

The two policemen turned towards the light and the sound, then moved to the gate, where they stood peering into the field. As they did so, Colleano and Purcell closed in from behind, so quietly that the policemen heard and felt nothing until they were on them. The older man went down like a felled tree; the younger man half avoided Purcell's attack and turned to offer resistance, but Colleano pivoted round and swung at his throat with the edge of his hand. The young policeman gurgled as the blow jarred home and fell beside his companion.

Barr squelched through the mud and climbed the gate behind Piotrowski. 'Listen,' he said, 'listen! I've had enough. I don't know what game you're playing and I don't much care. Just get me back to the main road and I'll find my way from there!'

'You've got an appointment with the guv'nor,' said Piotrowski.

'Tell him I can't make it,' said Barr.

'He may not like that.'

'Too bad!' Barr looked down at the unconscious policemen. 'I don't like this either, so that makes us square.'

It was then that he felt the gun in his back.

Chapter Seven

1

'Do you mean to say that the police have got absolutely nothing on these people?' The Prime Minister leaned forward in his chair and glared at the Home Secretary across the Cabinet table. The famous bushy eyebrows, so beloved of the cartoonists, quivered above the pale eyes and the slightly puffy face.

'Not as yet,' replied the Home Secretary calmly. 'Naturally they are following up a number of leads – '

'Leads!' The Prime Minister wrinkled his nose. 'Do you know that the Foreign Secretary has had three embassies on to him this morning? And I've had at least six calls. Some very important people were involved in that fiasco last night. They set out to go to a party and finish up in a field up to their necks in mud! And strange as it may seem, they didn't like it, Harry, they didn't like it one little bit!'

'Do you mean very important or very rich?' said the Home Secretary. 'There is a difference. I don't condone what happened but, in my view, they were asking for trouble. To spend that sort of money on a party at this time was stupid – a provocation of the worst kind.'

He looked thoughtfully at a fingernail for a moment, and then favoured the Prime Minister with a thin smile. The two men had been colleagues for almost thirty years, but there was no friendship between them: beyond their membership of the same party, they had little in common. Both were able, talented men and, as a result of working together, each had developed a grudging respect for the other's abilities; but it went no further than this, their partnership touched no deeper chord. They were like two powerful and hostile bears, continually circling each other, wanting to

91

strike but afraid to commit themselves to a struggle because neither could be sure of the outcome.

The door opened a few inches and the Principal Private Secretary's face appeared.

'It's ten o'clock, Prime Minister,' he said, looking diffidently towards the two men at the long coffin-shaped table. 'Everyone is here.'

'In five minutes,' the Prime Minister said. 'Give us five minutes.'

The face disappeared and the door, with its covering of baize, closed gently. The Prime Minister turned again to the Home Secretary. 'I don't like the smell of this Churchill Commando business.' He tapped his nose. 'I don't like the smell of it at all. That's all I'm trying to say. Right?'

'Politically, you mean? The political consequences?'

'Of course. What else? Look, in the space of little more than two days we've had four incidents. They've all been different in type and scale, but there is a single common factor. Each one has been designed to exploit a particular, popular prejudice and win the maximum public support and sympathy. Football hooligans, pornographers, extreme Left-wing groups, and last night, a bunch of long-haired pop singers and their jet-setting friends. Right?'

The Home Secretary nodded, but without enthusiasm. His colleague's habit of closing a statement with a question – his continual use of the word 'Right?' irritated him. He scratched at a tiny spot on the sleeve of his jacket and glanced up at the portrait of Sir Robert Walpole on the wall behind the Prime Minister. Then he became aware of the silence and saw that the other man was waiting for his full measure of attention. 'Go on,' he said, 'I'm listening.'

'Thank you,' said the Prime Minister. 'Well, suddenly it's happening. The backlash. Someone has come along and translated the fantasies of the man in the street into reality. Not us, not the police. But these Churchill people. And you've seen the result – right? Pictures of the Old Man going up everywhere. And this – ' His fingers drummed a brief rally on the pile of newspapers which lay on the table before him. 'In Gloucester, Bournemouth and Dundee groups of worthy citizens have announced the formation of what they call the Churchill Movement. They've disassociated themselves from the methods of the Commando, but declared support for its policies. Did you see that?'

'Yes, I did. The police are aware of the danger. They'll crack down on any attempt to organise vigilante groups.'

'I don't doubt the efficiency of the police. But this thing could spread, believe me. It could spread like a forest fire, and get beyond control. The silent majority on the march. It's been on the cards for a long time, Harry. It only needed something to trigger it off – and what happened this weekend has done just that. Don't underestimate the feeling or the danger. Unless we check it – and check it quickly – it could topple us. We're down to a majority of two now. A couple of bye-elections and we could be out. Right?'

'I'm not underestimating anything, Prime Minister,' said the Home Secretary, 'but on the other hand, I don't think we should allow ourselves to over-react. We've seen this sort of thing before – '

'Not like this, not like this,' said the Prime Minister, interrupting him.

'All right. Perhaps not quite like this. But we've had extreme minority groups to deal with, and all sorts of organised violence. In the end, these groups burn themselves out.' The Home Secretary spoke without conviction, rather out of the habit of opposition than anything else. He had never lost his respect for the Prime Minister's political instinct, for his ability to sense the mood of the country. and the strength of the other man's concern had shaken him. Was he being too complacent? He added quickly: 'All the same, I assure you that we're not treating this thing lightly. The police are giving it No. 1 priority. I'm in constant touch. But it's basically their job and we must let them get on with it. If you'd like to talk to the Commissioner – '

'No, no. I'm sure you're right. Just keep leaning on him, that's all.'

'I shall do that, don't worry.'

The Prime Minister nodded and sat for a moment without speaking. The only sound in the room was the faint rustle of newsprint as he fidgeted with one of the papers. Then he sighed, the long, deep sigh of a weary man.

'This is a funny one.' He spoke as though to himself. 'Perhaps the big one. I can feel it in my water. I don't like it.' His voice took on a firmer tone. 'No. This isn't just a bunch of cranks out on the loose. The tone of their manifesto, for example. Clever, very clever. All that stuff about supporting democratic institutions – and the bit about posing no threat to any decent citizen, whatever his age, race, colour or religion. There's a shrewd political mind somewhere in the background. Well, shrewd politicians only want one thing – and you and I both know what that is, right? Power, Harry, power. A politician without power is like a jockey without a horse. His number isn't even on the board – he's a non-starter. My hunch is that what we've seen so far is only the beginning – ' He checked and glanced at his watch. 'Better have the others in and get on with the meeting.'

'Do you want me to raise this business?'

'I don't think so. No point. If someone else brings it up, just tell them what you've told me – that the police are giving the matter top priority.' The Prime Minister stood up, squaring his shoulders as though for battle. 'Oh, one other thing,' he said softly. 'I'm proposing to postpone two Bills. They're both yours, I'm afraid. Prison Reform and the measure to widen the abortion laws.'

'Now, wait a minute!' The Home Secretary rose, his face pink with anger, and faced the Prime Minister. 'On what grounds?'

'Suppose we say lack of parliamentary time? Pressure on the legislative programme?'

'I was promised time – it had already been allocated!'

'It is only a postponement. You shall have your Bills. But not just now. For the moment, I think we should keep a low profile on this sort of social, reforming legislation.'

The Home Secretary made an effort to calm himself. The Prime Minister was one of the very few people capable of shaking his normally impeccable control and he had come to the meeting this morning determined not to be provoked; yet somehow the other man had found a way through his guard. In a controlled voice he asked: 'You're doing this because of what happened this weekend, isn't that so? What you're saying is that the Churchill Commando have won the first round!'

'Nothing of the sort!' said the Prime Minister sharply. 'I'm doing it because of the mood in the country. That's all. With our thin majority we can't take any chances. People think there's been enough prison reform – that we pamper the prison population too much as it is. As for abortion – well, you know what an outcry there has been already. Of course, if you want to challenge my decision in Cabinet – '

The two men stood staring at each other, the hostility and dislike flowing between them with the quivering force of an electric current. The thought of resignation leaped into the mind of the Home Secretary and he was on the point of putting it into words when he saw the glint of anticipation in the other man's eyes and drew back, avoiding the trap. When he did speak, his voice crackled with sarcasm like ice underfoot.

'Perhaps you'd like me to go a step further and introduce a Bill to bring back the death penalty?'

'I shouldn't joke, Harry,' said the Prime Minister coldly. 'It might well come to that.'

'Over my dead body!' said the Home Secretary.

'It could come to that too,' said the Prime Minister and then he smiled. 'Sorry. Nothing personal. I'm in my Cassandra mood this morning. I have forebodings of doom.'

2

There were three men in the room, standing with their heads together over a trestle table on which there was a large map. Two of them turned as Barr entered and looked towards him; nothing showed on their faces, not even curiosity. Neither could have been older than twenty-five but their hair, which was close-cut, gave them an odd, old-fashioned appearance. They were wearing dark-blue uniforms made in the style of the wartime British battledress; the taller of the two carried on his shoulder lapels the insignia of a captain, and the other man that of a lieutenant. Both men carried revolvers, the butts showing above the holsters which hung at their sides.

'Major Barr, sir,' snapped the escort, and at once the two officers stiffened, and their right arms rose and fell in a formal, military salute, their heels clicked. Barr hesitated, wondering whether to respond: in the end he compromised with a small, ironic signal of the hand.

'Thank you, sergeant,' said the third man without turning, and the escort saluted smartly and went out, closing the door. The man studied the map for a moment or two longer, and then turned towards Barr with a welcoming smile. He was dressed in a uniform of similar style to that of the young officers, except that his bore no insignia of rank and he appeared to be unarmed. He was tall, slim, with short, wiry, greying hair, and Barr judged that he was in his early fifties: the smile made wrinkles in his lean, tanned face, giving him a look of extraordinary charm, but it was the eyes that stunned Barr. They were the colour of amber, clear and lambent yet glowing with a magnetism which was almost overwhelming; force and strength seemed to flow from them in subtle, invisible waves, dominating the room.

'Major Barr,' said the man, extending a hand. 'Welcome, welcome.' He spoke with deliberation, in a deep, resonant voice. 'Allow me to introduce myself. Wilcox, Major-General Wilcox.'

Barr took a step forward and almost grasped the out-stretched hand, but he remembered his anger just in time, and pointedly ignored the gesture. The General looked down at his hand as thought surprised to see it there, and lowered it slowly.

'Is anything wrong, Major?' he asked softly.

'Oh, no,' said Barr. 'I like having a gun stuck in my ribs, I enjoy being locked up for the night.'

'I apologise, Major. I was anxious to meet you last even-ing but it proved to be impossible. I was detained else-where. As for the rest, I am afraid that your friend Piot-rowski disobeyed orders. He was instructed not to involve you in last night's affair.' He glanced at his watch. 'Dis-regard for orders and indiscipline is something we cannot tolerate. You will appreciate that, I'm sure. Piotrowski and the others have already been court-martialled and found guilty. Sentence will be carried out in exactly one minute.'

'Sentence?' said Barr.

'Of course. If you care to step over here – ' Wilcox motioned towards the window, still smiling, and Barr moved across.

He found himself looking down at a square-shaped yard, paved with flagstones; long, low buildings framed the area on three sides, and beyond these Barr could see green fields, dipping away at first and rising towards some wooded hills. One of the officers came up beside him and threw open the casement window, letting in a stream of cool air which stirred the papers on the desk behind them.

Seven men came into the yard, moving in brisk, military order. Four of them, two in the front and two at the rear, were armed with sub-machine guns, and between them marched three prisoners, their hands bound behind their backs; Colleano, Piotrowski and Purcell. Barr watched in growing bewilderment as, in response to a shouted order, the group came to a halt, crashing their boots smartly on the stone surface of the yard. Three of the armed men took up positions just below the window, while the fourth, who was wearing the stripes of a corporal, marched the prisoners across to the wall opposite and stationed them against it.

For a moment, Barr had the uncanny feeling that none of this was real, that he was watching a scene from an old film. The men standing by the wall with their hands tied, Colleano even accepting a lighted cigarette from the corporal, the other men waiting below him, their guns cocked in readiness – this was the stuff of Hollywood, he could not believe that it was actually happening. He turned and saw that the General was watching him, a glint of amusement in those extraordinary eyes, as though he was waiting for Barr to respond to the situation.

'What the hell is this – what are they doing?' Barr had to force out the words; they seemed to stick in his throat, and his voice sounded unfamiliar, as though someone else had spoken.

The General seemed unperturbed. He patted Barr on the shoulder as if to reassure him and turned to the window. In the yard below, Colleano took a long drag in his cigarette, blew out a column of smoke, and with a contemptuous gesture flicked the butt in the direction of the armed men. Piotrowski, half-lounging against the wall, looked equally unconcerned, but Purcell, the third prisoner, was standing erect, his eyes closed and his lips moving as though in prayer.

The corporal marched forward stiffly, came to attention, and looked up to the window. 'All present and correct, sir!' he shouted, his voice echoing across the yard. His arm rose and fell in a salute.

The General returned the salute and nodded once, with studied deliberation. Then, as the corporal turned towards the armed men and barked an order, Barr broke out of the strange spell which seemed to be holding him back and blazed into action. Swinging round, he plucked the revolver from the holster of the nearest officer, and shoved him aside so violently that he crashed into the map-table. In almost the same movement Barr turned and pointed the revolver at the General.

'Right!' he said. 'Call them off! Call them off. If you don't, you go with them.' He moved behind the General, using him as a screen, and prodded him forward. 'Call them off!' Again, Barr experienced this strong sense of unreality. The young officer he had charged aside was picking himself up from the floor, and he was smiling, as though in pleasure. Moreover, the other officer had made no attempt to go for his own revolver, and there was a look of amusement on his face also. It was as if they were enjoying a joke at Barr's expense.

The General took a step towards the window. 'All right, men!' he called. 'Fall out. I'm afraid Major Barr has a gun at my back. The party's over.'

And then an extraordinary thing happened. As Barr watched the three prisoners broke into broad smiles and brought their arms from behind their backs, with the cords which were supposed to be binding their wrists dangling loose.

'Good on you, Major!' Piotrowski shouted, and lifted both thumbs towards Barr in a gesture of appreciation.

The other men gathered in a group below the window, shaking their heads with amusement, some openly laughing. Eventually the corporal ordered them to break it up, and they strolled away, the execution squad and their erstwhile targets, still murmuring and laughing together.

Ignoring the revolver, the General turned to face the angry and bewildered Barr. 'That was excellent, Major,' he said. 'A very impressive display of loyalty to your old comrades. I apologise for the deception. It was a little juvenile, I admit – but we thought it might be useful to devise some sort of test.'

'With me on the sharp end!' snapped Barr. He looked down at the revolver in his hand. 'You'd have been in a bloody mess if I'd pulled this trigger.'

'Oh, no,' said the General. 'Even our sense of humour doesn't extend as far as that. It isn't loaded.' He smiled and this time, drew a wry smile from Barr.

'Bloody hell!' said Barr. 'It gets worse by the minute!'

He tossed the gun towards the officer, who caught it deftly.

'I have heard a great deal about you, Major,' said the General. 'Enough to know that you are a fine soldier. I have no doubt of your professional skills, but I needed to know a little more than that, to see for myself what kind of man you are. You see, I set a high price on a man's capacity for loyalty. It is a quality I prize above all else. No great enterprise can succeed without it – and we here are engaged in a very great enterprise indeed. We have pledged our lives to this cause, and that is the highest loyalty of all. I am glad you have come, Major. I hope, I hope very much, that we shall be able to engage your sympathy, your support, and your undoubted loyalty.'

The phrasing was oddly rotund and formal, like a speech prepared for a special occasion, but the man seemed to cast a spell over the words, endowing them with a sincerity which intrigued Barr, and dispersed the last remnants of his anger. But he was suspicious of speechmakers. He had learned that words could be more deadly than weapons, seen them rob decent men of all reason. Too often it was the wrong causes which used the right words.

'I'm not a great one for causes, General,' he said cautiously. 'I only ever found one in my life that I thought worth fighting for. It was a lost cause at that – a very painful experience.'

'Come outside,' said the General, 'it is a pity to waste the sunshine.'

3

It was an old house, and very beautiful. They walked in the garden, away from the yard and the modern buildings at the rear, over fresh, green lawns and long terraces draped with aubretia and daffodils. Fruit trees, pink and white with blossom, spread their arms along the red brick of the enclosing wall, goldfish brightened the clear water of an ornamental pond. It seemed a hundred years and a thousand miles away from the scene Barr had witnessed a few minutes before.

'How much do you know about us, Major?' asked the General.

'Very little. Whitaker told me that someone was recruiting men and that the pay was good – that's all. He put Piotrowski in touch with me – and here I am.'

'A true mercenary!'

'That's right,' said Barr. 'Have rifle, will travel. Anywhere, and for anyone. If the money is good.'

'A man I know, a good friend of mine and yours, would not entirely agree with that statement.'

'Then he doesn't know me.'

'On the contrary. He did know you very well. His name is Colonel Ojukwu.' As Barr stopped and stared in surprise, the General smiled and continued, 'I was in Biafra during the war. Quite unofficially and only briefly. I was a serving officer at the time and if the British army authorities had found out, I would have been cashiered. I went there to meet Ojukwu, and to give what help and advice I could. He often spoke of you, and always with respect and admiration.'

'I was paid to do a job. I did it,' said Barr.

'Oh, no. It was more than that. You do have a conscience, Major. Why be afraid to admit it?'

Barr made no answer but he bristled inwardly. He valued the privacy of his own thoughts and motivations, he was not prepared to have them analysed or discussed. The General seemed to sense this, for he made no attempt to pursue the subject.

He stopped by a magnolia bush, and parting the dark, green leaves, peered anxiously at a bird's nest which was perched precariously on the thin branches and put a careful finger on one of the small bluish eggs.

'Warm,' he said, and looked upwards. 'She'll not be far away.' And then suddenly, with a glance at Barr, 'You're not married are you, Major?'

'No,' said Barr edgily. This was a private area also, not

to be invaded. He had a momentary vision of Iris lying beside him in the house in Papua–New Guinea, sleeping as she always slept, with a hand under her cheek and her long, incredibly fine hair spread across the pillow, and his heart quickened . . .

'I lost my wife three years ago,' he heard the General say quietly, in a matter-of-fact voice. 'Odd, really. She was killed by a bomb on a London Underground train. I.R.A. Quite indiscriminate, I mean they weren't specifically aiming at her. She'd just gone to town for the day to do some shopping. And where was I? On active service in Northern Ireland. You might call it one of death's little ironies.'

As they walked on he pulled at the fingers of his left hand, cracking the knuckles. 'You say you know little about us, Major. But you must have learned something from that escapade last night – and you've probably guessed a good deal more. Am I right?'

'The Churchill Commando?' said Barr.

'You tell me,' said the General.

'I'm telling you. It wouldn't take a genius to work that one out. Whitaker was very cagey about the job, where it was, and so on – '

'He doesn't know,' said the General. 'We took care to tell him as little as possible. He deals through Piotrowski and then only indirectly. Whitaker is well-paid and I imagine that is all that interests him.'

'He's not an idiot. If I can put two and two together, so can he. If he decided to go to the police – '

'No, I don't think he'll do that,' said the General with a smile. 'Your friend Piotrowski has made it plain, in his own inimitable way, that the consequences of such a move could be very painful, even fatal. Let us leave Whitaker,' he continued more seriously. 'You said upstairs that you had only known one cause that was worth fighting for. I assume you meant Biafra?'

'I'm not even sure about that now,' Barr said.

'What about your own country, what about Britain?'

'What about it?'

'Is that not worth fighting for?'

'If there was a war – I suppose, yes.'

'We are at war,' said the General earnestly. 'That is the mistake people make. What we have in Britain today is merely the illusion of peace. We are at war, we are under attack from an enemy as ruthless as the Nazis and far more insidious. But the tragedy is that today we ourselves are the enemy, we have become our own Fifth Column. In the last twenty years I have watched this country grow shabby, lazy, greedy, and brutish. I have watched it happen with growing despair. There is no pride, dignity or vitality any more. Think about it, Major! At one time, we were respected throughout the world, for our industry, our craftsmanship, our political institutions, our way of life, our tolerance, our commonsense and – not least – for our courage. What has happened? We have become a stagnant pond in which the scum has risen to the surface.'

He stooped and plucked a tuft of couch-grass from the lawn, tugging at the obstinate root until it released its hold. He held it in his open hand for a moment, then closed his fingers around it, making a fist. 'Once you let this stuff take hold, you can say goodbye to your lawn.'

He turned abruptly to face Barr and there was a mixture of anguish and anger in his voice.

'Something has to be done, Major, it has to be done now, quickly, or it will be too late. We've tried to talk the problems away, we've passed pious resolutions, preached worthy sermons – all to no effect, like trying to cure a mental breakdown with an aspirin! I love this country, Major, I love this country and its people. Oh, I know it's not fashionable to talk in those terms but I don't care for fashion, I never have. I want to bring back courtesy, order, self-discipline, respect. I want to see this country – ' He stopped suddenly and as the tension left his face he smiled. 'I'm sorry. I didn't mean to get on to my soap-box.'

'Don't worry about me,' said Barr. 'If I wasn't interested, I wouldn't be listening.'

'Come over here and sit down.' The General led the way

to a seat on one of the lower terraces. As they settled back in the warm sunshine he seemed to relax and his voice assumed a quiet, conversational tone.

'About two years ago I was discussing this problem at a dinner party. The conversation went round and round, everyone grumbling about the state of the country, but it was like the gabbling of geese, without real meaning or purpose. And then, a very old lady who had remained silent up to that point suddenly pushed her chair back from the table and stood up. Everyone stopped, wondering what was going on.

' "I'm tired," she said, "and I think I'll go to bed. Would you like to know why I'm tired? It is because I'm bored. I'm bored because I've heard this same conversation a hundred times in the last ten years. I will tell you what is wrong with this country in one word. You. People like you. Talkers. Wind-makers. I am the daughter of a farmer, I was the wife of a farmer, and I know one thing for certain. You can't plough a five-acre field with your tongue or put out a forest fire by spitting on it!" '

The General leaned forward, chuckling. 'She was magnificent! Killed the conversation stone dead.'

He opened his fist and began to pluck at the piece of couch-grass, shredding it through his fingers. 'That marvellous old lady was the trigger for me. I decided that if I waited for someone else to act I might wait forever. I resigned my commission as soon as was possible and set to work. It was my intention to begin operations in the autumn, but when I read of the murder of that girl – Joy Clark – I felt I could delay no longer. When a girl can be buried alive – ' He shook his head. 'Monstrous, monstrous. And the murderers will simply go to prison, where they'll be fed at our expense and released after a few years. Well, we shall see.' He paused again and smiled. 'What you see here, Major, is the beginning. You have come at a good time.'

He brushed his hands free of the grass and cocking his head to one side he looked at Barr expectantly, as though awaiting a response. His eagerness was almost boyish, there was an element of ingenuousness, of innocence, in his manner, which both puzzled and disconcerted Barr. He found it impossible to identify this man, to classify and place him in a way which would make him easier to understand. A boy-scout playing an elaborate game? A soldier-politician ambitious for personal power? A simple patriot with a genuine, unselfish concern for his country? Or a brilliant man, burning with talent, who was just a little off balance, half-genius, half-crank? Whatever the answer, thought Barr, at least he cares, at least he is awake and alive!

All the same, because he was a practical man who liked to deal in realities, and because there was a perverse and obstinate streak in his nature, he said bluntly, 'If you want to put things right, it seems to me that you're going a very funny way about it, General.'

'You think so?'

'What have you done? Hosed down a few hooligans, shoved a man in with the pigs, stopped some of the pop set from enjoying themselves. What does it amount to? A rag. Like that bloody pantomime execution you staged for my benefit. What's the point? People think you're just a bunch of practical jokers.'

'You expect too much, Major. We have only just begun. And so far the operations have been more successful than I dared to hope. Let me explain. My first objective was to arouse some degree of mass support. For that reason, I deliberately chose to attack targets which would evoke the maximum public response. For example, the football hooligans – the whole country is tired of their animal antics. Again, I decided that the operations should, as far as possible, be non-violent – even contain an element of humour. To have gone too far at this stage would have alienated a good deal of support. Now, perhaps, we may sharpen our campaign – we shall show them that this is more than a practical joke, have no fear of that.'

'O.K. But how long do you think you can get away with

it?' Barr waved a hand towards the house. 'This set-up for instance. How long do you think it will be before the police find out what's going on, and move in?'

'We are not quite alone,' said the General. 'We have a few friends beyond that wall.'

'I can imagine,' said Barr. 'And I suppose they're putting up the money?'

'I like your directness, Major!' The General chuckled. 'Let us just say that we do not lack for friends or resources.' And as Barr shook his head, he added, 'Something else on your mind?'

'Why are you using mercenaries? It doesn't add up.'

'I needed some good professional soldiers quickly. It is as simple as that.'

'And, of course, they are expendable,' Barr said. 'If you lose one, you can always buy another.'

'Any officer who regards his soldiers as expendable is a bad commander,' replied the General sharply. 'I wouldn't give him house room! No. I have great respect for the mercenary, Major. He is like a gun, he asks no questions. He is your true professional. It is not difficult to fight, and even die, for an ideal or a cause; but to be prepared to lay your life on the line simply for pay – I admire that. It is the ultimate in professionalism!' He paused, then added reflectively, 'Do you know Housman's poem?'

'I don't even know Housman,' said Barr ruefully.

'I find that sad. Practical men sneer at poets, but they can often see farther than any of us. The good ones at anyrate. And Housman was good. He called his poem, *Epitaph on an Army of Mercenaries.*' He began to recite in a quiet, low voice as though he were running the verses through as a test of memory.

'These, in the day when heaven was falling,
    The hour when earth's foundations fled,
Followed their mercenary calling
    And took their wages and are dead.

'Their shoulders held the sky suspended;
    They stood, and earth's foundations stay;
What God abandoned, these defended,
    And saved the sum of things for pay.'

Barr nodded his head slowly as the resonant voice died away. The words echoed in his head and for some reason, which defied explanation, he felt saddened by them.

The General turned to him abruptly, dismissing the subject. 'Now to business. I have talked to you freely, Major, more freely perhaps than I should have done. But I believe that you are a man to be trusted. I now ask you the direct question – will you join us?'

Barr hesitated for only a fraction of a second. He still could not place this man and he wondered how much or how little he had been told about his real motives. But since when had that sort of thing worried him? He was bored, and the General was offering him the only certain cure for that condition – action and excitement. He looked into those clear, eager eyes and grinned.

'Why not?' he said. 'I've nothing special on at the moment.'

Chapter Eight

1

CHIEF Superintendent Charles Welwyn had lunched and wined rather well, and this, combined with the afternoon warmth of his office, had induced a certain drowsiness. He wasn't actually asleep at his desk, for he was a conscientious officer, but his eyelids were drooping and he found it difficult to concentrate on the monthly return of Crime Statistics which lay before him. There was an accumulation of other paper work to be dealt with also, and in anticipation of clearing some of this away, he had instructed the sergeant on duty in the station office downstairs that he was not to be disturbed, unless he were required by the Chief Constable, or some emergency situation arose.

The knocking startled him at first and he took a moment to bring his thoughts into focus. When he realised that someone was at the door, he shook his head, straightened up in his chair and adjusted his papers.

'Who is it?' he called irritably.

The door opened and a young, nervous face looked towards him. 'P.C. Hayes, sir.'

'Well?'

'I wonder if I could – if it is convenient – for me to have a word with you, sir. If it is convenient –'

'What about?'

'Something has come up, sir.'

'Is it important?'

'It could be, sir, I'm not sure.'

The Chief Superintendent sighed audibly, partly because he was annoyed, and partly to show the young policeman that he was intruding upon the time of a busy man. 'Well, don't stand there!' he said. 'Come in and shut the door behind you.'

'Thank you, sir.' Hayes came in, closed the door carefully and advanced towards the man at the desk. God, thought Welwyn, he looks like a schoolboy in uniform, they get younger every day! Despite his irritation he found himself regarding the young constable with approval. He disliked untidiness, and this one was neatly turned out, neither his uniform nor his shirt and tie could be faulted; the face, glowing with health, had the rugged, manly look of a sportsman, the eyes were bright and intelligent, the manner respectful without being obsequious. The flaxen hair was a trifle too long perhaps but it was clean and well-groomed and – a detail which Welwyn regarded as being of great importance – his fingernails were clean. It was Welwyn's view that you could tell a great deal about a man's character from the condition of his fingernails.

'Well, what's on your mind, Hayes?'

'It's rather difficult to explain, sir – '

'Why?'

'It – well – it could be important. On the other hand – '

'Suppose you start at the beginning? I'll soon let you know if you're wasting my time.'

'Yes, sir.' Hayes paused, gathering his thoughts; he was clearly nervous and to mask this he took refuge in safe, official language. 'As a result of observations I have made in the vicinity of Cresswold House at various times over the past three days, I have reason to believe that persons on those premises may be connected with certain recent activities of an illegal nature, sir.'

Welwyn was alert now, all his former tiredness gone, but nothing of this showed in his manner. He opened a drawer, took out a packet of menthol cigarettes and lit one. He leaned back, blowing a plume of smoke from between pursed lips, and shook his head slowly.

'And this is what you've come to see me about?'

'Yes, sir.'

'You do realise, Hayes, that Cresswold House is now an

109

official Government research station, and that the people there are engaged on work of a highly confidential nature?'

'With respect, sir – '

'Yes?'

'It calls itself the British Centre of Industrial and Technological Research – Transport Division. With respect, that is not an official Government organisation.' Hayes allowed himself a small smile of self-approval. 'I did some checking, sir. With the Department of Industry and the Department of the Environment. Neither of them has any knowledge of a British Centre of Industrial and Technological Research.' The smile disappeared as he spoke, to be replaced by an expression of great seriousness. The earlier nervousness had gone, and he stood before Welwyn with the air of a man whose initiative and perspicacity had now been established beyond doubt, and who was clearly a candidate for both praise and promotion.

The Chief Superintendent certainly seemed to be impressed. He sat for quite a long time without speaking, the blue smoke curling above his head, simply looking at Hayes, as though weighing the significance of the constable's statement. A motor-cycle began to roar in the car-yard below and Welwyn, with a gesture of irritation, rose from the desk and went over to close the window. Without turning he said, 'Tell me about these observations of yours.' He spoke so softly that Hayes only heard half the words.

'Beg pardon, sir. I didn't catch – '

Welwyn swung round and faced him. 'You said you'd made certain observations. Did you or didn't you?'

'Yes, sir. I mean, yes, I did, sir.'

'Then tell me about them!' Hayes slipped a notebook from the top pocket of his tunic, but Welwyn interrupted him before he could open it. 'Give me that!' he said sharply. He took the notebook, flipped through it casually, and then put it down on the desk. 'Never mind your notes. Just tell me what you saw in plain language.'

'Well, sir, as you know, Cresswold House was taken over by the Centre, as they call themselves, about six months ago.

They built three or four big huts in the grounds alongside the old house and surrounded the perimeter with that high wire fence. There was a lot of coming and going at first – transport and men moving in and out – but for the past couple of months it's been fairly quiet. They keep themselves pretty much to themselves up there. They're only three miles from the town but they never seem to go in – not even for supplies, or for a night out, or anything like that. My brother-in-law is manager of a grocery store in the High Street – '

'You said you'd made observations over the past three days,' interrupted Welwyn. 'Let's leave your family and get to that, shall we?'

'Yes, sir. Very good, sir. As I said, it's been quiet up there for the last couple of months. Until this weekend. I was up that way early Saturday morning and I saw two big trucks and a red Jag leaving the place. The registration number of one of the trucks is in the notebook, sir.'

'Wouldn't you expect to see trucks and cars up there, considering that they are supposed to be doing research into transport?'

'Of course, sir. In the normal way, I wouldn't have given the matter a second thought. But as one of the trucks pulled over to pass me, the canvas sheet covering the back came adrift. I noticed that the truck was filled with men and as far as I could see they were wearing dark blue overalls. And I caught a glimpse of something that looked like a searchlight. They put the sheet back quickly and that made me wonder. I mean, it was quite a mild day – you'd have thought they would welcome a bit of fresh air. Why should they want to hide themselves?'

'Go on,' said Welwyn.

'Well, I don't suppose I would have bothered much about it. But when I read about the Churchill Commando in the Sunday papers, I began to think. According to the reports, they used searchlights when they cornered those football hooligans – and the men involved were wearing dark overalls, rather like uniforms.'

'And you connected the two things – the Churchill Commando and the men you saw in the truck?'

'Yes, sir. In a sort of way – yes.'

'Why didn't you come to me straight away and tell me of your suspicions?'

'I wasn't sure in myself, sir. It could all have been coincidence. I mean, I thought – we all thought – that this Centre was some kind of official outfit, maybe working on top-secret projects. But I couldn't get it out of my mind – and that's when I decided to check with the Government departments in London.'

'How did you do that?'

'I've a friend who is a journalist in Fleet Street. He used to work for our local paper. I asked him to make some enquiries.'

'Did you tell him why you were asking?'

'No, sir. Definitely not. I said I knew someone who wanted to try and get a job there – and asked him to find out where to apply.'

'And he came back with the information that the Centre is not an official Government organisation, is that it?'

'He couldn't find anyone who knew anything about it, sir.'

'I see,' said Welwyn. He went slowly back to his seat at the desk. 'Is that all?'

'One more thing, sir.' Hayes took a deep breath, as if to emphasise that he was now about to reach the most vital part of his report. 'This morning, sir, I took some binoculars, went up to the Centre, and worked my way round to the back, through Heslop Wood. About two hundred yards from the perimeter fence, there is a big, old cedar. I climbed up as high as I could, and this gave me a view of a section of the yard behind the old house.' He paused to clear his throat and then, weighing every word, he continued: 'I saw men in dark uniforms moving about the yard, sir. Some of them were carrying arms – rifles. I couldn't see the whole yard, but it looked to me as if they were doing military drill. I counted ten men, but I'm positive there were more.'

'I see.' Welwyn nodded gravely. 'I see.' He rubbed his chin with a finger, making a circular motion. 'Well, I'm pleased you came to me about this, Hayes. You've shown commendable initiative. It will not be forgotten.'

'Thank you, sir.' The constable's face went pink with pleasure.

'What I am going to tell you now is secret and confidential,' Welwyn continued. 'It must not be mentioned outside this room – not to anyone, not even to your wife. Is that clear?'

'Yes, sir. Of course, sir.'

'Good. If it does go any further, I shall find out and I shall know who is responsible. And you could be in very, very serious trouble.'

'It won't, sir, it won't.'

'Right. The first thing I have to say is that you have been wrongly informed. The Centre operating at Cresswold House is a Government establishment, despite what your journalist friend told you. Naturally, the people he contacted had no knowledge of it – its existence and purpose is known only to a very few top people. Even we don't know what they do up there – we've simply been told to keep an eye on the place and to keep people away. The order came from the highest authority, Hayes. The Centre could be some sort of secret military establishment, it could be connected with intelligence, it could be anything. There are some times when it's wiser not to ask questions. Do you understand?'

'Yes, sir. I probably did wrong to go up there and start poking around.'

'Perhaps. But you weren't to know. And you have uncovered a weakness in their security system. I mean, that cedar tree and the approach through Heslop Wood. They must be warned about that. Now, have you anything further to add?'

'No, sir. Thank you, sir.'

'Good.' Welwyn picked up the notebook. 'I shall retain this, and see that it is destroyed. And you will forget this conversation the moment you leave this room. It didn't happen. If anyone asks why you came to see me, tell them it was on a personal matter, not connected with the job. Right. Off you go, constable.'

As Hayes moved away, Welwyn said, 'Tell me, Hayes, what do you think of these Churchill people?'

The younger man hesitated, as though he were deciding what was the right thing to say. 'Well, sir, they're breaking the law, aren't they?'

'Yes, of course,' said Welwyn. 'But aside from that – what do you think? Off the record.'

'I agree with a lot of what they said in their manifesto, or whatever you call it. It's time something was done.'

'So you approve, do you? Maybe not as a copper, but as a man.'

'I don't go all the way, sir. I don't like what they did to those two policemen last night – if it *was* them. But those football hooligans, and that rich mob at the party – people who have never done a day's work in their lives – I reckon they deserved all they got. That's my frank opinion, sir,' he added apologetically.

'Thank you,' said Welwyn. He waited until the door closed behind Hayes and then began to flip through the notebook. He studied the last two or three entries carefully, then he set it down and pressed a button on the inter-office communication speaker.

There was a brief buzz, the click of a switch, and a voice said curtly, 'Inspector Cantwell.'

'Welwyn here, Ronnie.'

The voice at the other end assumed a warmer and more respectful tone. 'Yes, sir. Anything I can do, sir?'

'Yes. Young P.C. Hayes – what do you think of him?'

'Anything wrong, sir?'

'I didn't say that.'

'Sorry, sir. He's a good enough lad. Got a way to go yet, but he'll make it. He's applied to go into plain-clothes with the C.I.D. on a couple of occasions, fancies himself as a detective, I think. But I reckon he's just a bit too raw. I can bring up his records if you want, sir – '

'No need for that. Ronnie, I want him posted to Rackham.'

'Rackham? But that's on the other side of the county, sir.'

'I know where it is!' said Welwyn.

'It's a good sixty or seventy miles from where he's living – he'd have to move or go into lodgings – '

'Ronnie,' said Welwyn, 'I've moved house nine times since I joined the force. Do it, will you?'

'If you say so, sir. Of course. What shall I tell him though? He'll want a reason.'

'Tell him nothing. Or maybe hint that going to Rackham is a step in the right direction for him – that it will be good for his career. But don't bring my name into it. O.K.?'

'Wilco, sir.'

'I want it done immediately, Ronnie. I want Hayes to report to Rackham within twenty-four hours.'

'Yes, sir.'

'One more thing, Ronnie. The prison escort for Fraser and Gladstone. Have you got the details?'

'That's all fixed, sir. No problems.'

'Send up the papers. The timing, route, everything. This could be a tricky one. I'd like to check it.'

'Yes, sir.' The Inspector only just managed to keep a sigh out of his voice.

Ten minutes later the papers were on Welwyn's desk. He studied them carefully, taking his time, and then, picking up the private telephone with a direct line to the outside, he dialled a number. While he waited for a reply, he lit another menthol cigarette, and noted, as he did so, that his hand was trembling.

Thirty-six hours later, at 8.15 a.m. on Friday morning, a blue prison van left Rockwell Prison. There were four men in the interior of the van, the prisoners, Ross Fraser and Monro Gladstone, and an escort of two police officers. Two police cars accompanied the van, one leading and the other bringing up the rear; the policemen in these cars wore civilian clothes and there was no marking on the cars to identify them as police vehicles. The convoy turned left outside the prison gates and began the fifty miles journey to London.

Fraser, aged 27, a carpenter from Paisley in Scotland, and Gladstone, aged 22, unemployed and of West Indian extraction, were due to stand trial at the Central Criminal Court on charges of having kidnapped and murdered Joy Clark. A third person, Sally May Ramsay, a garage attendant aged 19, was being held in the women's prison at Holloway on similar charges. The two men were being transferred from Rockwell to Brixton Prison in readiness for the trial which was set to open on the Monday of the following week.

The driver of the leading police car, a young officer named Stead, was a little puzzled by his travel instructions. He had been ordered to avoid the motorways and other main roads and proceed, via B-roads, across country until he reached the southern outskirts of London.

'Bloody daft!' he told his his companion, a stolid, long-serving constable named Chifley. 'It'll put at least thirty minutes on the journey.'

'The top-brass know what they're doing, lad,' said Chifley contentedly. He was enjoying this break from routine, and, in his view, the longer it lasted the better. 'Half the people in this country would like to lay hands on the pair of villains in that van. Given the chance they'd lynch the bastards.'

'For what they did,' said Stead grimly, 'lynching is too good. If I had my way, I'd make the punishment fit the crime. I'd bury them alive, the same way they buried that girl.' He drove on in silence for a while, and then added, 'Did you see the papers this morning? The result of that public opinion poll? Over ninety per cent in favour of bringing back the death penalty for murder and kidnapping.'

'Aye,' replied Chifley. 'We've had them polls before. Don't make no difference. You won't shift Parliament.'

'I'm not so sure,' said Stead. 'I reckon those Churchill Commandos have got the right idea. They've really stirred it up – got people thinking.'

'Maybe,' said Chifley enigmatically.

'Don't you think so, then?'

'Maybe. I'm not sure what they're aiming at, that's all.'

'It's obvious! Stands out a bloody mile. They're trying to clean things up, bring back a bit of respect for the law. And about bloody time too, if you ask me.'

'Aye,' said Chifley, and nodded, 'that's fair enough. Just seems funny to me. You say that they want people to respect the law – but they haven't shown much respect for it themselves, have they? And there's another point. If one lot take the law into their own hands, what's to stop another lot doing it? We'll be in a right mess if that happens, I can tell you!'

'We're in a right bloody mess now. Couldn't be much worse. Light me a fag, will you?'

Chifley lit a cigarette and handed it to his companion. To his relief, Stead made no effort to pursue the subject, and he was able to sit back and occupy his mind with more important and pleasing matters. Should he take a chance this weekend and plant out his tomatoes? If there was a late frost, of course, he might lose them all, but on the other hand –

3

Barr had positioned the unit on either side of the narrow road, at a point known as Axbridge Bottom. Here the road dipped between steep, wooded banks and the green arch of the overhanging trees held back the sun. From where Barr was standing, at the top of the right-hand slope, he could see the two cars and the blue van moving towards them; they were lost to sight for a moment, screened by a clump of scrub-ash and whitebeam, and then they appeared again, rounding the bend which would bring them on to the comparatively straight stretch of road leading downwards to Axbridge Bottom. He lowered the binoculars and scrambled down to where Piotrowski and Purcell were waiting.

'They're coming,' he said. 'All set?'

'Ready,' said Piotrowski. He grinned and brushed the back of a hand across his forehead, wiping away the sweat.

'Give them a bit of space,' said Barr. 'Wait until the car is well clear. We don't want anyone hurt.'

'You know me, Major,' said Piotrowski, 'I wouldn't hurt a fly.'

In the first car, Chifley had his eyes closed and was half asleep. Stead had forgotten all about the state of the country and was thinking about Doreen, his latest girl friend. He had a 48-hour weekend leave coming up and they were going to Bournemouth together. She was no beauty, quite plain in some respects, and her figure was all out of proportion – heavy breasts above an oddly narrow waist and thick thighs; but what she lacked in looks she more than made up for in enthusiasm and dexterity. He was not without experience himself but he had been amazed by Doreen; she had made him feel like an amateur, teaching him positions and techniques that he had never even dreamed of. He felt himself quicken and smiled in anticipation of the delights to come.

And then, suddenly, his mind leaped back into the present as he saw the great tree lying across the road just ahead and his body tensed in tingling fear as he stamped fiercely on the footbrake. He grasped the wheel, pulling back hard, as though willing the car to halt, and momentarily closed his eyes.

118

When he opened them again he saw that the car had stopped within inches of the obstacle, a huge, old pollard beech; the van had pulled to a halt a yard behind, but the second car skidding in a layer of rotting leaves, had slithered sideways and crashed into the right-hand bank.

There was a long moment of horrified silence, and then Chifley, moving fast for such a heavy man, heaved himself out of the car and hurried towards the crash, followed by Stead. The driver of the van watched but made no effort to move or help. His instructions were strict and precise; he was not to leave his post except in the most extreme emergency. He kept the engine ticking over and waited.

The men in the second car were shaken but uninjured. Stead and Chifley helped them out on to the road, and as they did so, Barr stood up.

'Stand where you are, gentlemen, please,' he called, 'and put your hands on your heads.' As he spoke, a half-dozen masked men emerged from the bushes on either side and levelled sub-machine guns at the astonished officers.

The driver of the van was quick to react. He thrust the gear lever into reverse, trod down hard on the accelerator, and the heavy vehicle shot backwards. It crashed into the rear of the second car, slewing it round so that it stood parallel to the bank, and opened up a space wide enough for the van to get clear. As the driver increased speed Barr ran into the middle of the road and shouted towards the spot where Piotrowski and Purcell were hidden.

'Let her go! Let her go, damn you!'

There was a moment's pause and then from Piotrowski there came an answering shout of triumph.

'Timber! Timber!'

Twenty yards so so beyond Barr, an ash began to lean forward; there was a rustling whisper of leaves, the branches quivered nervously, and then a space opened in the green arch above him as the tree toppled across the road. Its topmost branches came to rest halfway up the slope on the further side, so that the trunk was at least two feet above the surface of the road and spanned it like a narrow, improvised bridge.

It was still settling as the reversing van crashed into it and came to a shuddering halt. The driver was thrown forward by the impact and lay across the wheel, stunned and defeated.

Fraser, the first prisoner to be released, blinked nervously at the strange group of armed men and said nothing; he sensed their hostility and was afraid. His companion, Monro Gladstone had no such inhibitions. All he could understand was that, by some miracle, the prison gates had been flung open and he was free. He grinned cheerfully, his white teeth gleaming, as he jumped to the ground.

'Great man, great!' he cried, and thumped Piotrowski on the shoulder. 'Am I glad to see you!'

Piotrowski stepped back as though in disgust, his eyes dark stones behind the nylon mask. He transferred the sub-machine gun to his left hand, and with the back of his right struck Gladstone viciously across the face. The blow landed with such force that the West Indian almost fell, and blood from a split lip began to trickle down his chin.

'Don't you touch me, you bastard,' said Piotrowski. 'Don't you even look at me, do you hear? Keep your eyes down! If I catch you looking at me, I'll kill you!'

'Leave him, leave him,' said Barr gruffly. He stepped in between them. The West Indian looked at him, his bright eyes quick with fear, and Barr pushed him roughly away, towards his companion. 'Get them out of here!' he said.

'Bastards!' muttered Piotrowski. 'What they did to that girl! Bastards!'

'We're all bastards,' said Barr. 'It takes one to recognise another.'

Piotrowski glanced at him curiously, and Barr turned away abruptly. He was both disturbed and puzzled by his own feelings, which seemed to have no direction, no fixed point of reference, so that they veered and altered course without reason, like a rudderless boat. He had enjoyed the brief, fierce minutes of action, any doubts had been swallowed up by the tension and excitement he always experienced when in the field. This was when he felt most truly himself, when the questions had been settled and all that mattered was the answers. Other men drank or gambled or took drugs as their means of escape. Barr went to war.

It wasn't that his attitude to Fraser and Gladstone differed in any material way from that of the other mercenaries. The murder of Joy Clark, and the ruthless nature of the killing in particular, had filled him with the same loathing and contempt for her murderers. Certainly he had no sympathy for the politics they professed to hold, although his feelings lacked the fierce edge of Piotrowski and some others, for whom anti-communism was a crusade, a conflict that could only be resolved in blood. Barr was wary of such single-minded commitment, he distrusted it instinctively, from whatever quarter it came. The solutions were not as simple as the communists or their enemies supposed; people were too varied, the world too complex to be pinned down in a political blueprint.

He had tried consciously to stand aloof from all these things, to clothe himself in an armour of cynicism, to think of himself as a professional soldier following his trade, no more no less. He was a gun to be fired, his commitment was to fight well for whoever paid his wages, and otherwise to observe certain simple rules – rules which were dictated as much by expediency as by any concept of honour. You did not slaughter your prisoners or torture them, you treated them as decently as the circumstances permitted, you did not wantonly destroy people's homes or deliberately terrorise non-combatants. Barr had learned that such actions, in the long term, strengthened the enemy and often weakened your own side. In a dozen campaigns, Barr had imposed this code on the officers and men under his command with utter ruthlessness. He was aware that some of the mercenaries were thugs and criminals who had come to Africa in search of easy money and loot; he asked no questions about their past, that was none of his business.

But if they stepped over the invisible lines he had drawn, he dealt out swift retribution. Once, when three white soldiers had tortured and raped two twelve-year-old native girls, he had paraded the entire company and the local villagers, to witness their execution.

Beyond this basic code, he believed that there was no place in his chosen life for emotions, feelings, prejudices, opinions; they were no part of a soldier's equipment. Yet ever since Biafra, he had felt some change in himself, as if that part of his nature which he had kept so carefully locked away was hammering to get out. He had fled from Iris, the Australian girl, because of this fear of commitment; he was afraid that his emotions would take over and destroy his independence. It had been a near thing, for she had pierced all his carefully arranged armour, thrusting herself deep into him like a knife, and the pain was still with him . . .

Since then, certainty seemed to have deserted him; it was as though Iris, and to some extent Ojukwu before her, had left some gap in his defences which was beyond repair, and through which the doubts and the questions kept forcing their way out. Why, for instance, should he give a tinker's curse for the General and his motives? He liked the man, he was clearly a leader, and he was paying him well. Why not just take the money and soldier on, as he had done so often in the past? What else mattered? Yet the question mark was there in his head and stubbornly refused to go away.

And again, only a moment ago, he had felt the stab of doubt. A few years before, in Africa, he would have ordered the execution of murderers like Fraser and Gladstone without a single second of hesitation. They were scum, they were guilty beyond argument. Why, then, when he saw the terrible fear in the eyes of the West Indian, the look of mute, dog-like appeal, had he felt a small sudden spasm of pity, even of guilt? What was happening to him?

He shook his head. It must be a question of age; in a couple of years or so he would be forty, he was growing old. It was the only explanation he could think of, but it didn't convince him.

The two prisoners were being led along the lane towards the point where the get-away trucks were waiting. The men were talking and laughing among themselves, as soldiers do after a successful action.

'Cut it out! Cut it out!' shouted Barr. 'This isn't a bloody picnic! Get moving!'

The anger sounded in his voice like thunder, so that the mercenaries, as they fell silent, glanced at each other and made signs, wondering what was wrong.

Chapter Nine

1

THERE are times when those who hold ministerial office feel beleaguered, when everyone in sight appears to be either hostile or helpless, when each telephone call brings a problem and each problem spawns another. The world looked that way to the Home Secretary at this moment, he felt both angry and depressed. Moreover, as if the fates were determined to make his harassment complete, he had developed a sniffling cold and sore throat over the weekend and his normally clear, mellow voice was now little more than a painful croak.

It was now 6.15 p.m., on Monday. Over three days had gone by since the kidnapping of Fraser and Gladstone and there was still no news of any significance. The Churchill Commando had sprayed their familiar symbol on the side of the police van, leaving no doubt that they were responsible, but there had, so far, been no statement from them, no communique. From their point of view, the operation appeared to have been a complete success; the County police had mounted a comprehensive search of the area without any tangible result.

The Home Secretary had just listened to part of the early evening radio news programme of the BBC and it had brought him little comfort. The final editions of the London evening papers were on the desk before him. The main stories were devoted to the kidnapping, but there were several other related items which concerned him almost as much. Groups of the so-called Churchill Movement seemed to be springing up everywhere; the *Evening Standard* estimated the number at well over a hundred, the BBC had put it even higher. It had been a busy weekend. The Churchill Commando had been mercifully inactive since the coup on Friday morning, but the citizens groups had more than made up for this.

There was report after report. In a small coastal resort in Cornwall a group of local citizens had descended upon a colony of hippies, and driven them from the area. In Manchester, a meeting called to promote reform of the laws governing homosexual behaviour had been wrecked by a hostile audience and two of the speakers beaten up. In several places pickets had appeared outside cinemas showing pornographic films and defaced posters and photographic displays; the *Evening News* carried an interview with the owner of one such cinema in which he complained that his customers were being intimidated to such an extent that business had dropped by eighty per cent in two days. In Bristol, a man of thirty-five, the father of a large family, who had boasted publicly that he had not worked for five years and that he was quite happy to live on social security and welfare benefits, had been tarred and feathered and dumped in a ditch on the outskirts of the city by a group of unknown assailants.

In one or two places, there had been attacks on members of the immigrant community, an ominous development which suggested that other prejudices were seeking an outlet. All in all, the picture was one of growing national disorder, of rising fury and violence. The silent majority had found its voice and its fists. The backlash had begun.

The correspondence columns of the newspapers were almost entirely devoted to the subject; the overwhelming majority of letters expressed support for the aims of the Churchill Commando, though some qualified their approval by disassociating themselves from its illegal activities. A similar attitude had been adopted by a number of M.P.s and other people prominent in public life. No fewer than ninety-three M.P.s had put their names to a Parliamentary motion which demanded the restoration of the death penalty for murder and a range of other serious crimes. The Opposition was considering the putting down of a motion of no-confidence in the Government.

The loudest voice, and the one heard most frequently, was that of Patric Bierce, the Member of Parliament for East Devonshire. A volatile politician who generally leaned to the right, he had thrust himself forward as the spokesman for all those who sympathised with the new Churchill Movement, garnering enormous publicity in the process. Both evening papers headlined his call for a mighty demonstration in Trafalgar Square on the following Sunday at which he intended to demand the formation of a new Government, dedicated, as he put it, 'to the revival of the Churchill spirit in all aspects of our national life'. It was reported that thousands of people, from all over the country, were making plans to attend the rally.

And, as if all this wasn't enough, the first rumblings of apprehension and anger were beginning to rise from other quarters. The Communist Party was calling for a counter-demonstration and a mobilisation of the working-class against what it called 'this Fascist threat'. The Scottish Trade Union Congress and several miners' lodges had passed resolutions demanding that the authorities should take urgent steps to arrest the members of the Churchill Commando and bring them to trial: some of the protests accused the police of giving covert support to their illegal activities. But it was also reported that opinion in some trade union branches, and among the dockers in particular, was divided, and that many workers were openly supporting the new movement.

. The Home Secretary pushed the newspapers aside wearily and sneezed into a tissue. He could feel that heat in his blood, his skin was glowing, and his forehead and neck were damp with sweat. He dabbed at his face with a fresh tissue and as he did so, his eye fell on an item in the Stop Press section of one of the papers.

It was an announcement that one of the speakers at the Trafalgar Square rally was to be the distinguished soldier, Major-General Hugh Wilcox. There were no other details.

The Home Secretary looked at the words for a long time. Patric Bierce he could understand, he was the sort of politician who would exploit any issue, jump on almost any band-wagon, to satisfy his hunger for publicity and further his quest for power. In the past, he had always gone too far; on issue after issue he had finished by drowning in his own words and no doubt he would do so again.

But Hugh Wilcox was another kettle of fish altogether, and in this context, infinitely more dangerous. He had rolled up a distinguished record as a soldier, displaying not only a remarkable military talent, but a charisma and style which had led some people to compare him with Montgomery. And like Montgomery he was one of the few soldiers whose name was known to the public at large. In the sixties, during the troubles in Aden, he had personally led a small Commando group on a daring raid into the interior to rescue an army unit which was cut off and in danger of being wiped out. The operation was a brilliant success, over two hundred lives were saved, and Wilcox emerged as something of a national hero. His success, coupled with a habit of speaking his mind plainly, had not endeared him to certain brass-hats at the War Office, and they had to put a brake on the promotion his abilities deserved. Even so, his resignation from the army at the age of 55, and his virtual retirement to the country, had surprised his many admirers. Some said he had never recovered from the death of his wife.

The Home Secretary had met Hugh Wilcox on two or three occasions and each time he had been both puzzled and intrigued. He had intelligence, a shrewd political understanding, and his undoubted self-confidence was tempered by a wry sense of humour – but there was something more, some elusive, evanescent quality which made him stand out. Hard to pin down, it was a near relation of the enigma people refer to as personality. In the theatre and the cinema they called it star quality, the mysterious X-factor which neither the finest drama-school nor the most brilliant of directors can pass on to or draw from an actor.

If you have it, the Home Secretary told himself, you are an eagle. If not, not. And Major-General Hugh Wilcox has it. What puzzled him was that such a man should retire, play no part in public life, seemingly be devoid of ambition.

Had he merely been waiting in the wings for this moment?

The room seemed suddenly to have grown cold, as though a chill wind, blowing down Whitehall, had penetrated the sturdy Victorian walls of the Home Office. He picked up the green security telephone, on which all conversation was automatically scrambled, and called the Prime Minister.

'Prime Minister,' he croaked. 'I'm coming round. I must see you urgently.'

'You saw me this afternoon.' The Prime Minister had troubles of his own and he made no effort to disguise his irritation.

'I know. Something has come up.'

There was a pause at the other end of the line, and then the Prime Minister said: 'From the sound of it, you ought to be in bed. How is the cold?'

'The cold's fine,' said the Home Secretary wearily. 'I'm terrible. I've got a touch of your forebodings of doom. Listen, can we bring in the Defence Secretary?'

'What for?'

'I'd like to know if we can rely on the armed forces in the event of trouble.'

Another pause and then: 'Look, why don't we talk in the morning? Cancel whatever you've got on, take a couple of aspirin, and have an early night.'

'I'm not sick, I've just got a simple cold,' said the Home Secretary hoarsely. 'And it hasn't got to my brain, I'm not in a panic. But I believe you had the right instinct. This Churchill thing is spreading – at an alarming rate. And there are other aspects of it that worry me.' His voice was smothered by a rasping cough and a half-minute passed before he could continue. 'Sorry. Let me put a couple of things to you. First, a bunch of armed men have been moving around this country for the last week. All available police resources have been mobilised to track them down,

128

without result. Ask yourself why. Second, a police convoy is ambushed and two prisoners kidnapped. Ask yourself how.'

'I'm afraid I don't follow you.'

'The answer is obvious.'

'Thank you.'

'Isn't it? Isn't it obvious that this Churchill Commando must have inside information, that they have top-level contacts inside the police? The route the convoy was to take – that was highly confidential, known to only two or three high-ranking officers, and it was even changed at the last minute. Yet the Churchill Commando was waiting at exactly the right spot.'

'All right, I take your point. But I don't see – '

'Take it further. If these Churchill people do have links with top policemen, why shouldn't they also have connections within the armed forces?'

'I think you're the one who is over-reacting now.'

'Do you? Tell me, do you know Major-General Hugh Wilcox?'

'Of course. What's he got to do with this? He's been out of the army for over a year.'

'I know. All the same, how should you estimate his standing with the armed forces?'

'He was a very respected and popular commander, particularly with the younger officers. But I still don't – '

'Did you see that he has come out openly in favour of the Churchill Movement?'

There was another and much longer pause. 'It may not have any special significance,' said the Prime Minister carefully. 'I wouldn't read too much into it. Still, perhaps you'd better come round. And I'll see if I can get hold of the Defence Secretary.'

2

The General came into the room and led the way to the table, which was covered in a cloth of green baize. He was

129

followed by Piotrowski and one of the young officers Barr had met on his first day at the camp, Captain McKinnon. They sat on either side of the General. Piotrowski winked at Barr, who was standing by the door, and gave him a small grin, but the General and McKinnon looked stern and serious. About a dozen men in blue overalls stood along the sides of the room, watching in silence.

'I declare the court to be in session,' said the General. 'Bring in the prisoners.'

Fraser and Gladstone were brought in under escort and led to the centre of the room, where they stood facing the General and his two companions. The West Indian kept his head down, staring at the floor, and Barr saw that he was trembling. Fraser looked ahead defiantly, but it was clear that he was doing it only by a great effort; he held his hands clenched, pressing them against his thighs, as though by this means he could hold his body in check. The purple bruises on his temple and face glistened in the stark, white light. The squat shadows of the two prisoners, darkening the floor, almost reached the table.

McKinnon handed the General a sheet of paper. He gave a curt nod of acknowledgement and placed the document on the table before him, smoothing it carefully. The faint, crackling sound made by the pressure of his fingers seemed to fill the room. The General studied the paper for ten slow, long drawn-out seconds and then looked up. He began to speak and as Barr listened he became aware of something new in the voice, a small rasping sound which seemed to come from the General's throat. It occurred only three or four times, and it was just audible, but it added a strange emphasis to the words.

'Ross Gregory Fraser and Monro King Gladstone,' the General said. 'You have been charged before this military tribunal with the kidnapping and murder of Joy Rosemary Sheila Clark. We find you guilty on both counts. That verdict is unanimous. It is now my duty to ask you if you have anything to say before sentence is handed down.'

Gladstone looked up for the first time and half-turned

towards his companion. He was trembling more violently now and his voice was little more than a whisper.

'What are they saying? What are they saying? I don't understand, I don't get it! What are they saying?'

Fraser shook his head several times, his face blank. It was impossible to tell whether he was simply baffled by the proceedings or replying to his fellow-prisoner. Then, as if some invisible string had tightened inside him, his head went back so that his face pointed upwards, and he slowly closed his eyes.

'Do I take it that neither of you wishes to speak?' asked the General. He leaned forward slightly, and cocked his head to one side. His voice was smooth and gentle now, the odd little rasping had gone; he seemed to have assumed the manner of a sympathetic uncle.

The West Indian whimpered and shuffled his feet. He looked again at his companion, but Fraser remained silent and motionless, as though he had deliberately cut himself off from what was happening. The General waited a moment longer, looking from one to the other.

'Very well,' he said. He leaned back, clasping his hands across his chest. 'The crime to which you have both freely confessed was one of the most savage and brutal in our experience. We can find no mitigating circumstances. It is the sentence of this court, sitting on behalf of the British people, that you, Ross Gregory Fraser and you, Monro King Gladstone, be taken from hence to a place of execution and that you shall there be hanged by the neck until you are dead. And may the Lord have mercy on your souls.'

Barr found it hard to check the dry laugh that rose in his throat. He had the feeling that he was standing at the back of a school hall watching the fifth-form act out a Greek tragedy, he could not escape the thought that the performers were juveniles solemnly trying to behave as adults. In other hands the words and the ritual might have the authentic ring of tragedy, but here they came too close to absurdity to sustain belief.

He glanced towards the General. Was this yet another example of his odd sense of humour, like the mock execution of Piotrowski and the others? The General looked back at him, but there was no smile in the eyes. They were bright and hard, in a face that seemed set like a mask.

Colleano and three other men closed in on the shocked and silent prisoners. The West Indian seemed suddenly to have thrown off his fear, for he pulled himself erect and walked with dignity to the door, but Fraser went suddenly berserk. He broke free from his captors, charged towards the table and flung himself across it, reaching for the General. His momentum was such that he managed to grasp the General's shirt with one hand and bring the other up in a flailing movement that raked the other man's face.

'Fascist!' he screamed. 'Fascist, fascist! You stinking fascist bastard! All of you – bastards – fascist bastards!' He sucked in his breath and hissing like a snake, ejected a stream of spittle which splashed on to the General's forehead and began to trickle down his nose.

The General pulled away in disgust but Fraser held on desperately. There was a tearing sound as a piece of the shirt came away in his fist and as he fell across the table the General brought a hand down on his neck. It fell like an axe in a short, chopping movement; the air exploded from Fraser's lungs in a fierce gasp and he lay silent.

'Take him out!' The General's voice was scarcely audible but Barr noticed that the faint rasping sound had returned and that, as he fingered the bleeding furrows on his face, the hand was trembling. He took a handkerchief from his pocket and wiped away the gleaming bubbles of spit, rubbing the skin hard as though it were stained. He looked at the handkerchief for a moment and then dropped it to the floor. Looking up, he saw that Barr was watching him and suddenly, as though triggered by some internal switch, the self-control returned and a tiny, ironic smile widened the mouth.

The police patrol car cruised slowly past the silent station at Chislehurst and turning left into Summer Hill headed upwards towards the Common. The two policemen in the car sat in silence; it had been a quiet night and they had more or less exhausted conversation. Boredom had added weight to their tiredness. The driver, a man named Wells, glanced towards an old sports car which was parked to one side of 'the road, opposite the slope leading down to the Rambler's Rest, a popular local public-house, but he did not stop. They had checked the car an hour or so before; it was not on the list of stolen vehicles, it no longer concerned them.

His companion, Stephens, took off his cap, scratched languidly at his thick ginger hair and yawned. 'Roll on six o'clock,' he said.

They turned right at the crossroads into Watts Lane, a thin belt of shadowy woodland on one side and the cricket field on the other.

'A bird stopped me along here once,' said Stephens. 'Middle of the bloody night. Wanted a lift. It was summer and she was wearing a mini-skirt – '

'Mini-skirts,' said Wells, with a sigh of regret. 'I wonder if they'll ever come back.'

'Don't suit everyone,' said Stephens. 'They've got to have the legs.'

'And the thighs.'

'This kid had them. Mini-skirt up to her handbag, you could practically see what she'd had for breakfast. And she made no bones about it – if I'd give her a lift to Swanley, I could have the lot – '

'Wait!' said Wells suddenly, and pulled the car to a halt.

'What is it?'

'A light. I thought I saw a flash of light over by the cricket pavilion.'

'I didn't see anything.'

'You were too busy yacking on about your piece of crumpet. I saw something.'

'Kids,' said Stephens. 'That place is broken into twice a bloody week.'

'Let's take a look anyway.'

Wells turned the car to the right and entered an unmade road. The tyres rasped on the rutted gravel as he braked and stopped. The dark outline of the pavilion was just a few yards ahead and nearby, on the edge of the field, there stood a truck. It had a big, high enclosed body, of the kind used by removal vans.

'What the hell is that doing there?' whispered Stephens.

They watched for a full minute. From somewhere in the woods, some distance away, a fox howled and was answered by the faint barking of a dog, but that was all. From the area around the truck there was no sound or movement.

'It's just been parked there for the night,' said Stephens. 'Convenient. Off the road.' He pulled out a packet of cigarettes, and held it towards Wells. 'So long as we're here, we might as well have a fag.'

'Better take a look,' said Wells. 'Check the number.'

Stephens sighed, replaced the cigarettes, and climbed wearily from the car. As he did so, two men in dark overalls emerged from the shadows and closed in on him. A sharp beam of light hit his face and he blinked, momentarily blinded; before he could recover, the hard snout of a sub-machine gun was jammed into his stomach, and a voice hissed: 'Stand where you are. And keep quiet; absolutely quiet. One sound and you're a dead 'un.'

The second man covered Wells. 'Don't try and touch that radio, son,' he said. 'Get out of the car – slowly, carefully.'

The two policemen were lined up against the car, their hands clasped at the back of their heads. A third man appeared, masked and armed like the others. 'Take them into the pavilion,' he said. 'Tie them up and shove on a gag.' He turned towards Wells and Stephens. 'Sorry about this, gentlemen. Your bad luck to come along at this moment. Behave yourselves and you won't get hurt.'

Stephens, who was an impulsive young man, lowered his hands and swung round, but as he did so the gun went into his stomach again, there was a sharp, metallic click, and he stopped abruptly, his heart thudding with fear. Slowly, very slowly, he lifted his hands to their former position. The gun was pulled back and he felt his stomach heave with relief, the bitter taste of vomit rise in his throat.

The third man shook his head sadly and said, in a pained voice, 'No, please. Don't be foolish. We're on your side, we really don't want to hurt you.'

4

An hour later, concerned by his failure to make radio contact with the patrol car, the duty officer at Bromley police station despatched another car and two men to make a search. They cruised around without success for a good thirty minutes. At one point, they saw a large removal van moving down Perry Street in the direction of London and the police driver wondered vaguely what it was doing on the road at that early hour, but his attention was on the other things and he put the thought from his mind.

It was early dawn before they discovered the police car parked on the edge of the cricket field. Its radio had been put out of action, and there was no sign of Wells and Stephens. The light was still grey and uncertain, and looking out across the field, the driver could just see a blurred outline in the centre of the field, where the cricket pitch cut a smooth swathe through the longer grass surrounding it. Leaving his colleague to make radio contact with Control, the driver moved across the field, treading warily.

'Hey! Hey!'

The interruption was so unexpected and sharp that his heart gave a sudden lurch and he stopped in mid-stride, looking around. And then, sighing at his own stupidity he realised that it was the call of a waking bird. The sound appeared to act as a signal, like a conductor tapping his baton on the rostrum, for at once the dawn chorus began:

the calls were isolated and muted at first, but gradually they grew in volume and blended until the field seemed to be surrounded by a great, unseen orchestra and the air shimmered with sound.

It was still cold and, shivering slightly, he moved forward. The sky behind the fringe of trees brightened suddenly as though a blind had been raised, and the outline in the centre of the field took on a clearer shape. He stopped once more, sucking in his breath, his body tightening like a stretched wire.

In front of him was a rough wooden gallows. It consisted of a sturdy beam, supported at each end by two thick poles, set at an angle to the ground like inverted V-signs. A narrow plank ran the length of the structure; it rested on struts nailed to the end supports and was about two feet from the ground.

Two nooses hung down from the top-most beam and in each noose there was a man. Their heads were covered in thick, black hoods, their hands bound behind their backs. One man stood on the plank as though frozen to attention, his head tilted upwards by the pressure of the rope: the other, by contrast, stood with his head slumped forward in the noose, his knees bent, his body moving slightly like a branch stirred by the wind.

A dog came running across the field, and circled the gallows, barking fiercely. The noise startled and roused the driver. Savagely, angrily, he kicked out and the dog scurried away, its yelps of pain dwindling into the distance.

It was twenty minutes before reinforcements came and it was possible to cut down the two men. When the hoods were removed they were immediately recognised as Fraser and Gladstone. As it turned out, neither of them was hanged; and it seemed that this had never been the intention. The plank had given them the precarious support necessary to prevent this. Fraser was in a condition of acute shock. Ashen-faced, he kept turning his head in tiny circles as though to convince himself that the noose was no longer holding him; his lips moved ceaselessly but no words came.

Gladstone, the West Indian, was unconscious and appeared to be in a coma. Both men were rushed to Queen Mary's Hospital in Sidcup.

Wells and Stephens, the two policemen from the first patrol car, were found in the changing room of the pavilion, bound and gagged but otherwise unharmed.

The police discovered a typed communique from the Churchill Commando nailed to the gallows, and it confirmed their responsibility for the deed. The communique ended with these words:

> We do not believe in lynch law. That is why we did not hang these murderers. Ours was a demonstration. By an overwhelming majority the British people have demanded the restoration of the death penalty. Parliament must now give effect to that opinion.

Two hours after being admitted to the hospital, Gladstone came out of his coma. He opened his eyes, pulled himself up in the bed, and began to scream. His eyes rolled in panic as the screaming rose in intensity, his body quivered with terror. He fought wildly with the policeman and nurses who tried to restrain him and then, as suddenly as he had woken, he collapsed. Every effort was made to revive him, but without success: his heart would not respond.

The doctors couched their verdict on his death in official, medical terms, but one newspaperman put it more succinctly when he wrote that Gladstone had died of fear.

There was some speculation about why the Commando had chosen a cricket field in Chislehurst as the place for their so-called demonstration. It was ended when a reporter discovered that, in the distant past, highwaymen, footpads, and other criminals had been hanged within a few yards of the field. A stone commemorating this piece of history had been erected on the site. It bore the inscription:

HEREABOUTS STOOD A GIBBET

Chapter Ten

1

As it happened, Barr did not go with the men who carried through the bizarre demonstration at Chislehurst for he had been ordered by the General to hold himself available for a special assignment. Nor had he been told that Fraser and Gladstone were to be submitted only to a mock execution; when the unit returned safely, in the early hours of the morning, and he heard the full details from Piotrowski, his reaction was one of bewilderment, coupled with an odd sense of relief.

One of the huts at the back of the house had been fitted up as a mess and recreation room; a dozen men sat there eating thick, hot bacon sandwiches, swilling mugs of strong tea, and talking over the events of the night.

'I don't know why we didn't hang the bastards,' said Piotrowski.

'I bet they wish you had,' said Barr. He refused a sandwich but took one of the mugs of tea. 'I know I would. If someone put a rope round my neck I'd want them to bloody well pull it.'

'You wouldn't like to be left hanging around, you mean?' said one man, laughing coarsely at his own joke.

'It's not funny!' Colleano said sharply. He chewed with noisy concentration for a moment as he pulled a thin strand of rind from between the slab-like slices of bread and dropped it on the table. 'I'll tell you the truth, I didn't like it. It was sort of – you know – weird. You know? I seen a lot of death in my time. It's not a joke, something you joke about. If a man deserves to die, okay. Kill him. But make it quick. Don't prolong the bleeding agony.'

'I'm not arguing!' said Piotrowski. 'Am I arguing? I

said we should have finished the job, I said that. I don't like playing these games any more than you do. All right, the Old Man has had his bit of fun. Now it's time we did something for real.'

'Like what?' asked Onslow. He was a new recruit who had been sent down by Whitaker two days before, a thin, languid man, with the drawling echoes of an English public-school background in his voice, and a face which, from the pale eyes to the jutting chin, seemed to wear a look of perpetual boredom. The languid manner and the thin body were deceptive. Barr had fought with Onslow in Biafra and knew the inner strength that was enclosed in the bony frame, the speed and energy with which the man could react in a crisis. He had never liked him, never penetrated beyond the cynicism which Onslow wore like a second skin, but he had learned to respect his quality as a soldier. And for Barr, that was going a long way.

'Christ Almighty,' said Piotrowski savagely. 'The country is crawling with communists. They run half the bloody unions, they're everywhere. We could shoot up a few of them for starters.'

'My dear old chap,' said Onslow, 'this is England. One doesn't go around shooting people, it just isn't done.'

'Maybe that's what's wrong!' said Piotrowski.

'No,' said Onslow. 'The General has the right approach. Spot on. The British will join a revolution only if it has the correct note of respectability, if they can wear their bowler hats and carry their umbrellas. The General has judged it perfectly. Using the Churchill label, for instance. That was a touch of genius. Personally, I think old Winnie would spin in his grave at the idea, but what does that matter? His name gives the whole business the right sort of ring. Gutsy, patriotic, respectable, with just the faintest touch of melodrama. And that first manifesto! Magnificent. Beautifully balanced. It went just far enough, made all the right noises, without going over the top. Calculated to get them cheering in every golf club and semi-detached from Land's End to John O'Groats. Exactly what the worthy citizens have been saying for years. What they needed was a focal point, a lead. Well, now they've got it. Someone has been clever enough to put a few of their pet prejudices and frustrations into the pot, season with a dash of humour, and stir gently. And, by God, it's working.'

'A very penetrating analysis, Mr. Onslow.' They turned and saw the General standing in the doorway. As they pushed back their chairs he smiled and waved a hand. 'At ease, gentlemen, please. Don't let me break up the party. In fact, I'll join you if I may.'

He pulled up a chair and someone brought him a mug of tea. He took a tentative sip and made a wry face. Someone passed a half-bottle of rum down the table towards him.

'Like to liven it up, sir?'

'It needs something,' he said. 'I had a sergeant in the Western desert who used to brew tea like this. So thick that the spoon stood up in it. He once gave some to a captured German colonel and the poor devil was sick. Said he intended to complain under the Geneva Convention about mistreatment of prisoners of war!'

The men responded with a few muted chuckles as he stirred the mixture of tea and rum. Barr watched him in admiration. The man had an extraordinary ability to adapt to the colour and tone of his surroundings, to put people at their ease, to mingle without patronising. At this moment he was a soldier relaxing with other soldiers, no more no less.

'Were you out there with Montgomery, with the 8th Army, sir?' asked Colleano.

'Oh, yes,' said the General. 'Indeed. That was quite a man. Wavell was a fine commander, but Monty left him standing. One of the greatest generals in all our history. And don't let any of these so-called military experts tell you otherwise!' His eyes glowed with enthusiasm. 'Do you know the first thing he did when he took over as C-in-C? Made a bonfire of all the plans his predecessor had made for withdrawal. Then he ordered everyone at HQ to take a half-hour of physical training every morning! You should have seen those fat-arsed staff officers running around in their vests and pants, puffing and blowing, their bellies quivering like jelly, their faces the colour of claret! And those who couldn't make it were fired. Kicked out. It was tremendous.'

This time the laughter was strong and uninhibited, and Barr joined in.

'Monty was shrewd. He knew, he knew very well that the word would soon get through to the other ranks,' continued the General, 'and, of course, it did, with electrifying results. You have to remember that, for the most part, he was dealing with amateurs, not professionals like yourselves. He had to motivate them, build up morale, and by Jupiter, he did it!' He shook his head. 'I was a young captain at the time, not long out of the egg. I'd have gone to hell and brought the devil back under close arrest if Montgomery had asked me.'

He sipped his drink, looking at them over the rim of the mug, his eyes moving from one face to another until they came to rest on Onslow.

'Well, Mr. Onslow,' he said, 'what do you think of things so far. To your liking, are they?'

'No complaints, sir,' Onslow said.

'Well, I've got a complaint!' Piotrowski said bluntly. 'I think it's time we stopped playing games, that's what I think.'

'Ah,' said the General. 'You disapprove of our tactics so far, do you?'

'I'm not saying that, sir,' answered Piotrowski, 'that's not for me to say. O.K. Maybe Onslow was right. You've just been stirring the pot, getting people going. But going where? And for what? That's the bit I don't understand.'

'Perhaps Mr. Onslow can answer that. He seems to understand these things,' said the General softly. He leaned forward, his head slightly to one side and fixed Onslow with his clear, bright eyes. He was smiling, but the smile had no depth, and there was an odd feeling of menace in his manner which puzzled Barr. It was as if the General were stalking the other man, offering him some obscure kind of challenge, as though the area around the table had suddenly become an arena in which two adversaries faced each other. The men seemed to sense this change in the atmosphere also, for they sat back like spectators, looking from one man to the other, but taking no part.

Onslow spread his hands, palms upwards, in an uneasy, deprecatory gesture. Had he been a stranger Barr would have said that he was afraid, but he knew the man and he had never seen him reveal a hint of fear or, indeed, of any other emotion.

'Sorry. Can't help,' he drawled. 'I'm the new boy around here. I'd rather listen and learn.'

'You disappoint me,' said the General coldly. He stared at Onslow for a moment longer as though he were measuring him, weighing him up, and then he turned brusquely back to the others.

'You'll get your action, Mr. Piotrowski,' he said. 'All you want and more. The games, as you call them, are over. Phase I has been completed, and completed successfully, thanks to you, gentlemen. We shall continue to stir the pot, as Mr. Onslow so picturesquely put it, but Phase II will be a little more serious, I promise you.'

He paused, sipped at the mug of tea, and then lowered it slowly to the table. There was a wet ring-mark on the bare surface, and he rubbed half of it away with his finger, leaving behind a rough outline of the letter C. He seemed amused by this, his face eased into a little smile. The others watched in silence, waiting for him to continue.

'How do you save a country?' The General spoke so softly that he seemed to be talking to himself. Barr leaned forward, straining to catch the words. 'Above all, how do you save a country from itself? How do you give it back the will to live, to work, how do you restore its pride, its self-respect, its courage, its sense of purpose? Once, gentlemen, less than a half-century ago, it was possible to find many, if not all, of those qualities in these islands.' He shook his head. 'No more, no more. We have lost our place in the world, and with it our faith in ourselves, in our standards, our traditions. We are in decline, as the Romans were, and unless we look to ourselves we shall die as surely as Rome died, not because we have lost an empire, but because we have lost our heads. We shall be taken over by the barbarians – barbarians of our own making! The Romans are remembered for their roads, and perhaps, with luck, we shall be remembered for the English language. That will be all. Nothing more. Nothing.'

His voice, which had grown stronger as he went on, again sank to a whisper, but in the silence that followed his eyes held them fast. Clear and fierce as the eyes of a tiger, they glittered with a power which was almost hypnotic. Even Barr found it impossible to look away or remain unaffected; his skin quickened as though it had been pricked by needles. He was reminded of an American who, after meeting Orde Wingate, the British general who fought a guerilla campaign behind the Japanese lines in World War II, had remarked: 'Christ, the way that guy looks at you, it's like a sunglass burning a hole in your guts!'

The General leaned back and smiled again, his eyes softening, as if the power behind them had been turned down. 'However, we shall not follow that scenario, gentlemen. We will not fail. Let me tell you a story. When I was a young man – a boy really, no more than sixteen or seventeen – I went to Germany on a holiday. It was just before the war. One evening I went into a beer cellar with some friends, and as the evening progressed, there was singing. I suppose there were a couple of hundred people there, a few visitors, but mainly German and most of them young. And then, at one point, a young Nazi began to sing the German national anthem, *Deutschland, Deutschland Uber Alles*. In a light-hearted way, we began to counter this with *Land of Hope and Glory*. The effect was electric. Within moments they were all on their feet, roaring out their song, drowning our voices. I tell you, I have never seen such fervour, never felt such intensity. It was as if

143

those young people were possessed. I saw the same thing a few days later at a Nazi rally in Munich. Thousands of people animated by one will, flaming with pride. I was overwhelmed and terrified. It seemed to me that I was surrounded by a storm, a hurricane which could never be diverted from its course.'

A little knot of unease began to tighten in Barr's stomach, and something of his feelings must have showed on his face, for the General looked at him and shook his head, as if disappointed.

'No, Major, no. I can see what you are thinking. I am not a fascist or a Nazi. I saw the fruits of that philosophy towards the end of the war, at Belsen and other concentration camps, and the memory still disturbs my dreams. It wasn't until then that I understood the word evil. And that, in a sense, has become the dilemma of decent men. Hitler perpetrated such vile crimes in the name of patriotism, discipline, order, that these concepts have become suspect. Today, if we dare to say we love our country we are called chauvinists. If we suggest that there must be more discipline in the factories, the schools, the family, we are told that we are a threat to the liberty of the individual; if we speak of the need for order, the need to enforce and strengthen the law, we are branded as neo-fascists; if we say people should work harder we are told that we are anti-working-class; if we talk of virtue, decency, courtesy, civilised values, we are mocked as squares, or worse. And so decent men are intimidated. They stand aside, watching in despair, as the mobs, the muggers, the louts, the extremists, the merchants of porn and perversion, the money-grabbers, run riot. They look towards Westminster, only to see one tribe of mediocrities succeed another, neither of them with the courage or know-how to check the slide to decadence and disaster.'

The General stood up abruptly, scraping his chair on the hard surface of the floor.

'I'm sorry, gentlemen. You have had a long, hard night and this is hardly the moment for speeches or lectures. I

144

apologise. Let me make one more point. The last tonight, I promise you.' He looked directly towards Barr. 'You seemed uneasy when I mentioned the Nazis, Major. I did so only to illustrate my argument. A nation can only be saved if it has the will to survive, to rise again. But why is it that only the extremes, either of the Right or Left, seem able to create that will, to build the sense of purpose, the dedication, the enthusiasm, the pride which I felt in that beer cellar that night? Why is it that we British can only generate a national will when we are fighting a war?'

He brought his fist down on to the table, rattling the crockery, and his eyes gleamed with their former intensity.

'What is crippling this country, strangling it? It is not the balance of payments, the falling value of the pound, our economic or industrial troubles. They're the symptoms. The cause lies elsewhere. It is apathy! Indifference! Cure that, and all the other problems will sort themselves out. Apathy! That is the enemy we have to destroy. We have to take Britain by the scruff of the neck and shake it until it comes to its senses! We must bring the ordinary, decent man out of the shadows and show him that he is not helpless, give him the will to act.'

He stopped suddenly, drew in a deep breath, and continued in a more controlled even amiable tone. 'That's what it is all about, Mr. Piotrowski. We are going to create a revolution, a revolution neither of the Left or the Right, a revolution unique in history, a revolution not to destroy the democratic system but to purge it, to revitalise it.' He smiled. 'I don't suppose you have read Lenin, have you?'

Piotrowski shook his head, his face creased in a puzzled smile.

'You should,' said the General. 'Lenin was the expert. He said that a revolution was necessary not simply to change the system, but to change people. *Change people*. That is the key. Do that, change our people's outlook, forge a national will and we shall be on the way to solving all our problems.'

The others turned to Onslow in surprise as his voice broke the brief silence which followed.

'May I ask a question, sir?' he said.

'Why not? We've been hoping to hear from you,' said the General. Once again, Barr noted the faint mockery in the tone, and was surprised by it.

Onslow was either unaware of this, or chose to ignore it. 'A revolution can only succeed if it takes power. There's no point otherwise. So those who lead the revolution must somehow acquire the means, the machinery of government. You've said that you're not out to destroy the democratic system. O.K. But at the moment we have an elected government, and there is no General Election in sight. How do you propose to handle that situation?'

'A good question, Mr. Onslow. Right on the button, as they say,' answered the General coolly. 'I could answer it, but I won't. Even Montgomery didn't tell his troops everything he had in mind.'

There was some laughter at this, in which Onslow joined, but Barr noticed that there was no smile on the General's face.

'Get some rest, gentlemen,' he said, 'we have a busy weekend before us. Captain McKinnon will brief you in my absence.' He looked at Barr. 'You will join me in my office in thirty minutes, Major. Wear civvies and bring your overnight gear. We shall be away for two or three days.'

He moved to the door and stopped, his back to them, holding a hand to his jaw as though in thought, then he swivelled round to face them again. 'There is one more thing. A problem. We have a problem. Not entirely unexpected. We could hardly expect the enemy to remain inactive, could we?'

He came back to the top of the table and his eyes moved around the watching faces, searching them.

'MI5 has placed an agent in our ranks. We have a spy on our hands.' He spoke softly, almost amiably, he might, thought Barr, have been speaking about a problem no more important than a passing headache, or greenfly on the roses.

'There is, I'm afraid, no doubt about this,' the General continued. 'I wish there were. I received the information an hour or so ago, from a very reliable source.'

'Tell me who it is, and I'll strangle the bastard!' said Colleano. He held up two huge hands and made a circle with them.

'Who is he?' growled Piotrowski. 'Tell us who he is!'

'Well,' said the General, 'it isn't you. And it isn't Mr. Colleano.' His eyes travelled round the table again and stopped at Barr. 'And it certainly isn't Major Barr.'

Barr was only half-listening to the almost casual words. He was watching Onslow, knowing it was him, feeling an invisible rope tighten round the man's neck. And as the General paused, halting his game of cat and mouse, the others realised it too, and one by one they stood up and faced Onslow. Once again, Barr had to admire the man.

Onslow pushed his chair back and rose languidly to his feet. He smiled as he looked around the ring of accusing faces, and as Piotrowski made to move towards him, he brought up his right hand and waved him back. The hand was holding a pistol.

'No, Pete, no. Don't. Please,' said Onslow.

Barr was to remember afterwards, with a degree of wonder, that his initial reaction was strictly professional. Part of his mind registered the information that the pistol was a Beretta 90, but as Onslow backed off and he saw the weapon more clearly, he realised that he had been wrong. The pistol was the SIG P–230, a fairly new type of pocket gun developed in Switzerland and manufactured in West Germany. Barr had tried one the year before on the factory range at Eckernforde and had been impressed by its performance.

At the same time he was estimating the distance between himself and Onslow. If he were to push the table over and if he moved very quickly –

Onslow anticipated him. 'Back from the table,' he said. 'All of you. Slowly now. Nothing hasty.'

'You bastard!' Piotrowski said. But, like Barr, he knew Onslow and he shuffled backwards with the others. Only the General did not move. Instead, he held out a hand.

'I'll take the pistol, Mr. Onslow,' he said.

'I don't think I want to part with it – not for the moment,' Onslow said.

'Please don't be foolish. You are a sensible man. If you use it, you will alert the camp, and your chance of getting out alive will be non-existent.'

He took a step forward. Barr saw the muscles of Onslow's hand tighten on the gun, the trigger finger move almost imperceptibly. He began to calculate again. The firing-pin of the SIG P–230 had a built-in safety factor, an automatic block which prevented the weapon from being fired until the very last fraction of trigger pull.

'Onslow,' he said sharply, 'for Christ's sake! You haven't got a chance.'

'You never know, old chap,' said Onslow. He moved around the table, waving them back, edging towards the door. He reached it safely, and stood there for a moment, the familiar mocking smile playing on his lips.

'If we're talking about chances,' he said, 'I reckon mine are as good as yours. Out in Africa, if you killed a man, you could call it war. But this isn't Africa, comrades. This is stuffy old England. And here they have a name for that sort of thing. In this country, they call it murder.'

Colleano reached a cautious hand towards a rifle that was stacked against a chair just behind him, but in the same moment Onslow fired. The bullet scorched past the out-stretched hand and thudded into the wall. Colleano straightened up sharply, like a marionette operated by invisible strings, and looked down at his hand in wonder.

'Naughty, naughty,' said Onslow. He stepped back through the door and slammed it in their faces.

'Get him!' snapped the General.

Barr's reactions were instinctive, ice-cold, automatic. As

the others rushed the door, he snatched up the rifle and smashed the butt against the window, shattering it. He saw Onslow running across the yard, and he shouted a warning.

'Onslow! Hold it! Hold it!'

Onslow checked for a moment, and then continued his run, ducking and weaving, heading now towards the corner of the house. He was moving into the sun, and his shadow fell behind him, a black silhouette against the grey slabs of stone. As Barr hesitated, he heard an exploding crash nearby, and turning, he saw Piotrowski standing in the doorway, a rifle at his shoulder. When he looked out of the window again, he saw Onslow lying face downwards on the ground, his fingers opening and closing as if he were grasping for something beyond his reach.

He was dead when they reached him, the blood already staining his shirt, and even in death the look of mockery was still fixed on his face.

2

An hour later Barr was sitting in the back of a car with the General, on his way to London. Drage, the young lieutenant whom Barr had seen at his first meeting with the General, was at the wheel. He and McKinnon were the General's aides, they seemed to be closest to him.

Barr sat tense and silent, looking ahead, the anger burning within him. The General seemed at ease as he studied maps and papers, looking up only occasionally to glance at Barr or to admire the sun-lit countryside.

Once he said quietly: 'I've been all over the world in my time, you know. And I really do believe that this is the most beautiful country in the world. Just look at it.'

But Barr did not look and he did not answer. Not so bloody beautiful for Onslow, he thought savagely, not any more! You knew he was a spy, you could have disarmed him, put him under close arrest, but no! You had to work one of your bloody jokes, play the old cat-and-mouse game, and now the poor bastard is dead. Onslow's voice echoed in his head: *In this country, they call it murder.*

Now the bar in Singapore seemed like a refuge, the crashing boredom of the life he'd lived there like an elusive, beautiful dream. He cursed the impulse which had driven him back to his old trade, the hunger for action which, at regular intervals, seized him with such force that it overwhelmed all his other instincts. Drug addicts could be cured, alcoholics dried out, a compulsive smoker could learn to kick the habit. There was hospitals, nursing homes, for such people, there were doctors who could help them. But for his particular addiction there was no help, no treatment. Iris had come near to working the miracle, only Iris. Iris. And because he had become afraid that she was succeeding, because he could feel the change in his nature, he had left her, packed his bag and walked out. Fled. Iris, he thought, oh Christ, Iris, Iris, Iris.

He lowered the window, gulping in the flow of air, glad to feel its coolness on his skin. The trim suburbs of outer London slid by the car window, ordered flower-beds, compact lawns, laburnums in tidy, yellow bloom, patches of blue aubretia hanging in an organised manner from careful rockeries and neat, low walls. In one garden a woman in a dressing-gown was already at work with a sprinkler. There was a portrait of Churchill in the window of almost every house in the row.

At some traffic lights they pulled up alongside a small car. His radio was on, and Barr could hear an announcer spelling out the details of the Churchill Commando's latest exploit. The driver, a man of about thirty, wearing a smart executive-type suit, caught Barr's eye and smiled.

'They've done it again!' he said. 'You've got to hand it to them! They've done it again!'

Yes, thought Barr, lovely morning for a killing, don't you think? But he said nothing, he did not even return the smile.

As the lights changed, the other man accelerated away and Barr saw that he had a picture of Churchill fastened to one side of his rear window. The General shuffled his papers, stacked them neatly in a worn brief-case, and glanced at his watch.

'You've friends in London, Major?' he asked.

'None that I can think of,' Barr answered, and then he remembered Noonan and added, 'Yes. One.'

'I shall be occupied most of the morning,' said the General. 'I thought you might like a couple of hours to yourself. After that, I will brief you on this special assignment. Where would you like to be dropped?'

The tone was conversational but Barr was being given an order and he knew it.

'Marble Arch will do,' he said.

Ten minutes later the car stopped on the corner of Great Cumberland Place and Oxford Street. As Barr got out, the General said, 'I have a press conference lined up for 12 noon. I suggest we meet up again there. At the Churchill Hotel.'

Where else, thought Barr. He nodded and watched the car ease its way into the morning traffic and head towards Park Lane. He stood there for a full minute, trying to adjust to this new situation. Clearly, the General was going to an important meeting, and equally clearly he did not want him to be there, or to know about it. No doubt he would be discussing Phase II with those powerful friends on the outside, about whom he had hinted, making contact with that 'reliable source' which had informed him about Onslow.

Out of this thought there sprung another, and Barr's anger came welling back. The card Benedict had given him was in his top pocket. He went into the Cumberland Hotel, found a phone booth, and called the number. Benedict answered almost immediately.

'Where are you?' asked Barr.

'Why?'

'Because I bloody well want to see you, that's why!'

Benedict did not react to this. He gave the address of an

apartment in Great Portland Street. 'Have you had breakfast?' he asked.

'Yes,' Barr said savagely. 'I had a beautiful breakfast.
A real gutful!'

He slammed the receiver down and head down, pushed
his way through the crowded lobby into the street.

3

'What do you think of Barr?' said the General.

The car was negotiating Hyde Park Corner and Drage
replied over his shoulder, without turning.

'Good chap, sir,' he said. 'Bit odd, in a way. Seems to
have no feelings. At least, doesn't show them. Still nothing
wrong with that, I suppose. For us, it could be an advant-
age.'

'Yes,' said the General thoughtfully. 'Yes, I suppose so.'

'When Phase II is finished, sir – and if all goes well –
what will you do about them?'

'How do you mean?'

'I mean, we'll have no further use for the mercenaries.
And we can't just pay them off. They know too much.'

'If all goes well, as you put it,' said the General tersely,
'what they know will not matter. I shall not only find a
place for them, but I shall expect them to be treated as
soldiers who have served their country well – with respect
and honour.'

'Of course,' said Drage. But he spoke without conviction.

Chapter Eleven

1

HARRY BENEDICT'S apartment was on the second floor of a building near the Oxford Street end of Great Portland Street. Below it was a sandwich bar, and as Barr paused outside he saw a stout woman in a blue overall spreading butter on to slices of bread. He smiled grimly, recognising the style, and wondered if she had ever worked in an army canteen, for she worked with enormous economy laying the butter on with one swift, scraping movement of the knife and removing most of it as she brought the blade back. By her side stood a tall, thin youth with an incipient moustache peeling rectangles of yellow cheese from a cellophane packet, slapping them between the slices of buttered bread, and cutting the resulting sandwiches diagonally across with a thin, sharp knife. Customers sat on high stools facing the brown walls, sipping coffee, nibbling at buns, and reading newspapers.

The woman looked up and caught Barr's eye. She gave him a weary smile. A small bead of sweat dropped from her forehead into the basin of soft butter, but she seemed not to notice. She pursed her lips in a silent whistle to indicate to Barr that it was hot, and then, tearing the wrapping from a sliced loaf, she set to work again, the knife sliding back and forth, back and forth across the thin slabs of pasty-looking bread. As Barr turned away he saw a portrait of Churchill on the glass door; the Sellotape had come away at one corner, and the picture was beginning to curl up, giving a lop-sided effect to the round, pugnacious face.

The door leading to the rooms above the shop was locked. There were three bell-buttons, and Barr, as instructed, pressed the one bearing the name R. J. LENNOX. A moment later a voice, heavy with distort, came through the tiny speaker below the bells.

'Yes? Who is it?'

'Barr.'

'Come on up.'

The locking mechanism purred, and with a sharp click the door responded to Barr's pressure. He heard it swing behind him and close as he mounted the stairs. Benedict's face, thin and yellow, peered over the banister, looking down at him, and all Barr's anger came seething back.

Benedict led the way into a room which was half office, half sitting-room. Barr caught a faint drift of perfume on the air, noticed a brown handbag on the floor beside one of the armchairs, and pushing past the surprised Benedict he threw open a door to the right of the desk.

By the side of a kingsize double-bed a young girl was putting on a pair of white knickers. She looked at Barr in astonishment, her thumbs in the elasticated waistband, and then, snapping on the brief pants, she straightened up.

She was not as young as her body suggested. There was nothing wrong with the face, but it was the face of a woman, mature and experienced, and Barr guessed that she was in her mid-thirties. The figure was superb, youthful; long legs, slim hips, firm breasts, a skin which gleamed like milk.

'Have you seen enough?' she asked. She stood with her hands resting loosely on her thighs, a tiny, sarcastic smile on her face, making no attempt to move.

Barr looked round the room. There was only one other door, half-open, leading to a bathroom. Benedict spoke from behind him.

'If you want to talk come into the other room,' he said quietly, and to the girl he added, 'Sorry about this, love.'

'You've got some funny friends,' she said.

'Get her out of here,' said Barr.

'Who the hell do you think you are?' said the girl angrily.

154

'Get her out!'

Barr went back into the other room, slamming the door behind him. He heard their voices raised in argument, and then Benedict came out of the bedroom. He glanced at Barr, his eyes sharp with curiosity.

'What's wrong?' he asked.

'Wait till she's gone.'

'Coffee?'

'No.'

Benedict went through to a kitchenette and Barr heard the chime of crockery. In the bedroom, the door of wardrobe slammed twice and he heard the girl swear. He crossed to the window and looked down into the street. The sun glinted on the glass and metal of cars wedged together in a tailback from the traffic signals in Oxford Street, the pavements were crowded with hurrying people. Below him a girl dropped her handbag as she collided with a man going in the opposite direction, and a little circle of space opened up around her as she crouched down to retrieve the bag and the half-dozen things which had spilled out. No-one stopped to help, and after a moment or two she stood up, her face red, and continued on her way.

Suddenly Barr hated everyone down there in the street, he felt an urge to open the window and spit his venom down upon their heads; but the impulse passed almost as soon as it came and he turned away. His anger and contempt was not for them but for himself, and he knew it.

Benedict came back with a cup of instant coffee and sat down behind the desk. He stirred the coffee thoughtfully, watching Barr, but saying nothing. On the wall behind him, the face of Charlie Chaplin looked down from a framed poster advertising the film *Gold Rush*. On another wall there hung a group of autographed photographs of actors and actresses, including one of Charlton Heston in the role of General Gordon, and a large framed montage of old theatre programmes. Some of the photographs were signed *To Ronnie*.

'I've rented the place furnished,' said Benedict. 'From a writer. He's in New York.'

Barr grunted, showing no interest, and Benedict resumed his former silence.

At length, the bedroom door opened and the woman came out. She was wearing skin-tight jeans, a loose top decorated with the names of French cities, and carrying a shoulder bag. She went to Benedict, tilted his face upwards and kissed him – not a farewell peck, but a long, full kiss over which she took her time, and when she broke away she looked at Barr mockingly.

'See you this evening, Harry?' she said. The words were addressed to Benedict, but she kept her eyes on Barr.

'Of course,' Benedict said. 'I'll be here.' He glanced at Barr as he spoke, as though expecting him to challenge this statement, but the other man simply looked away impatiently.

The woman ruffled Benedict's hair in an affectionate gesture, picked up her handbag, and went out, closing the outer door quietly behind her, and as if this were a signal, Barr swung round.

'Right! Now talk – start talking, Harry!'

'What about?'

'Onslow!' Barr almost growled the name.

'What do you know about Onslow?' said Benedict warily.

'Don't fart around, Harry! I'm not in the mood!' Barr flicked out a hand which sent the cup of coffee flying and a brown stain spread like a scar across the fawn carpeting. 'You couldn't get me to work for you, so you put in Onslow. And then you shopped the poor bastard, you set him up. Right? Right?'

Benedict sat with his hands resting lightly on the edge of the desk, his calmness contrasting with Barr's anger.

'Hadn't you better begin at the beginning?' he asked quietly.

'I'll begin at the end!' said Barr. 'Onslow is dead. He

was shot, a couple of hours since. How does that grab you, Mr. Bloody Benedict?'

'It doesn't. Who killed him?'

'You knew Onslow then, you admit that?'

Benedict hesitated, then hunched his shoulders. 'Yes. You turned the job down – you didn't expect us to stop trying, did you?'

Their eyes met and Benedict's did not waver. His coolness, his air of quiet certainty, disconcerted Barr and drained off much of his fierceness. Now he felt only confused and bitter; he combed fingers through his hair and sat down.

'Oh, hell,' he said, 'oh, bloody hell.'

2

Some thirty minutes before this encounter, a young Fleet Street reporter, his mind bubbling with the thought that he had pulled off the scoop of the year, was climbing down from the old cedar tree where he had been keeping observation for some three hours.

He was there in the first place because his friend, P.C. Hayes, was a worrier, a man not easily put off. The sudden transfer to the other end of the county puzzled him, he could see no reason for it, and he was not convinced by the Inspector's assertion that the move would be in his best interests. Hayes could not get out of his mind the thought that all this had something to do with his interview with Chief Superintendent Welwyn, during which he had reported the presence of armed men at Cresswold House. It didn't make sense, it went against everything Welwyn had told him, but he couldn't help thinking that there was some connection between all this and the ambush in which Fraser and Gladstone had been kidnapped by the Churchill Commando.

It was a very mysterious business altogether and the constable had brooded about it since the interview, wondering what he should do, if anything. By chance, on the

Saturday afternoon, his journalist contact from Fleet Street, a man named Jeffrey Pilling called on him. It was Pilling who had made the enquiries about the British Centre of Industrial and Technological Research at Cresswold House. He was more than a contact. He had been through school with Hayes and they had kept in touch after Pilling left the local newspaper for the richer pastures of Fleet Street. Now, back in the town on a visit to his parents, one of his first actions was to look up his old friend.

It wasn't long before Hayes told him of his impending transfer and of the other matters which troubled him. The element of coincidence puzzled Pilling, arousing all his instincts as a journalist, and he decided to carry out a little investigating on his own account.

He spent part of the following day making discreet enquiries in the area and keeping watch on the front entrance of Cresswold House. He saw the odd closed truck come and go, but very little other activity and certainly none of a suspicious nature. It looked very much like other government or semi-official institutions, with a lodge just inside the high, locked gates and custodians in dark blue uniforms. But what was going on inside? And what was this high-sounding Institute which, according to his researches in London, did not even exist?

Early the next morning, while it was still dark, he made his way to the back of Cresswold House, following the route through Heslop Wood which Hayes had taken previously. He had known the wood since boyhood and he located the magnificent old cedar without difficulty. It stood on open land between the house and the wood, sheltering the ground beneath like a huge, green umbrella, and before first light, equipped with binoculars, he was safely settled in the higher branches, with a good view of the rear of the house and of part of the drive leading from the gates.

Within a few minutes, his vigil was rewarded. A truck rumbled down the drive, coming from the direction of the main entrance, and drew up in the yard. It was still too dark to see anything in detail, but in the light which streamed out from the open door of one of the huts, Pilling made out the shadowy figures of about eight men. Clearly, they were returning from some mission. From where, he wondered. And what sort of mission could it have been to take them out under cover of darkness?

He felt his heart quicken with excitement. He was an ambitious and slightly romantic young man, and in his mind's eye he could already see his name writ large over an exclusive story in which, for the first time, the world would learn the inside story of the Churchill Commando. He saw himself stepping up to the podium to receive an award as Reporter of the Year.

Sternly, he put these thoughts aside, chiding himself. So far he had little to go on, it was all conjecture. The truck with its cargo of passengers might well have been out on some perfectly innocuous and legal journey. What he needed, as his editor was always telling him, were facts, facts, and yet more facts, hard evidence. He settled back to wait for the light to strengthen.

The sun, unaware of the young man's impatience, took its own majestic time to rise over the line of distant hills. Unfortunately, Pilling was facing almost due east, and he was forced to change his position slightly to avoid looking into the strong, direct sunlight. Nevertheless he still had an almost perfect view of the back of the house, of the huts which huddled round it, and of part of the drive to the main gates.

A long hour passed, with very little happening, and then time seemed to explode around him. What he saw, in fact, was the death of Onslow – saw the man run from one of the huts, heard the sharp crack of the rifle, saw the running man stumble, fall and lie still. Within moments, the fallen figure was surrounded by armed men wearing dark uniforms who lifted him up and began to carry him back into the hut.

It all happened so quickly that Pilling fumbled awkwardly with the binoculars, tangling up the leather strap around his neck, and missed some of the action, but he saw enough with the naked eye to set his heart racing. He had to steady himself on the branch, feeling a sudden eerie sensation of weightlessness as if his body had suddenly been emptied of bone, muscle, fluid, and was filled only with air. What he had just seen was beyond his experience, and he was torn between fear and excitement; despite the sweat on his face and neck, his skin suddenly grew cold, the dank, chilling cold of an old gravestone, and he shivered violently.

Gathering himself, he focused the glasses on to a tall man who appeared to be ordering operations. The face was vaguely familiar, but Pilling could not put a name to it. After a while, the man went into the house and after that, apart from some general movement of men about the yard, there was a further lull.

The fear had subsided now, and the excitement returned. How right he had been to follow his instincts, his nose for news! He had no doubt at all that he had uncovered the main operations centre of the Churchill Commando, and that had to be the story of a lifetime. He considered whether he should leave his perch and contact his editor in London, but he decided to keep observation for a further hour or so. He began to compose the lead paragraph of his piece in his head, shuffling words around so as to create an opening with the maximum impact.

A car left the house some time later, but Pilling was unable to get a clear view of the three occupants. He lowered the binoculars and scribbled the registration number of the vehicle on the back of an envelope.

It was as he put this back into his pocket and lifted the binoculars again, that Piotrowski, looking out of the open window of the hut, saw a flash of light come from the upper branches of the cedar tree. As he watched, it was repeated two or three times, as though someone was signalling with a mirror, and then, high up among the dark green foliage, he made out the figure of a man.

Within less than a minute Pilling guessed that he had been sighted. He could hear shouts from the yard, see men running towards the perimeter fence and pointing in his direction. He eased himself back along the branch towards the shelter of the centre of the tree, cursing the binoculars as they swung from his neck, impeding his progress. He waited in the shadow by the dark trunk for a moment, gathering his senses, wondering what his next move should be. He could no longer see the buildings, and all he could hear was the familiar, comforting sounds of the woodlands, the rustle of leaves, the whisper of the breeze through the old tree, the fluting call of a blackbird.

He began to feel that he had allowed himself to panic without need, but the hard knot of fear remained and he decided that it was time to beat a decent retreat. He worked his way downwards, keeping as near the trunk as possible until he reached the lowest branch.

And then, suddenly, he stopped, his eyes shining with excitement, his hands trembling. With its usual perversity and odd sense of timing, memory had responded to his earlier prompting, and the name he had been seeking leaped into his mind. Wilcox! There could be no doubt, no doubt at all! Pilling had seen enough photographs in the press, seen the face on the television news-bulletins often enough. It had been some years ago, around the time when Mrs. Wilcox had been killed in a bomb incident, but the man looked just the same, he had scarcely altered. Wilcox! Major-General Wilcox!

He wrote the name down on the envelope, as if afraid that it might elude him again, and then edged himself carefully, inch by inch, towards the end of the branch, trying hard to control his excitement. Near the end, where the branch thinned out and began to sag under his weight, he twisted the binoculars round so that they dangled at his back. Rolling over on his stomach, he took a grip with his hands and allowed his body to slide into space. He swung from the branch for a moment, preparing himself for the drop to the soft earth beneath.

In this position he presented a perfect target and Piotrowski made no mistake. When Pilling hit the ground, he was dead.

'A drink?' asked Benedict.

Barr nodded and Benedict went to a side table and poured a large measure of Scotch. Barr drank half of it in a single, desperate gulp, and choked slightly as the neat whisky tingled in his throat. As Benedict went back to his seat behind the desk, Barr closed his eyes for a moment, trying to get a grip on himself, to order his thoughts. He felt the hardness of the pistol between his body and the chair and he reached into his pocket and drew it out.

'I came here to use this on you, Harry,' he said.

'Charming!' said Benedict, with a little smile.

Barr weighed the pistol in his hand and then tossed it towards the desk. It fell into a wire basket, on top of some papers, and Benedict picked it up.

'A souvenir,' Barr said. 'Onslow's pistol. Recognise it?'

Benedict nodded. 'A little beauty.' He laid the pistol on the desk between them. 'What happened to Onslow exactly?'

Barr shook his head, recalling the scene, and then swallowed the remainder of the whisky. He seemed more relaxed as he continued: 'How much do you know, Harry?'

'I'm not sure. Something. But not enough.'

'Tell me,' Barr said.

'It's not strictly my area,' Benedict said carefully. 'I was brought into it in the first place simply because I happened to be here. My department was curious about Whitaker – we wanted to find out if he was recruiting mercenaries for service abroad. But strictly speaking, this is MI5 and Special Branch territory, not mine.'

'I don't want to hear about your bloody departments,' Barr said. 'Tell me what you know.'

'A lot of it is guess-work. MI5 is playing this one very tight. George Lydd doesn't say much – or he doesn't tell me very much, shall we say. But I know the mercenaries are operating in this country, not abroad. My guess is that they're the backbone of the Churchill Commando.'

'Brilliant!' said Barr heavily. 'Do tell me more.'

'Six months ago – maybe seven – we received a report from one of our men in South Africa. A retired British army officer, Major-General Wilcox was out there on a visit. He had talks with certain wealthy and influential people in Johannesburg, Durban and Cape Town. We know that they pledged themselves to give him substantial sums.'

'For what?'

'We didn't know – then. And our man couldn't find out. Our guess was they they wanted him to form a special unit of volunteers to fight against the black nationalists in Rhodesia.'

'Wrong.'

'Yes. Wrong. But we had nothing else to go on at the time.'

'Why should the South Africans give him money?'

'It's not only the South Africans. We're pretty sure he has received funds from other sources also – from this country, and from one private source in the United States. A sort of Randolph Hearst character, very rich, very powerful. The South Africans almost certainly have a specific, political purpose. The present British government is pretty hostile towards them. They might feel that a change would be in their interest. Or simply that if the General could stir things up a bit over here – which he has done – make it sticky for the British government, it would help to take the heat off their own situation.'

'You mean, they're using the General?'

'In a sense. Except that he's not a man who can be easily used.'

'You can say that again.'

'What we do know now is that he put some of the money into a group called the Organisation for the Study of Subversive Activities. OSSA. All quite legal. They issue pamphlets, hold conferences, send out speakers. OSSA is run by a colonel who used to be on Wilcox's staff. And the

Council is pretty high-powered. A couple of former ambassadors, a sprinkling of rich industrialists, an ex-Commissioner of Police. They're the official ones – unofficially they have close links with highly-placed people in the Foreign Office and other key ministries, and with top men in the police, the services, the press, the other media, and in politics. A very powerful set-up.'

'And the General is top-dog?'

'Top-dog? That's something I'd like to know.'

'This organisation – what did you call it? – OSSA. What does it do?'

'A great many things. Its main function is to study the nature and impact of communist, marxist, and other subversive movements in Britain. It issues a Special Report each month to about 5,000 subscribers.'

'Nothing wrong with that.'

'No. As I said it's quite legal. What OSSA has done is quite legal – so far.' He stopped, and then changed direction suddenly. 'What do you make of the General?'

'He's a hard man to fathom.' Barr said slowly. 'When you're with him, when he starts talking about the things he believes in, he really does get through to you. He's got – what's that phoney word?'

'Charisma?'

'Yes. And energy. Christ, he's got enough of that to power ten Concordes, and there'd still be some left over to light up the run-way.'

'He did get through to you, didn't he! Surprise, surprise!'

'In a way. I don't deny it,' said Barr defensively. 'But not all the way.'

'Ah.'

'When you're not with him, when the light goes out, you start to wonder. I mean – what he's really after? I can't make up my mind. He's like one of those cocktails, so many things mixed up in it, so much fruit salad floating around, that you can't pick up the flavour. He's vain, in a controlled sort of way, it's not unbearable. I think he

164

really does see himself as a sort of hero riding up in the nick of time to gun down the villain and rescue the innocent. No, maybe not quite that. More as a kind of General de Gaulle, the soldier-statesman – that sort of thing. At the same time, there's a kind of old-fashioned innocence in him too – when he talks of honour and loyalty and decency he really means it. All very nice and sweet-sounding but not very practical maybe. Not when he meets up with the real politicians.' He shook his head. 'I just don't know.'

Benedict smiled. 'What was it the man said? As a matter of fact, it was your General's very own hero, Winston Churchill. He said once that it is a fine thing to be honest but it is also very important to be right. Or words to that effect.'

'Oh, the General hasn't any doubts on that score, believe you me.' Barr paused, and then continued: 'One thing I don't understand. What are you blokes doing? Why haven't you picked him up? And Whitaker, come to that – why haven't you put him through the wringer?'

'We needed Whitaker. It was through him that we planted Onslow. Not that he knew, of course. As for the General – well it's not yet illegal to go to South Africa and talk to a few rich people.'

'O.K. But for the past week he's been charging around the country with armed men, holding up trains, kidnapping people, hi-jacking police vans and all the rest. What about that? Is that legal?'

'You should know the answer to that,' Benedict said drily. 'That's what you've been doing, isn't it? What made you go in with them after all? You told me you were no longer for hire.'

'Impulse. Curiosity. Money. Most of all, boredom.'

'Didn't you know what you were getting into?'

'Christ, Harry, you didn't know, with all your resources.'

'But when you found out, why didn't you quit?'

Barr hesitated before replying. 'I don't know. I'm not sure whether they would have let me go. In fact, I'm bloody sure they wouldn't. But I suppose the real truth is – well –

the General. I was curious about him – still am.' He paused, then added defiantly: 'What he says makes a hell of a lot of sense. This bloody country is going to the dogs, it does need a shake-up. And he's the only man I've met who could be big enough to do it.'

Benedict looked at Barr for a moment, then rose, shaking his head. 'I haven't met the man, so I wouldn't know. By all accounts, he's pretty formidable. But I distrust these instant Messiahs. They either end up as live dictators or dead martyrs. And the cures they offer are usually worse than the disease.' He went to the whisky bottle and gave Barr an enquiring glance.

'No, thanks,' said Barr.

Benedict twisted the bottle in his hands and put it down with evident reluctance. 'I've been ordered to stay off the juice,' he said. 'This damned jaundice.'

'I could cry for you,' Barr said, without expression. 'Big tears.'

'What happened to Onslow?'

Barr told him.

'Can you remember the General's exact words?'

'Not exactly. But how did he know about Onslow? He was so sure. No doubt in his voice. Listen. Someone warned the General about Onslow. Someone who knew. And that same someone must have told the General that I was O.K. Told him that I'd refused to work for MI5 or MI6 or what have you. Now, you tell me. How many people knew about that?'

'Only two. Myself and George Lydd.'

'How about those fellows who came to pick me up? One of them was a sergeant – name of Chandler.'

'Errand boys. They didn't know why we wanted to see you.'

'Then it's down to you and Lydd,' said Barr.

'That's right,' said Benedict. 'And it isn't me.'

A long silence fell between them. The atmosphere in the room felt stuffy and oppressive and Benedict, rising wearily, his face drawn, threw open a window. A gust of air fluttered the papers on the desk, bringing with it the blare of traffic from the street below. Benedict slammed the window shut, a frown on his face.

'Anyway, that answers your question,' he said.

'Which one? There's several you haven't answered.'

'Why the General hasn't been picked up. I told you, it's not my pigeon. It's a domestic operation. Lydd's department.'

'What about the police – Special Branch?'

'Listen – if Lydd is in with the General there must be others. A hell of a lot of others, I'd guess.'

'OSSA?'

'OSSA,' said Benedict.

4

'For God's sake, man, you didn't have to kill him!' said McKinnon, his voice icy with anger.

'What else was I supposed to do?' Piotrowski faced the other man defiantly, and there was a touch of contempt in his tone. 'He was getting down from that tree! In another few seconds he would have been off through the bloody woods! He was a reporter, he'd got the General's name written down and the car number. If he'd got clear, it would have been splashed all over the papers and we'd have all been up the sodding creek! If you want someone to use a catapult, get yourself a Boy Scout.'

'Do you suppose he came here without telling anyone? How long do you think it will be before someone starts wondering where he is, and begins to ask questions? You're a first-class shot, Piotrowski, you could have put a bullet into his leg or his shoulder – then we could have taken him alive and found out just how much he had learned, who he had told. Now – ' McKinnon lifted and dropped a hand and sighed. 'Get the N.C.Os. Tell them that I want all the stores and equipment loaded ready to pull out in one hour.

You will personally supervise the operation. I want nothing left here, not even a wet dishrag. Clear?'

'Clear,' said Piotrowski. 'Where are we going?'

'You'll know that when I'm ready to tell you. Now – get on with it!'

Piotrowski moved to the door, and stopped. 'What about the bodies – Onslow and this other laddie?'

'Wrap them up in blankets and stow them in one of the trucks.'

'Right.' Piotrowski smiled. 'My trouble is that when I shoot, I shoot to kill. Always been the same. Can't seem to break myself of the habit.'

'I'll remember that,' McKinnon said coldly.

When Piotrowski had gone, McKinnon lifted the telephone and dialled a number. He tapped the desk impatiently as the ringing tone went on for some time, but eventually a man's voice came on the line.

'Chief Superintendent Welwyn.'

'Dalton's Hi-Fi Service here, sir,' said McKinnon carefully. 'I'm afraid we've mislaid your order for the recordings. Would you mind giving me the details again?'

'There were two. A song recital by Kathleen Ferrier, that's on the Decca label, I think. And a Louis Armstrong record – a new issue by C.B.S.'

'Can you talk?'

'Not easily. Not now.' Welwyn's tone was guarded, careful.

'Then listen. We're pulling out. Contingency Plan B.'

'When can I expect delivery?' asked Welwyn in the same cautious voice.

'In ninety minutes, two hours at the most.'

'Right. Thank you for calling.'

Within the prescribed time, the first truck left Cresswold House, heading for a destination known only to the driver and the N.C.O. who travelled with him in the cab. Both men wore their civilian clothes, as did the mercenaries who sat among the stores in the darkness of the sealed interior.

Thereafter, the other trucks left at staggered intervals, taking different routes towards the same destination. McKinnon was in the last truck to go. He was careful to lock the main gates behind him.

At noon, the Chief Constable of the County, together with Chief Superintendent Charles Welwyn, led a task force from the local police to Cresswold House. His officers had been assembling the force, calling the men in from their routine duties and from leave, and briefing them, for the past three hours. At least twelve trained marksmen, armed with Parker-Hale .222 rifles, were in the assault group. One party of ten men approached from the rear, through Heslop Wood to cover the rear gate and the perimeter fence.

Young P.C. Hayes had been called in from the far side of the county to take part in the operation. He felt a sense of pride, believing that but for him, the fake Institute would never have been exposed. He hoped that the Chief Superintendent would remember that he had shown commendable initiative.

It was a matter of some disappointment to him and to most of the others to find, when the entry was effected, that the place was deserted. There was no shoot-out, no sensational arrests, no Churchill Commando. Nothing.

Well, perhaps not quite nothing. There were sufficient indications of recent occupation, tyre tracks, prints, and other clues, to suggest that the house and the area within the perimeter fence had been used by the Commando. One policeman found a used cartridge in the grass by the fence, and in one of the huts someone had scrawled the motif of the Commando on the wall – the letter C in a triangle.

The Chief Constable left a squad of men to complete the search and went back to headquarters where he summoned the press. He was justifiably proud that it was his force which had made this first, important break-through, but he was a modest as well as an honest man, and he left the assembled reporters to draw their own conclusions. He was a little brusque with one man who asked why the police had allowed their quarry to slip so neatly away. Why had they not acted sooner?

The Chief Constable parried this by pointing out that valuable evidence had been found which would assist further investigation. The Commando had been flushed out of one base – they would find it more difficult to settle in another. And he added, for good measure, that the charges against them now included that of murder, since Gladstone, one of the victims of the mock hanging had died as a direct result of this experience.

'I know that many people in this country have shown great sympathy for these so-called "Commandos",' he said sternly. 'They admire their daring, the skilful way they have carried through their operations. Perhaps they see it as a sort of a joke, a rag. But make no mistake, gentlemen, it is a joke no longer. The police of this country do not treat kidnapping and murder as a laughing matter. We shall get these people and they will have to answer to the courts for their actions.'

He concluded with a tribute to Chief Superintendent Welwyn, who had played a key part in the investigations leading to the raid on Cresswold House. Welwyn, not to be outdone in modesty, gave full credit to P.C. Hayes, describing that young officer's initiative as 'being worthy of the highest traditions of the police force'.

It was very pleasant and exciting for Hayes. When the formal proceedings broke up he was interviewed by some of the pressmen, and several photographers took his picture.

What a pity, he thought, as he tried to look suitably stern for the cameras, that Jeff Pilling isn't here to write up the story for his paper.

5

'We need a replacement for Onslow,' said Benedict softly. He picked up the pistol and began to turn it in his hands.

'No,' said Barr, 'oh, no.'

'Someone Lydd doesn't know about. Someone the General trusts.'

'I said no.'

'You owe us that.'

'Christ!' said Barr, 'I owe you bloody nothing! Nothing!'

'Then let's say you owe Onslow.'

'I didn't set him up!' said Barr. 'He knew what he was doing. He went in with his eyes open, he knew what to expect if his cover was blown. He was a stool pigeon, and he would have turned us in without a second's thought. All he got was the rate for the job – a bullet.'

'I'm sorry,' Benedict said calmly. 'I thought you'd come here to avenge him, I thought that was the idea.'

He drew back his arm and tossed the pistol at the other man. Barr put a hand to his face in an instinctive movement of self-protection and fielded the gun neatly.

'You've missed the point,' said Barr. 'It could have been me. If I'd taken your bloody job, I'd be where Onslow is now. I don't like that, Harry, I don't find it funny.' He slipped the pistol into his pocket and stood up. 'Where can I find Lydd? I'd rather like to talk to him.'

'No,' said Benedict, 'no. You leave him to us. We'll deal with Mr. Lydd.'

'Not if I get to him first,' Barr said. He moved to the door.

'Tommy,' said Benedict urgently, 'leave this one alone. Lydd, the General, the lot. It's too big, too rich for your blood. If you won't help us, get out. Take your gear and go fishing. Don't try and play a lone hand, for Christ's sake.'

'Thanks for the drink, Harry,' said Barr amiably.

Down in the street the pavements seemed to be less crowded, although the little sandwich bar was busy with customers. The stout woman in the blue overall was still at her task, the knife moving mechanically across the slices of pale bread. Barr smiled to himself, wondering if she would ever stop, imagining her at the end of the day surrounded by mountains of sandwiches.

As he turned away, he saw a girl moving towards him, and he stopped in astonishment, his heart thudding. Iris! He took a half-step towards her, the name was on his lips, and she looked at him in surprised amusement.

'Wrong lady,' she said, and stepped neatly round him. A few paces further on, she glanced over her shoulder, still smiling, to see that he was still watching her. She bore a superficial resemblance to Iris, no more: she was a stranger, and he turned away, heavy with a sense of loss.

He glanced at his watch. It was still only 10.20, he had an hour and more to kill before joining the General at the Churchill Hotel. That was something he was still uncertain about. Maybe, as Benedict had said, it was too rich for his blood. Well, he had a little time yet. He decided to pay Noonan a call.

Looking down from the window, Benedict saw him cross the road, picking his way between the angry cars. Don't get yourself killed, chum, he thought, don't get yourself killed just yet.

He went to the telephone and called George Lydd. To his relief, Lydd was in his office and he was put through immediately.

'I have to see you at once,' he said.

'What about?'

'Something in which we have a mutual interest. It's hot, very hot. Can you come to my office?'

'Why not here?'

'It'll be easier at our place. I've stuff to show you.'

'I've a departmental meeting in ten minutes. That will take the best part of an hour. I can be with you just before twelve.'

'Fine,' said Benedict. He smiled as he pressed down the bar of the telephone, cutting off the call. He waited for a moment, then lifted his hand and dialled another number.

A woman's voice answered the call. 'Conroy International,' she said brightly. 'Good morning. Can I help you?'

Benedict gave a code word and his name and her tone changed. 'Yes, Mr. Benedict?'

'Put me through to Special Duties Section, will you, Millie?' he said.

Chapter Twelve

1

THE boardroom was on the top floor of one of the city's newest and most splendid buildings. From the windows it was possible to look down on the Stock Exchange, or to look across to the dome of St. Paul's and, in the further distance, to Big Ben and Parliament. It was said that Lord Leggatt, on seeing the view for the first time, had remarked: 'A perfect arrangement! The Stock Exchange, St. Paul's, Parliament. We are on top of the city, not too far away from God, and we can still keep an eye on those damned politicians!'

In their first draft sketches the architects had suggested that the top floor should be laid out as a penthouse for the personal use of his Lordship, but Leggatt had calculated in an instant what this would cost per square metre of floor space, and rejected the idea. Apart from a modest two-room apartment at one corner, the area had been put to productive use as executive offices. He used the boardroom as his own office, working at the centre of the long, elegant, 18th century, mahogany and satinwood table, or from an equally beautiful rosewood writing-desk of the Carlton House type which was set at a right-angle to one of the windows. Leggatt had a passion for antique furniture and most of the offices of his top executives were furnished in similar, if somewhat less expensive style.

'Buy modern stuff and its value drops every year. Buy good antiques – put them to productive use, don't just look at them – and you've got an investment.' It was a view he expressed often; he was very fond of talking about productive use.

He was sitting at the centre of the long table now, a tiny,

spry, balding man with a brown, mischievous, gnome-like face and alert, slate-grey eyes. His feet only just touched the thickly carpeted floor. The General was at the head of the table to Leggatt's left, and around them sat eleven other people, ten men and one woman. No-one had noticed that they were thirteen in number; they were too occupied with the business in hand to be concerned with superstitions or omens.

The discussion had been going on since nine o'clock and it was now well past ten-thirty. A buzzing sound came from the direction of Leggatt's left wrist and with a little smile of apology to the others, he switched off the alarm on his watch. He believed firmly that no meeting, however important, should last longer than two hours; he considered that any decisions reached after this period tended to be hastily conceived and basically unsound.

'Well, ladies and gentlemen,' he said, 'I think we have covered the business. We all have a good deal to do, so I suggest we go and get on with it. Are there any questions, anything on which you are not clear, anything you wish to ask the General?'

His eyes went round the table, moving from face to face. One by one, they responded with a little shake of the head.

'Excellent,' he said. 'I would simply like to stress one point, which is crucial to our whole campaign.' He looked across at the two men sitting directly opposite. 'This particularly concerns Ian and Allen, but of course, we are all involved. I have already given the necessary orders to the people running my papers, and I've had a discreet word with two or three key television people. Beginning with the press conference at noon, we must ensure maximum coverage for the General. Total, but total saturation, in all media. We haven't much time. We ought to aim to get a quarter of a million people in Trafalgar Square on Sunday week to greet him – the biggest demonstration of modern times. In the next eight or nine days his name must become a household word. We're already half-way there, he's by no means an unknown quantity – and there's plenty to build on. The soldier, the man of action, the patriot, the leader of men – that's the picture we need to present.'

The General winced and moved uneasily in his chair.

'I know, Hugh, I know,' said Leggatt. 'I know how you feel about the personality bit. But – with respect – you must look at it objectively. Thanks to you, we have the beginning – only the beginning, mark you – of a mass movement. We must draw that movement together behind a leader – and do so quickly or it will disintegrate as fast as it was built. And I'm afraid that means putting you under the spotlight.'

'I'm worried about overkill,' said the General. 'If we go too far we could provoke the wrong reaction. The British tend to be suspicious of instant-heroes.'

'They love 'em,' said Leggatt, 'believe me, they love 'em. And at the moment, they're hungry for a big one. Present company always excepted, they're fed to the teeth with the blotting-paper politicians at Westminster. There isn't a real personality in the entire bunch, and they know it.'

The rippling chuckle that ran around the table died away into an uneasy silence before the cold gleam in the General's eyes. Leggatt, reacting quickly, rose to his feet.

'Perhaps you and I can have five minutes together, General. There are one or two points to talk over. Thank you, friends, and good luck. We're only at the beginning, but at least, we know that the support is there. This last week has proved that.' He pressed down on the table with the palms of his small, neat hands. 'If we can mobilise it behind the General, then we must succeed. And succeed more quickly and more completely than any of us thought possible. Thank you again.'

'Yes, thank you, friends,' said the General.

As the others filed out, Leggatt said: 'Please leave in the usual way. At intervals and by different exits. You will be notified of our next meeting.'

As the last one closed the door, he went to a bureau and took out a glass and a jug of orange juice. He held the jug up to the General, who shook his head. Leggatt filled the

176

glass and drank the contents without pause. As he refilled the glass, he said, 'I drink a gallon of this stuff every day. I've got a thing about Vitamin C.' He replaced the jug and came back to the table. 'Hugh, there is one issue we didn't cover this morning. There was no point in bringing it up before the whole meeting. But I'd like to put it to you. In my view, it is of prime importance.'

'What is it?' The General's voice showed some impatience. The truth was that he missed his usual rigorous morning exercise; the meeting had been stimulating enough, but now that it was over he felt a certain sluggishness, a need to be on the move.

The sun, suddenly striking through the wide, panoramic window, blazed directly into Leggatt's face and shielding his eyes with a hand he crossed the room and pressed a white button. There was a gentle swish and the heavy maroon curtains moved together like tabs in a theatre, shutting out the sun. Light still flowed in from the windows in the other wall, but the room seemed to have assumed another personality, altogether more sombre than before.

The General watched Leggatt as he adjusted a fold in the curtains and wondered, not for the first time, how such a diminutive body could contain so much power and energy. The man was a bantam, scarcely more than an inch or two over five-foot tall and probably weighing no more than 110 pounds. Yet the bigger men had all gone down before him, heavyweight after heavyweight: in thirty years he had made himself one of the six most powerful men in the country, a man with commanding influence in commerce, industry, the press and politics. He was the key figure in OSSA, an organisation dedicated to the struggle against socialism and communism; its members, all carefully screened and selected, were men and women of high authority in the fields in which they operated, and by virtue of this, OSSA exercised an influence far beyond its numerical strength. When the General began to develop his ideas, Leggatt was the first person he had talked to, and

177

it was through him that the resources of OSSA had been mobilised to support the campaign.

A man to be reckoned with, thought the General – and also a man to be wary of. There was no question that Leggatt was capable of utter ruthlessness, that was something he could understand. What puzzled him was that after all these months of working together he still did not know whether the man was motivated by self-interest or principle, or just how far he would be prepared to go down the road they had chosen together.

He sighed inwardly. How much easier things would be if it were possible to choose one's allies, instead of having to accommodate oneself to those who were available! He needed their strength now to build his own; but when the time came, when he was strong enough in his own right, they would learn that he was not a man to be pushed or manipulated!

He suddenly realised that Leggatt was speaking, and pulled himself away from these thoughts.

'Sorry – what did you say?'

'I said that we have to win this one. There won't be another chance. And to do that we must play every card in our hand.'

'I thought we were already doing so.'

'Not quite.' Leggatt moved back to the table. 'Listen. We're agreed that we can only win if we arouse the maximum mass support – yes?'

'Agreed.'

'And that so far, though we've done well – you've done well – we've only scratched the surface?'

'Agreed.'

'Good. Now what is the one single issue that arouses the most discussion, the fiercest passions – the one thing people feel most strongly about?'

'The state of the country.'

'No, no. People – ordinary people – don't think in such general terms. They're more specific – they think in terms of their own situation. I'll tell you what's on my mind in one word – immigration.'

'In what sense?' The General stiffened.

'Don't get up-tight. Hear me out. I'm talking about prejudice – about the West Indians, the Asians, the coloured problem.'

'We issued a manifesto,' said the General. 'Or have you forgotten? In it we said – and I quote: "We pose no threat to any decent citizen, whatever his age, race, colour, or religion." '

'Who is talking of threats?'

'You spoke of prejudice.'

'That's the point. Unless we do something it will look as if we're the ones who are prejudiced.' The little man smiled impishly, but the General did not respond.

'I'd be glad if you would come to the point,' he said coldly.

'Very well. Take the Brixton area of London. It's practically a West Indian ghetto, and it's notorious. Almost impossible for anyone with a white skin to walk there at night without being mugged. If your Commandos were to make an example of some of the muggers – '

'I've thought about it,' said the General, 'but there are difficulties. Our motives would almost certainly be misunderstood. The black community would see it as a deliberate provocation, for a start. No, I'd rather not take that particular tiger by the tail.'

'You're exaggerating. And you're avoiding the issue. Look, Hugh, so far you've directed your operations against white targets – apart from that one West Indian kidnapper. That's discrimination if you like! There's a very real problem in places like Brixton – the law is laughed at, the police can hardly cope. It's a situation custom-built for the Commando.'

At that moment a telephone rang, its tone muted and almost musical. Leggatt crossed to the rosewood writing desk and picked up the receiver. As he listened he saw that the General was getting ready to leave and he held up a delaying finger.

'Interesting,' said Leggatt as he put down the telephone. 'We've just had a call from one of our contacts. There's been a sudden flurry of activity at the Ministry of Defence. Your old regiment, for instance. It's being shifted from Aldershot to West Germany. Some high-ranking officers at the War Office – including this particular contact – are being posted abroad to various military missions. And other things. Quite a shake-up.'

'It could be coincidence.'

'No,' said Leggatt, 'no. It means that they're beginning to work things out. The Prime Minister is a wily old bird. He's shrewd enough to get the drift of what's happening. Either way, it adds emphasis to the issue we were just discussing.'

'Does it?'

'For God's sake, we're not playing at toy soldiers, man!' Leggatt's voice grated harshly, and his eyes glittered.

Although the General did not move or speak, he seemed to draw himself apart from the other man in distaste. There was a moment of chill silence, and then, slowly, Leggatt's brown face creased in a smile.

'Sorry,' he said, 'sorry, I didn't mean that.' He put out a hand as though to touch the General's arm, but changed his mind, as though deciding that the gesture would be inappropriate or unwelcome. 'Listen,' he went on, 'when we first talked you spoke of a revolution, a new type of revolution. Fine. But revolutions are not made by the fastidious. The people out there, the vast majority of them at any rate, know as little about the real issues as the mob which stormed the Bastille or the peasants who followed Lenin and Trotsky. They don't think in terms of romantic ideals, they see only what is in front of their noses. How, then, do we turn them into a force? How do we unleash all that latent power? Well, you've shown what can be done in the past few days. A virtual miracle. But we can't stop there, Hugh, we can't. We have to use any and every weapon that comes to hand. Once we have the power we will draw the lines, we will control the situation, you above all will choose the road we must travel. But to win that prize we must be bold. We must strike now – and quickly. We have to use the hopes and fears – yes – and the ignorance and prejudice of the masses to achieve our purpose. In the next three or four days we have to bring millions on to the streets, generate a situation in which the government will find it impossible to survive. And to do that, to do that, we must let the wolf out of its lair!'

'Race riots,' said the General.

'Yes!' said Leggatt emphatically. 'You want it on the line, I'm giving it to you. The prejudice is there – exploit it! Later, when it's all over, when we've won – '

'We can change course?'

'We can do anything we damned well like.'

The General turned away. He seemed to have shrunk inside himself, he looked a tired, dispirited man.

'Well?' asked Leggatt.

The General took a long, deep breath and shook his head. 'No.'

Leggatt opened his mouth to speak, but the General over-rode him.

'Wait. You've made your point, let me make mine. I'll set up an operation against the muggers – '

'That's all I ask.'

'No. You asked for a good deal more. That I won't give you. I shall make it quite clear in the communique that our action has everything to do with restoring the right of the ordinary citizen to walk our streets in safety, and nothing – nothing! – to do with race or colour. I shall say that and keep on saying it. I shall attack prejudice, not encourage it.'

'Of course. Don't misunderstand me. It's all a question of tactics. Personally, I don't care whether a man is black, brown, or khaki – '

'Please,' said the General. 'I appreciate your advice and support. I have great respect for your political know-how. But please – spare me the hypocrisy.'

Noonan gave Barr the same advice as had Benedict. 'Cut and run,' he said. 'Jesus, man! This is England, not Africa. There's no war on. Sooner or later they'll crack down on your bloody General, and then where will you be? Twenty, thirty years inside. You'll be an old man by the time you get out!'

'Can you see me running?' asked Barr.

'You ran fast enough when we were in that business with the Selous Scouts in Rhodesia.'

'That was different.'

'What was different about it?'

'I don't know,' said Barr. It was the truth. He did not understand his own uncertainty, the strange loyalty which bound him to the General. Why should he feel that this would be tantamount to an act of desertion? There was no sense to it, he ought, as Noonan said, to think of his own skin, but he found it impossible, distasteful.

'I can't just walk out on him,' he said, shaking his head.

'Why not? Would he do as much for you?'

Barr considered this carefully, and then nodded slowly. 'Yes. I think so. I think he would.'

'Think?'

'Look, I've met him, you haven't. He didn't have to lay himself on the line. He could have stayed home fishing, sat on his arse like all the others. Maybe he's doing this the wrong way – I don't know. But one thing I can tell you for sure. He's not doing it for himself, or the loot, or anything like that. He's old-fashioned in a funny sort of way, and maybe a bit innocent. But he's straight, I'll lay odds on that.'

'Quite a Boy Scout.'

'Yes. In a way. It's not a bad description, a grown-up Boy Scout. Anyway I don't want to be the one to kick him in the guts. There'll be plenty lining up to do that. I just don't want to be one of them.'

'O.K.,' said Noonan with a sigh. 'Just watch it, will you?'

'I'll watch it,' said Barr.

'I mean, watch yourself,' Noonan said.

'That too,' said Barr.

3

Barr arrived at the Churchill Hotel at a few minutes before noon to find the foyer crowded with reporters, cameramen, television crews. The management had underestimated the interest in the General and was hastily making arrangements to transfer the press conference to another, larger room.

Barr pushed his way through to the desk and eventually managed to pin down a harassed clerk.

'Where can I find General Wilcox?'

'The conference will now begin at 12.15 in the – '

Barr interrupted him. 'I don't want the conference, I want the General. Is he in the hotel?'

'I'm afraid he isn't available,' said the clerk.

'Ring him,' said Barr. 'Ring his room. Tell him that Major Barr is here.'

The clerk looked at Barr and decided not to argue. He picked up the telephone, dialled a number, and after a brief conversation he directed Barr to a room on the second floor.

The General opened the door himself and greeted Barr with a smile of welcome. 'Ah, you made it, Major!'

'Did you think I wouldn't?'

The General covered a momentary hesitation by closing the door, then smiled again. There was genuine warmth in his voice as he held out a hand.

'I'm glad you're here,' he said. 'How did you kill the time?'

'I looked up an old friend,' Barr said, and quickly switched the subject. 'You said you wanted me for a special assignment, sir.'

'I've something in mind,' the General said lightly, 'but that can come later. For the moment, I should be grateful if you would simply stick as close to me as possible.' He nodded towards the young lieutenant, Drage, who was standing by the window with a briefcase under his arm. 'Both Major McKinnon and Lieutenant Drage seem to hold a low opinion of London. They think I should have a bodyguard.'

'You never know, sir,' said Drage.

'Totally unnecessary,' said the General, 'but who am I to argue?'

'We ought to go down now, sir,' Drage said.

'You have the statements for the press?'

'They're being distributed as the people go in,' Drage patted the briefcase. 'And I have a few spare copies here.'

The General fastened the zip on his dark-blue casual jacket and pulled it up to his chest. Beneath the jacket he was wearing a thin, white, high-necked sweater; his trousers were of linen, in a slightly lighter shade of blue than the coat. Exactly right, thought Barr. There was nothing there that could not be bought fairly cheaply in any high street multiple store; the clothes were clean and pressed, but they looked lived in. The tanned skin showed up against the white of the sweater, giving the General a rugged, outdoor look, the stamp of a man of action, while the deliberate worn casualness of the outfit suggested that this was someone who had more important things on his mind than clothes.

'Will I do?' asked the General, catching Barr's look.

'You don't look much like a politician,' said Barr.

'Good! That was rather the reaction we'd aimed for.' He squared his shoulders, bracing himself. 'Right,' he said, 'let's get on with it, shall we?'

Barr was surprised to catch a note of nervousness in the tone.

At about this time George Lydd was in a taxi on his way to a building in Kennington, near the Oval. He was annoyed that he should have to make the journey: Benedict was his inferior in rank and properly speaking the arrangements ought to have been the other way round – Benedict should be coming to see him.

That, he thought, was typical of MI6 where the organisation was far too slap-dash and happy-go-lucky for his taste, and typical of Benedict's own cynical attitude towards authority.

He allowed himself a small, grim smile. In a few weeks at most, things would be different. He would be in charge of the security of the nation, in total command of British intelligence, both at home and abroad; indeed, he had already prepared a complete plan, setting out the steps necessary to effect a complete re-organisation. It was sitting in the safe at his home, waiting for the day when he could present it to the General. Yes, Benedict and his sort would be in for a shock then! There would be no place for people like him, no place for cynics and adventurers; he would surround himself only with true patriots, dedicated men and women who believed in the new Britain.

It was strange how people, even quite intelligent people, seemed to have no real conception of the basic problems of security. Even the General, brilliant man that he was, didn't really understand. It was all very well to talk about democracy and freedom, but there had to be limits. Unbridled liberty could only lead to anarchism and disaster. Who should know better than he? He had spent twenty years in MI5 and he had seen it all. Reds, extremists, and – almost the worst of all – woolly-minded liberals and do-gooders had been allowed to gather like a malignant cancer, preying on the nation's flesh, sapping its vitality, paralysing its will to act. He had watched them at work, chronicled their activities, noted the results – but he had been denied the right to take action to root them out.

Well, that too was going to be changed, he told himself grimly. It was all so simple, so logical. It was only necessary to remove about five thousand people, the real trouble-makers, from circulation, put them away somewhere safe where they could do no harm and might even be taught to do some useful work. Take the knife to the cancer, one swift, clean-cut operation and the entire outlook of the country would be changed overnight.

He rather liked the name he had coined for his detailed plan. He had called it the JUDAS OPERATION. It was apt, it had the right feel to it. The files, the lists of names, were in the safe together with his plans for re-organisation. No-one knew about them as yet, they were his secret, his contribution to the cause. He imagined the look in the General's face when he laid them before him, and smiled to himself again.

The taxi drew up at the Oval station and Lydd paid off the driver. It was a quarter of a mile away from Benedict's office but it was better to be cautious. He walked at a brisk pace with his shoulders back and his arms swinging, filling his lungs with air and releasing it slowly through pursed lips. It was a habit he had developed over the years, he believed that deep breathing freshened the body and enabled a man to think more clearly.

The building was modern, only two or three years old, designed in an unobtrusive yet pleasing style. From the outside it looked rather small, but Lydd knew that this was a deliberate deception; the part which showed above ground was only the tip of the iceberg. A small polished brass-plate beside the entrance bore the legend Conroy International, Marketing Consultants.

Lydd was met in the lobby by a cheerful, burly young man in floral, open-necked shirt and worn jeans. A Maltese cross on a thin silver chain swung from his neck. Another example of their sloppiness, he thought. He had nothing against such clothes, but there was a time and a place for everything. It was essential in his view for the service to maintain certain standards of personal appearance, they were essential to discipline.

'Mr. Benedict is downstairs, sir. I'll take you to him,' said the young man. He led the way to an elevator. As Lydd got in, he added, 'He's having a crack on the range. Trying out a new hand-gun.'

Lydd nodded but said nothing. The elevator took them to the bottom of the building, three floors down, and the young man led him along a wide brightly-lit corridor. In the background he could hear the steady hum of air-conditioning. They turned a corner into another corridor and the young man stopped at the second door along and opened it.

'If you wouldn't mind waiting in here, sir, I'll find Mr. Benedict.'

Lydd stepped into a small, square room not unlike the one at his own headquarters in which he had interviewed Barr. It contained a single bed, a small table and a chair, and through a half-open plastic curtain he could see a toilet and a shower. Why the hell should he have to wait in such a place? He turned angrily to the young man, but it was too late. The heavy door had already snapped into place behind him and, to his utter amazement, he heard the sound of bolts sliding into place.

Chapter Thirteen

1

HALF an hour after he had put Lydd under lock and key, Benedict began to have doubts about the wisdom of what he had done. He was used to taking the law into his own hands, that was often part of the job, but this time, without consulting his own bosses, and on what seemed now to be very insecure grounds indeed, he had virtually kidnapped a high-ranking officer from another security department.

In his own mind he was sure that Lydd was guilty, but proving it, persuading the man to talk, that was a different matter. If he failed, if in the end he had to release Lydd, there would be the devil's own outcry! And there was the additional problem that he did not know whom he could talk to, whom to trust, even in his own section. How far had OSSA penetrated the security services, who else beside Lydd was involved? Certainly, in terms of political outlook, there would be many who would sympathise with the General's ideas; he had heard many of them comment with approval on the activities of the Churchill Commando.

His mood was not improved when two men he had sent to the East End to pick up Whitaker, the man responsible for recruiting the mercenaries, returned empty-handed with the information that the premises were locked and deserted, and that the bird had flown.

He ordered the two men to arrange a round-the-clock surveillance of the General, starting with the press conference at the Churchill Hotel. He wasn't sure whether Barr would show up there or whether he would take his advice and get out, but for good measure, he gave the men a detailed description and told them to keep an eye on him also.

This done, another thought occurred to him. Lydd was a meticulous, highly-organised man, and he would almost certainly have told someone at MI5 about his movements. It wasn't a thought that did anything to alleviate his doubts and he considered carefully what he should do. Lydd had now been in the room downstairs for less than an hour, it wasn't too late to release him and to explain, with apologies, that it had all been a mistake.

In a sense, this particular problem was resolved when Lydd's assistant at MI5 rang through to ask if he could speak to his chief on an important matter. Without quite knowing why, Benedict plunged in with a lie, thereby compounding his offence and cutting off his only escape route.

'As a matter of fact,' he told the assistant, 'I was just going to call you. He hasn't shown up yet.'

'He isn't there?'

'No. He was supposed to be here around noon, but there's no sign of him.'

'He left at 11.30. He said he was going to your place and that he expected to be back in the office at 1.30.'

'Perhaps something else came up?'

'No. He would have told me. Or telephoned in. I can't understand it.'

'I'll call you if he shows up,' Benedict said, and hung up. You're in it now, he told himself, you're right in it!

An hour later, just as he was about to do down and question Lydd, the door opened and the Director of Operations, Benedict's immediate superior, came crashing into the office. Swarbrook never entered a room quietly, it was against his nature to do so. Benedict had long ago decided that it was part of a deliberate policy, as if Swarbrook was trying to emphasise his lack of furtiveness. No need of that, thought Benedict; it would be hard to imagine anyone more direct, less secretive in manner.

They were about the same age and had known each other a long time. Once, in Beirut, Swarbrook had saved his life and later, in West Berlin, Benedict had repaid the compliment. On neither occasion had any comment been passed or any word of thanks exchanged, but the passing of such small change was outside their characters and unnecessary. They respected each other and that was enough; friendship was not a popular word in their trade. In the final resort, a man, even a friend, was expendable and it was better, therefore, to keep at a distance from one's colleagues so that personal feelings did not intrude when a decision had to be made.

Swarbrook had lost his right arm on an assignment in Hong Kong some four years before, otherwise he would never have agreed to take a desk job in London. But having done so, he tackled it with all the no-nonsense, gritty directness which had characterised his work in the field, and within eighteen months he was put in sole charge of operations.

A stocky, swarthy-faced man, he planted himself like an oak in front of Benedict and said bluntly, 'The big white chief of MI5 has just been on to me. They've lost one of their Deputy-Directors, George Lydd.'

Benedict tried to keep it calm, to stop his jagged nerves from showing. He put on a wry smile and said: 'That's very careless of them.'

'He was supposed to be coming here to see you,' said Swarbrook. 'What about?'

Under the bushy eyebrows, the dark eyes were fierce and accusing. Benedict looked into them, hesitating, his mind racing. He had to talk to someone, he could not keep this thing to himself or hold Lydd downstairs without anyone knowing. And if there was one man he could trust, it was Archie Swarbrook. It was unthinkable that he should be tied up with Lydd, with the General, with this OSSA outfit. The man wore his honesty like a badge.

'I think I'm in a bit of a bloody mess, Archie,' he said, with a thin smile. 'Sit down and I'll tell you about it.'

Benedict expected an explosion of anger, surprise at the very least, but Swarbrook listened quietly, his face showing no feelings. When the other man had finished, he sat in silence for a full half-minute, pressing the thick fingertips of his one hand down upon his knee.

He looked up at last, and said: 'Barr. I met him in Beirut when he handled that Martov job for us.'

'That's the one.'

Swarbrook nodded. 'Good bloke. I wanted him to join us on a regular basis, but he wouldn't.'

'He's an independent bastard,' said Benedict.

'He'll be a dead bastard if he's not careful,' said Swarbrook. 'He's in bad company.' He stood up, the chair creaking with relief as he lifted its burden. 'We've only got Barr's word that Lydd set up this other character, Onslow.'

'I believe him,' Benedict said. 'There was no need for him to come to me, he could have kept his mouth shut.'

'Bit late for him to have an attack of conscience, wasn't it?'

'It wasn't conscience,' said Benedict. 'He wanted me to say where he could find Lydd.'

'That sounds more like it.' Swarbrook walked to the window, looked out for a moment, and then swung round. 'Well, don't sit there like a cup of cold tea! Let's go and talk to this bloody man downstairs, see what we can squeeze out of him.'

'You don't have to get yourself involved. I can go it alone a bit longer – and then you won't have to take the rap if it comes to pieces in my hands.'

'Balls!' said Swarbrook aggressively. 'This is my Section and I run it. All of it. And if this thing goes wrong – well, it won't be the first bloody time we've been in the consommé together, will it?'

In the lift going down, Swarbrook said suddenly: 'Harry, you're a bastard!'

'I know,' said Benedict, 'it's an established fact.'

'You know what I mean. I've been asking myself why you didn't come to me after your meeting with Barr. Why didn't you?'

'I don't really know,' said Benedict.

'You're a bloody liar! You didn't come to me because

you thought maybe I was in with Lydd, part of this OSSA operation. Right? Right?'

'I suppose so. I'm sorry. I was a bit thrown by the whole business.'

'It's O.K. I don't blame you. But then you did tell me. Why? Why did you take the chance?'

Benedict grinned. 'Maybe I realised that you'd find out anyway. Or perhaps it was because I couldn't resist your look of natural innocence.'

'Well,' said Swarbrook, 'I have this golden rule, see. I work for only one master at a time. So, if it's any consolation, I'm on your side.'

'I just hope to hell it's the right side,' said Benedict.

2

After the press conference, the General decided to move to new, pre-arranged headquarters in a penthouse in Knightsbridge. With Barr at his side, he slipped out of the hotel down the emergency stairs and through the staff entrance, where Drage was waiting with a laundry van. They moved away unobserved but to make certain they took a circuitous route and double-checked that no-one was on their tail.

When they were safe inside the apartment, the General briefed Barr on his special assignment. As usual, the planning had been immaculate. He was given a plan of the ground floor of a house in Westminster, a sketch map of the surrounding area, photographs of five men and a woman, and a timetable of the operation worked out to the second.

The six people in the photographs were to be kidnapped.

The General did not put it quite like that. He said that they were to be taken into custody and held until further notice, but neither he nor Barr had any doubt about his meaning. As always, the General's instructions were direct and clear, but Barr detected a faint note of weariness in his voice. It was not surprising. The journalists at the conference had given him a gruelling time, and although he had finally won most of them over, the effort must have taken its toll.

'Tonight,' continued the General, 'you will carry out a thorough reconnaissance of the house, make yourself familiar with the street and so forth. You will then come back here to me to discuss any problems. I do not anticipate any difficulties, I may say. We have been planning this operation for some time. At 10.00 hours tomorrow, you will meet Piotrowski and Meysell at the agreed rendezvous – it is there in the brief. They will have the necessary transport. Between 12.30 and 13.00 hours you will effect an entry to the house and hold these six people.'

'Hold them at the house, sir?'

'Yes. There will be two servants there, a man and a woman. Naturally, you will detain them also. No violence is to be used unless absolutely necessary. The threat of force should be enough. And these people are to be treated throughout with the utmost respect and courtesy. Is that understood?'

'Who are they, sir?' asked Barr.

'It is not necessary that you should know that,' said Drage, who was standing to one side of the General.

'I like to know what sort of people I'm dealing with,' said Barr drily.

'And why not?' said the General. 'As it happens, Major, they are all Members of Parliament. I don't think they will offer much resistance.'

Fifteen minutes later, Drage looked up from the newspaper he was reading to find the General standing in the doorway in his dressing-gown.

'You should get some sleep, sir,' he said.

'Listen,' said the General, 'that other operation. The one in Brixton. It's on my mind. Get hold of McKinnon – have him postpone it. Postpone it for twenty-four hours. I'm worried – I want to give it more thought.'

Drage glanced at his watch. 'Too late, sir, I'm afraid. The detail was due to leave twenty minutes ago.'

'Twenty minutes ago! Why so early?'

'It's very much a speculative operation, sir. They have a lot to learn about the area – they'll have to improvise, work things out on the spot.' He added reassuringly: 'It'll be O.K., sir. Colleano is in charge, he's a good man. He knows what we want.'

'Then he knows more than I do,' said the General slowly. 'I'll give you some good advice, Drage. Always listen to the voice of your own instinct.' He hesitated a moment, shaking his head, and then went on: 'It's one thing to say that we should slap a ban on all further immigration. There's sense to that, we're a small island, and we've taken in more than we can digest. But to set people at each other's throats – ' He shook his head again. 'What has that to do with our aims, our manifesto? No, take the lid off that particular pot and it won't be easy to screw it back on. I saw enough of that senselessness in Northern Ireland. The decent people retire to their homes and sleep with loaded guns by their beds, while the gangs rule the streets. God forbid that we should be the instrument of that!'

'I see that, sir,' said Drage, 'but the way I look at it is this. Without power, we are helpless, we cannot fundamentally change the course of events. If taking the lid off the pot, as you put it, helps us to get that power, surely we are justified in doing so?'

'The end justifies the means?' said the General.

'Yes, it's a cliche, but isn't it true?' Drage smiled. 'If I may say so, sir, we haven't shown too much respect for the law ourselves so far. Surely that's another instance of means and ends?'

'Perhaps. If it were simply a question of dealing with the people who terrorise our streets, I wouldn't mind. But there are under-tones I don't like. We run the risk of setting up the black population as Hitler once set up the Jews.' He shook his head. 'No. Go back to your history, Drage. See how often the use of the wrong means has corrupted the ends. Ring McKinnon. There may be some way of recalling Colleano. Do it now!'

The Commando Unit was now established in a transport

depot on the Great West Road, only a few miles from the centre of London. The depot stood alone in two acres of ground, and since the movement of trucks in and out went virtually unnoticed, it provided almost perfect cover.

Drage spoke to McKinnon in guarded terms, and as he put the telephone down he looked up at the General and shook his head.

'Like I said, sir. Colleano left with a detail of three men thirty minutes ago. There is no way they can pull him back.'

3

The little cafe was almost deserted. Mr. Billy Bramble, the proprietor, his black face gleaming with sweat, was anxious to close up for the night, but there were four customers sitting at a corner table and although at least an hour had passed since they had ordered anything he lacked the courage to tell them to leave. They would go when it suited them and not before; he knew that in any argument he would come out the loser, and that the experience could be painful.

He consoled himself with the thought that it was already growing dark outside. The shadowed streets were their territory, their possession; it would not be long before they slid into the night in search of prey. Then he could lock up, go home to Chrissie. Meanwhile, the pop music poured out from the radio and they lingered on, playing their interminable game of Twenty-One with a pack of greasy cards, drinking nips of white rum out of his cups. The coffee they had ordered an hour ago had long since gone and they had curtly rebuffed his offer to bring them more.

Three of them were around seventeen, eighteen years old at the most, while the eldest, Marvin Clay, was maybe twenty-one. A few years ago, he thought wistfully, I could have told them to leave and they would have gone, given me some cheek, but no more than that. But in the last ten years something seemed to have got into the young ones. They had no respect for their elders or for the old ways;

they were hot-eyed, angry, rebellious, and some of them, like those sitting in his cafe, using it as if it were their property, had grown mean, vicious, cruel.

In 1953, when he had first thought of leaving St. Lucia to come to England, his grand-daddy had warned him against it. 'A man is like a tree, son. It grow in its own place, roots in its own soil.' He could hear the tired, sing-song voice now. He hadn't argued – you didn't talk back to your grand-daddy or your daddy in those days – but he had come just the same. After all, wasn't England his home just as much as St. Lucia, her Queen his Queen? Year after year, morning after morning, in that ramshackle shed they called a school, he had stood to attention with the others and sang 'God Save the Queen'. The teacher had taught them that Britain was the mother-country, that they were free and equal citizens of a great Commonwealth: and to prove it beyond any possible shadow of doubt, he was given a beautiful blue passport bearing his name and photograph and the inscription: BRITISH SUBJECT.

It hadn't been so bad for him at first. After the initial agonies of homesickness he had settled in, worked hard at his job in the plastic factory, even saved enough to get married to a girl from Barbados, buy a good, used car. But in the past four or five years, things had gone sour. The factory had closed, he'd been unable to get other work. He had sold the car, put all he had into this little cafe, and soon even that would be gone for he was up to his ears in debt for supplies, just clinging on.

Thank God, thank the good Lord, that Chrissie had given him no children! What at one time had seemed a curse had turned into a blessing. For there was nothing for the young ones, little hope. The three teenagers sitting at the table had never worked, never been able to find jobs and nowadays they didn't even bother to look. Two of them had been born here, the other had been brought over as a child in arms, but still there was no place for them. British subjects! They were like aliens, displaced persons. If he'd had sons, perhaps they would have walked the same road, their bitterness and frustration exploding into hatred of authority, and of white authority most of all.

Mr. Bramble picked up the evening paper and glanced through it for the fourth or fifth time. It was filled with stories about a man they called the General, pictures of him on the front page, articles about his career. At a press conference that day he had said that no more immigrants should be allowed in for at least five years, not one single person for whatever reason. Well, that make good sense, thought Mr. Bramble, too many here already.

The bell over the front door gave a warning tinkle and Mr. Bramble turned towards it, his irritation changing to astonishment as he saw a white man standing in the doorway. He could scarcely believe the evidence of his eyes. Occasionally, but more rarely in the past year or so, a white man might come in during the day for cigarettes or a cup of tea, but never in the evening, never so close to the hours of darkness. The police, when they came, were always in pairs, and a car was never far away. But he hadn't heard a car draw up.

The man certainly didn't look like a policeman. He was thick-set, he looked as if he could take care of himself, but all the same there was a certain nervousness in his manner. His eyes flickered uncertainly between Mr. Bramble and the young men at the table. They had stopped their game and sat tight in their chairs, tensed like coiled springs.

'We're closed,' said Mr. Bramble, praying inwardly that the man would go away quickly, before there was trouble.

'Sorry,' said the man. 'I'm a stranger round here. Lost my bearings. How do I get to Coldharbour Lane?'

Before Mr. Bramble could reply, Marvin pushed back his chair and stood, sniffing the air in an exaggerated manner.

'Terrible smell in this place, Billy,' he said. 'Like something crawled in and died.'

'Smell?' echoed Mr. Bramble, his heart thudding.

'You mean your nose can't smell it, man?' He sniffed again and turned to his companions. 'Funny. I can smell it.

You can smell it. But Mr. Billy Bramble can't smell nothing.'

Marvin moved forward, snuffling the air like a hound on scent. The others stood up and began to follow his example, making an elaborate play of sniffing each chair and table. The stranger waited in the half-open doorway as though uncertain of what to make of this strange pantomime. The fellow must be stupid, crazy, thought Mr. Bramble. He wanted to scream at him, tell him to run but he was afraid, the words wouldn't come.

Marvin reached the counter and then turned slowly towards the man in the doorway. He twisted his face into a grin, though there was no laughter in his eyes, and the man smiled back, tentatively, nervously.

'Got it!' said Marvin. 'Got it.' He touched his nose. 'This old hooter don't never let me down. Do you know what that smell is? I'll tell you, Billy boy. White trash! You got white trash in this place.'

'Please, please,' breathed Mr. Bramble.

The others ranged themselves just behind Marvin, and in unison, as if in response to a signal, each of them drew a knife. There were four tiny clicks and four pointed shining blades sprung out towards the stranger. Mr. Bramble closed his eyes in despair. What he heard next made him open them again immediately, and they widened in amazement.

'Well, what do you know! Knives. Didn't your mammy ever tell you piccaninnies that you shouldn't play around with such things?'

A different man seemed to be speaking. The white man's air of diffidence and uncertainty had gone; his eyes were sharp with contempt, his body poised and tense. The youths were momentarily stunned by this change; as they hesitated, he stepped back through the door and slammed it in their angry faces with such force that the cups hanging behind the counter rattled against each other in protest. The door was stuck and Marvin struggled to open it; eventually it responded and he ran into the night, followed by the others, pocketing the knives as they went.

With a sigh of intense relief, Mr. Bramble closed the door once more, bolted it, and clipped the protective wooden screen into place over the glass panels. The bottle of rum was still standing on the table amid the litter of playing cards, and it was still a quarter full.

He took a clean cup and poured himself a stiff drink, feeling that he had earned it, then – just in case Marvin should remember and come back – he topped the bottle up with water to its former level.

As the rum warmed his throat, he looked around the dingy cafe and shook his head. Oh, Lord, he prayed, take me away from this place. Bring me a big win on the football pools, please. No, not even a big win, just enough to buy two tickets to St. Lucia. Dear Jesus, do this thing for me and I won't be no more trouble, I won't ask another favour for the rest of my life.

4

The stranger had no more than an eighty-yard start on the four West Indians but he did not seem to be pushing himself unduly; he ran at a gentle, loping pace, as though saving himself. As he turned a corner he even paused as thought to check that they were still in pursuit.

They came up on him fast, shortening the distance between with every stride. A burly coloured man stepped out of the shadows and tried to block his path. The white man paused, feinted, and his fist thudded into the other man's stomach. He fell back grunting and gasping and the white man ran on, with his pursuers now only a few yards behind.

A truck was parked on the opposite side of the road and he crossed towards it; but when he reached the far pavement he swerved away, and ran into a darkened alley.

Marvin checked the others. 'No hurry,' he said breathlessly. 'We got him. Ain't no way out, it's a dead end.'

One of the youths took out a glove, put it on his right hand and wound a length of bicycle chain around it. The others drew out their knives and waited, listening. Through the open windows of a nearby house the voice of Ella Fitzgerald floated into the night, telling the world in song that Manhattan Island should be given back to the Indians. From further away, a woman's scream hung on the air for a moment and then died away.

They moved forward in line, shoulder to shoulder, so that they covered the width of the alley, their eyes peering in the darkness. The engine of the parked truck started up behind them and Marvin halted the others with a gesture: after a moment, the truck moved away, its headlights briefly illuminating the entrance, and they continued their careful progress.

There was no way the white man could escape. The alley was bordered on either side by a high brick wall, topped with jagged glass, and at its furthest limit it ran head-on into the rear wall of a derelict sausage factory. The alley had once served as a service road to the factory, but now its only function was to provide an uncomfortable refuge for lovers with nowhere else to go.

Helped by a spill of irregular light from the houses beyond the walls, their eyes gradually adjusted to the darkness and they saw the shadowy figure of the stranger ahead of them, backed against the end wall. They moved more confidently now, their feet crunching the loose ashy surface of the ground.

And then, suddenly, a blaze of white light flooded the alley and they heard the roar of the truck at their backs. As they swung round the headlights stabbed at their eyes, momentarily robbing them of vision, and the truck was almost upon them before they recovered their wits sufficiently to spread themselves against the walls.

It stopped a yard or so away, and a man in dark blue overalls, his face masked, jumped down and came towards them. Two other men, dressed in similar fashion, came from the rear of the truck. All three were holding automatic pistols.

'All right, my bonny lads,' he said. 'Drop the blades.'

The three younger men obeyed, but Marvin gave a snarl

of anger, and threw himself forward. The stranger, taken by surprise, was too slow to avoid the full force of the rush, and he gave a cry of pain as the knife slashed into his shoulder, its point jarring the bone. He reeled back against the wall, and the West Indian turned to renew the attack.

As he did so, one of the masked men fired. It was a single shot but the blast, magnified by the confined space, echoed and reverberated like a clap of thunder. The knife dropped from Marvin's hand, his mouth opened in a silent scream, and he fell face downwards, his forehead resting on the stranger's shoes.

One of the men moved forward and turned Marvin over. He crouched over him for what seemed a long time, and then stood up.

'He's had it,' he said, in a matter-of-fact voice.

'He asked for it, the black bastard!' said the stranger savagely.

The white men seemed uncertain now, and as they stood looking down at the dead body, one of the West Indian youths began to edge away from them, squeezing himself between the truck and the wall. He moved inch by inch until he reached the cover of the rear of the vehicle, and then, his heart hammering with relief and fear, he ran for the entrance and the safety of the dark streets beyond.

A clamour of voices began to rise from the houses beyond the walls as, roused by the noise of the shot, people opened windows and called to each other.

'Let's get out of here,' said the stranger.

'We taking them with us?' said one of the men, jerking a hand towards the two remaining West Indians.

'Not this time,' said the stranger. Clutching his shoulder, he moved across to the youths. 'You're lucky. You're getting off light. Pass the word round. Pass it round good. You saw what happened to your mate. From now on, that's what will happen to scum like you. And if you don't like it, you know what you can do. Bugger off, get out, go back to banana land, where you came from.'

He raised his uninjured arm as if to strike them and as they cowered away he dropped it with a laugh.

As the truck backed out and drove away, the West Indian youth who had escaped was already pouring out the story to a crowded audience of young blacks in a local Disco. Within minutes, the body of Marvin Clay was discovered; a door was torn from a shed as an improvised stretcher and he was borne in procession through the streets to his home, a dead hero, all his sins forgotten. With each pace, the crowd around the body grew and the murmurs of shock and grief turned to angry shouts for revenge.

Attempts by community leaders to cool the atmosphere were thrust aside. In an hour, an army of West Indians, men and women, most of them young, swarmed into Brixton High Street, blocking off all the traffic. The hastily mobilised police patrols were forced to withdraw, though not before some of their number were injured, one so seriously that he died on the way to hospital.

Thousands strong, smashing lamps and windows, setting fire to stores, overturning parked cars, they marched on the nearest white area.

Word of the death of Marvin Clay had been phoned through to West Indians in other London suburbs and to those provincial areas where there were large coloured communities. Their reaction was almost as violent.

A pendulum swings both ways, every backlash provokes a response. Before long, gangs of white youths gathered, many of them wearing the insignia of the Churchill Movement, and began to take their revenge in turn on any coloured people who came their way. Barricades were thrown up in some streets and were the scene of bloody battles. A passenger in a plane flying over London reported that huge fires were burning in a dozen places – he had seen nothing like it since the war-time blitz. Fire engines found it impossible to get through to the blazing buildings, and the ambulances fared no better. Hundreds lay injured in the streets and in improvised casualty stations, and the tally of those dead had already reached double figures.

By 7 a.m., with the rioting showing little signs of diminishing, and as the rest of the nation roused itself from sleep, the BBC news commentator told his listeners that in some districts the situation seemed to be out of control and that the Commissioner of Police had asked for troops to be sent in to restore order.

Chapter Fourteen

1

'No troops,' said the Prime Minister. The sleepless night showed on his face, but his voice was wide awake. 'I have given orders to the army that they are to remain on the alert, ready to move in, but for the moment that is as far as I'm prepared to go.'

He looked round the long, coffin-shaped table of the Cabinet Room, waiting with tired eyes for a word of dissent from his ministers. There was a long, sombre silence. God, what a bunch, he thought. A half dozen of them sitting with their heads down, making meaningless scrawls on their papers or simply avoiding his look. They had the dispirited appearance of refugees; mentally, they were already packing their bundles.

'If I may say so, I think you're wrong, Prime Minister,' said the Home Secretary. The cold was still troubling him, his voice sounded as if it had been dragged through gravel.

'You may so,' said the Prime Minister. 'You might also like to tell us your reasons.'

'I believe – ' The Home Secretary paused and blew his nose. 'Sorry,' he said. 'I believe that the country will expect strong and decisive action. To hold the troops back now will be seen as a sign of weakness. The latest reports show that the coloured population have barricaded whole areas of S.E. London, North London, Leeds, Nottingham, Wolverhampton – '

'We have the reports,' said the Prime Minister impatiently.

'They have declared these places No-Go areas, rather along the lines of what the I.R.A. did in Ulster some while back. They have refused access to the police, and other authorities. The police report that in many districts both whites and blacks are preparing themselves for a full-scale resumption of violence tonight. The police can just about hold the line during the day, just about. But this evening – tonight – that will be the crunch point. I don't think the police will be able to contain the situation without help.'

'The dockers have called a one-day strike and are marching on Parliament this afternoon,' said the Secretary of State for Industry. 'You can bet they'll be joined by others. They're demanding – '

'We know their demands,' said the Prime Minister.

'Will we have enough police to control the march – that's my point.'

'We must find them!' said the Prime Minister tersely. 'Can you imagine how the docks would react if we surrounded the Palace of Westminster with the Brigade of Guards?'

There were nods from some of the others, but there were those who still kept their heads down. The Prime Minister sucked in his breath and released it in a long sigh of irritation.

'Look,' he said, 'that's my decision. No troops for the time being. I'll keep the situation under constant review. We can have the army at the key trouble spots within a half-hour if it becomes necessary. That is my decision, right or wrong.'

He leaned forward, his fists on the table, and waited for his words to sink in. The silence came back again, heavier than before; the air itself seemed to be dejected.

'Thank you for your enthusiastic support,' said the Prime Minister drily. The heads came up at this, and a sardonic smile gleamed in his eyes. 'Look,' he went on, seriously. 'We've got to keep our nerve. If we don't, the country won't. There is some evidence – it is scrappy as yet – that last night's fighting in Brixton was provoked by the Churchill Commando. What happened last night was the culmination of an organised campaign designed with one purpose, and only one purpose in mind. To create such unrest and disorder that this government will become discredited and be forced to resign. The Opposition have already put down a Motion of No Confidence for this afternoon. That's the first step.'

'You're not going to let them get away with that, surely!' said the Secretary of State for Scotland.

'I have very little choice, Secretary of State. In any case, I believe that we should meet the challenge, the sooner the better. If only to demonstrate to the country that we are determined to overcome this crisis. Even with our small majority, we should win, I think.'

'Don't worry, Prime Minister,' said the Chief Whip in a booming Lancashire voice. 'I'll have the buggers on parade, every man jack of them.'

His cheerfulness seemed to lift some of the depression; shoulders went back and there was an exchange of cautious smiles.

'Good,' said the Prime Minister. He subjected a fingernail to a careful scrutiny and when he continued his voice was low and intent. 'Let us all remember this. If – I say if – if by some miracle or chance they should carry the vote in the lobbies tonight, I shall have no other alternative but to see the Queen and hand in my resignation. Our resignation, in effect. Shall I tell you what I think will happen then?'

'A General Election, of course,' said the only woman minister present.

'No. I don't think so. I believe that they will argue that this is no time for the country to be without a government. And there's some force to that, it makes sense. There will be strong pressure to form a Government of National Unity to see us through this crisis. They will propose the bringing in of the best brains from outside. And I tell you, it will a damned difficult thing to argue against.'

'The bloody Trade Unions won't stand for that!' said the Chief Whip. 'No way!'

'Maybe they want a confrontation with the unions,' said the Prime Minister. 'Have you thought of that?'

'They tried that back in 1974 with the miners,' said the Chief Whip. 'Reckon they learned their lesson then.'

'I wouldn't be too sure,' said the Prime Minister. 'You see, I don't think this would be like anything we've seen before.' He did not enlarge on the thought.

'They. You keep going on about they. I'd like to know who they are,' said a voice from the end of the table.

'Certain members of the Opposition. The people behind the Churchill Commando. Other powerful, influential people. You know many of them, I don't have to spell out their names.'

'Who would lead this new government?' asked the Secretary of State for Trade.

'You haven't been reading your papers, Secretary of State,' said the Prime Minister in mock reproach. 'What about the General? They're not grooming him just for kicks. He's been given the full treatment by the media. And he has openly placed himself at the head of this Churchill Movement. These things don't happen by accident.'

'Why don't the police arrest him?'

'What for? I'm informed that he has a handful of cast-iron alibis covering all those times when the Commando were on the rampage. We'll nail him, I've no doubt of that. But in the meantime, I would be wary of making a martyr of the man.'

'I always liked him,' said one minister.

'Yes. A lot of people do. That's part of the problem.'

The mood, as the ministers left, was slightly more cheerful and determined. Some of those who had sat with their heads down at the beginning of the meeting, went to far as to assure their leader that they would fight every inch of the way with him. He thanked them politely for their confidence.

The last one to leave was the Foreign Secretary, the Prime Minister's most senior colleague and oldest friend. At the age of 69, he had taken on his cabinet post with genuine reluctance and had already announced publicly that this was to be his last term in Parliament.

'Well, John,' said the Prime Minister, 'that was quite a session.'

'You handled them. But then you always do. You're a bastard when things are going well, but when you hit a bad streak, it's a pleasure to sit back and watch you play the cards. I suspect you deal from the bottom of the pack sometimes, but I must admit, I've never actually caught you at it.'

'Thank you,' said the Prime Minister. 'Well, I didn't tell them everything. Half of them would have wet their underpants. But it's still true – the old saying. It's amazing how the threat of execution concentrates the mind.'

Suddenly he sniffed, lifted his head, and pulled out a handkerchief just in time to enfold a violent sneeze.

'Damn it!' he said. 'That's all I need. I think I've caught the Home Secretary's bloody cold!' The old man showed no sympathy. Clutching an elderly briefcase, he moved to the door and paused. A frown increased the lines on his forehead.

'I wonder,' he said, 'I wonder if this General knows what he is doing.' He held up a thumb and finger, and measured a centimetre of space. 'That's civilisation. That thick. Underneath it, we're animals. It took us five thousand years to grow that skin, and it can be destroyed in five minutes. Put a fist through it, and bang! – we're all back to the jungle. I wonder if he realises that he is playing tip-and-run with a nuclear bomb?'

He sighed, the sigh of an old, sad man, and as he went out his words hung in the air.

2

Lydd was obstinate, but not too difficult.

At the beginning of the interview he warned Swarbrook and Benedict in icicle tones that they were in deep trouble and demanded that they release him forthwith. Such an acknowledgement of their error would not absolve them from punishment, he said, but it would be counted in mitigation. They had his word for that.

After this initial salvo, he folded his arms and sat on the bed, with his face turned away from them, his chin thrust upwards and his lips clamped together, indicating that he had switched off, that the lines of communication were closed.

Benedict found it difficult not to laugh. There was something absurd in the man's manner, and he drew comfort and reassurance from it. It was a rehearsed pose, there was no real strength in it.

Swarbrook was surprisingly polite and unruffled. 'Look, Mr. Lydd,' he said, 'there is no problem. You are free to go.'

Lydd turned and stared at him, but said nothing.

'There is just this one outstanding point,' said Swarbrook. Lydd turned away again. 'Two people knew about Onslow, you and Benedict. One of you blew his cover. Result – one dead agent. Naturally, we want to know which of you was responsible. That's reasonable, isn't it?'

Silence.

'I think it was you,' said Swarbrook softly. 'You see, I know Harry, I don't know you. Well, we've met, but I can't say I really know you, can I? But I'm a fair-minded man, I think even my worst enemy would say that I was a fair-minded man. So, if you can say the word that will put you in the clear, and lay the finger on Harry – and prove it – you'll be doing this department a big favour. I'll tell your boss how grateful I was for your co-operation. And when we execute Harry, you can have a front seat. How's that?'

Silence.

Swarbrook turned to Benedict. 'Doesn't seem that he's prepared to clear you, Harry. Or himself for that matter. Pity. What do you suggest?'

'He seems to have difficulty in speaking. Perhaps we could arrange some treatment?'

Lydd's mouth opened slightly and the flesh around his jaws quivered, but he said nothing.

Swarbrook nodded thoughtfully. 'That's worth considering,' he said. 'Yes, indeed. Let's think about that.' He paused as though considering another idea. 'By the way, did you search him?'

'No, I didn't, as a matter of fact.'

'Well, that's wrong, for a start. You know the Department rules.' He turned to Lydd. 'Sorry about this. But we do have a strict rule and it applies to all our guests without exception. You won't mind turning out your pockets, will you? Just a formality.'

Lydd moved his head round further, towards the wall, in a sharp, indignant little movement.

'We've got a tough one here, Harry,' said Swarbrook, with heavy irony. 'Not surprising really. I mean, he's a professional, a trained man. You don't get to be a Deputy-Director unless you've got something, that's for sure. Handling all those files, records, checking the petty cash – a big, big job.'

He dropped a big hand on Lydd's shoulder, and pulled him around. 'Pockets,' he said, 'pockets!'

'Don't you touch me!' said Lydd, his voice quivering.

'Pockets.'

'You'll be sorry for this.'

'Tut-tut,' said Swarbrook. 'You've got the wrong approach. Too negative. Don't they teach you that at MI5? Over here we don't have the word sorry in our vocabulary. Never use it. Fatal. Now, pockets. On the bed.'

Lydd stood up and began to empty his pockets, placing the contents on the bed. He tried to maintain a show of indignation as he did so, but it was clearly becoming more difficult.

There was nothing unusual about the articles he produced. A bunch of keys, a wallet, a handkerchief, three ball-point pens (black, red, and green) and some money. Swarbrook gathered the stuff up and moved to the door.

'Right,' he said. 'That seems to be it for the moment. We'll leave Mr. Lydd to himself – he has a lot of thinking to do.'

Lydd swivelled round. 'I demand my immediate release. I protest in the strongest possible terms – '

But the door had already closed behind them.

It was then early in the afternoon. Hour after hour crept by, but no-one came for him. The only sounds he heard were the murmur of the air-conditioning, an intermittent drip of water from the shower in the alcove, and the pounding of his heart, which seemed to beat like a drum as his incredulity and indignation were smothered by his growing fear. He used the lavatory a great deal, and in between he sat staring at the heavy door, willing it to open.

He knew these men, and he was frightened. They were almost a law unto themselves – certainly more so than his own department. They were ruthless in pursuit of their objectives, and it was the thought of that ruthlessness – the thought alone – that tingled the back of his neck and iced the spine. It was not that he objected to violence; he had discussed the morality of it with his colleagues on several occasions, usually over after-dinner drinks at private dinner parties, and he had always taken the view that it was a useful technique which, in the right circumstances, could be a definite aid to an interrogator. But for him, such discussions had always been academic: interrogation of subjects did not come within the scope of his particular job. He remembered some of the things he had heard, and the recollection did nothing to relieve his feeling of foreboding.

They did not come back until after midnight, almost ten hours after the first interview. A last desperate manikin of courage stirred in the depths of his stomach, and he faced them indignantly, forcing out a quavering protest.

'Shut up!' said Swarbrook harshly. He had just heard that the General had given the slip to the men on watch at the Churchill Hotel, and he was in a less amiable mood.

211

'This is ridiculous – scandalous! I have never in my life been subjected to – '

'Shut up!' Swarbrook tossed Lydd's keys on to the bed, where they fell with a little ominous chink. He drew up the solitary chair and straddled it, facing Lydd.

'Now,' he said, in a less aggressive tone. 'Let me tell you why we've kept you waiting. We've been out, paying a call. We've been down to Ashford, in Kent, all the way to Ashford, to visit your home.'

Lydd's eyes went to the bunch of keys and Swarbrook nodded.

'That's right. We let ourselves in – I hope you don't mind? And we cooked ourselves some scrambled eggs and had a couple of nips of your Scotch. Very nice place you have there, neat but not gaudy. I don't think we did any damage, did we, Harry?'

'Only the safe,' said Benedict.

'That old thing? Hardly worth mentioning.'

'This is preposterous!' said Lydd.

'Shut up! I shan't tell you again,' said Swarbrook softly. 'Where was I? Ah, yes, the safe. We couldn't find the key or the combination, so we had no choice. Very careless, you know, a man of your experience of security keeping his stuff in a safe that could be opened by a one-handed Boy Scout with a tablespoon. Very interesting collection of papers we found. Kept us amused for hours. Ambitious little bugger, aren't you? I must say, I enjoyed reading your ideas on how you'd run our Intelligence services. You've been busy too, haven't you? All those lists of names, plans for work camps, the lot. You must have spent hours going through the files. All the same, we hoped to find more. So – you'll have to fill us in. Now, you have my permission to speak.'

'I have nothing to say.'

'I want to know where the Churchill Commando has moved to. I want to know what it plans to do next. I want to know who is behind it – I want names, names. You're in it – up to your ears. Who else? Who else is working with you? Ah, yes, and I want to know about the General. Where is he now? Where are the others? What's next on his agenda?'

Lydd set his lips in a thin, tight line and turned away. Swarbrook sighed and looked at Benedict.

'Harry, the point you raised earlier on about Mr. Lydd's speech defect. I seem to remember – haven't we got someone in the Department who could help him?'

'Of course,' said Benedict. 'As a matter of fact, I took the liberty of asking a couple of chaps to stand by. They're experts, the best. Shall I ask them to come in?'

Both men turned to Lydd, their faces creased into polite, enquiring, artificial smiles. His mouth opened like a hole, and he blinked nervously, looking from one to the other as though he hadn't quite caught their meaning.

Benedict opened the door. Two men in black sweaters and trousers appeared at his signal: their broad, expressionless faces looked as if they had been chipped out of granite.

'The gentleman has a little trouble with his voice,' Benedict said. 'Finds it difficult to speak. See if you can help him.'

As the first man moved in, Lydd stood up. His voice squeaked a little.

'Wait.' He put a hand to his forehead and squeezed, as if he were trying to push the words through his skin. When he lowered the hand he gave them a tepid smile. 'Look. I think we'd better have a talk. I mean, basically, basically, we're on the same side. Perhaps – perhaps, if I put you in the picture, you'll understand.' He inclined his head in a confidential manner. 'This is big. Very big. Top secret. You do understand?'

'Completely,' said Benedict.

He motioned to the two men, and as expressionless as ever, they retreated into the corridor and closed the door.

'We're listening,' said Swarbrook.

'General,' said Barr. 'I'd like a word. It's urgent.' It was the second time he had spoken and again there was no answer. Barr looked at Drage, who lifted his shoulders in a gesture of helplessness.

The General seemed not to be interested. He sat in front of the television set watching an extended edition of *First Report* on the independent channel, and he was like a man mesmerised.

A shot of a young West Indian woman, her eyes dazed with shock, looking down at her dead baby. A white couple, cramped with age, watching in bewilderment as the flames danced on their home. A bus lying on its side, one wheel revolving slowly.

A crowd of blacks chanting, demanding justice, vengeance. A crowd of whites with banners, GET RID OF THE BLACKS – BRITAIN FOR THE BRITISH.

The police outnumbered everywhere, the thin, blue line, trying to hold the ring. Burning cars. Burning shops. Burning houses. Emergency clearing stations.

Appeals by the Prime Minister and the Archbishop of Canterbury to end the violence. The views of pundits, politicians, the comments of the man in the street. Dockers preparing to march on Parliament, carrying huge posters of Churchill, one of their leaders demanding that the blacks be sent back where they came from.

News of new riots in Bradford, in the Chapeltown area of Leeds, and in Lewisham. A dozen lesser outbreaks in other towns. West Indian and Asian bus-drivers and conductors walking away from their vehicles in protest against the attitude of some passengers. Half the London Underground trains not working.

The huge barricades marking the No-Go areas . . .

Barr tried again. 'General – '

'Major?' The General turned, as if hearing him for the first time. The eyes that looked at Barr were momentarily without life, and then something of the old brightness flickered in them and took hold. 'What are you doing here? You have your orders – '

'It's not on, General. The house is staked out. We couldn't go in – we'd have walked into a trap.'

'How do you know that?' asked Drage fiercely.

'I know it,' said Barr coldly. 'I met Piotrowski and Meysell as arranged. We did a quick recce of the house in St. John's Wood and decided to back down.'

'You decided!' shouted Drage. 'Who the hell are you! You're paid to obey orders!'

'All right, Drage,' said the General calmly. He turned to Barr. 'Why?'

Barr tapped his nose. 'Smell. It stank, the whole set-up. They were in there waiting for us, I'll lay odds on that.'

'Do you know what you've done!' screamed Drage. 'After all our planning – everything – you've loused up the most crucial operation of all!' He turned to the General. 'We needed those people out of the way so that the Government would lose its majority, and be defeated! And he's screwed it up!'

'That's enough,' said the General, 'that's enough!' His voice cracked like a whip, sharp with authority. 'What happened to Piotrowski and Meysell?'

'I sent them back to warn the others.'

'But you came back.' A glow of warmth deepened the bright eyes.

'You've run out of road, General. You've been blown, somebody, somewhere is singing. Listen to me. You've frightened the hell out of them.' He waved a hand towards the television screen. A policeman, his face scarcely visible for bandages, was being interviewed in hospital. 'All this. It's too much. They're frightened, and frightened men get desperate – turn dangerous – '

The General held up a hand to cut him off and turned back to the television. The programme had been interrupted for a special news item. The Prime Minister was at that moment on his feet in the House of Commons making an important statement. Details were still coming in, but the studio commentator said they were now going over for a preliminary report from their Westminster correspondent.

A young man appeared on the screen, his hair slightly ruffled by the wind. In the background it was possible to hear the chanting of demonstrators. One man with the symbol of the Churchill Movement pinned to his jacket rushed forward to seize the microphone, but he was quickly and none too gently hustled away by policemen. He was shouting WE WANT THE GENERAL – WE WANT THE GENERAL as they hauled him off, and the call was echoed by the crowd.

'A few minutes ago,' said the young man, 'the Prime Minister rose before a packed and expectant House to make, as he put it, a very grave and important statement. There were calls of "Resign, resign," from the Opposition benches and some angry rejoinders from his own back benchers. Throughout this the Leader of the Opposition, and the leaders of the smaller parties sat in what can only be described as a grim silence. As is customary, they had been given prior notice of the contents of the statement and clearly they were shocked.'

A young woman entered the shot and passed the speaker a sheet of paper. He glanced at it and nodded, then continued speaking, the words coming out with machine-gun rapidity as he tried to crowd it all in. From time to time he consulted his extensive notes.

'The Prime Minister began by saying that during the course of the morning he had received information which indicated that the wave of disorder now sweeping the country was the result of a deliberate campaign of provocation by a highly organised group of powerful men, whose aim – whatever their pretensions – was to destroy democratic government in Britain.

'These men had formidable resources, he told the House, which by now was listening intently. There was reason to believe that a substantial proportion of their funds had been subscribed by sympathisers abroad. In the first instance these funds were used to set up bases in this country, to purchase arms and supplies and to recruit a number of mercenary soldiers who were formed into what has now become notorious as the Churchill Commando.

'At this point the Prime Minister looked up from his notes to comment that it was an insult to the memory of a great Parliamentarian, a man who believed deeply in democratic institutions, that his name should have been soiled in this way. Winston Churchill would have been the first among us to denounce this conspiracy, he said. There were murmurs of assent from both sides of the House.

'These mercenaries, these hired gunmen, many of them veterans of wars in Africa, men without principle, with no loyalty except to their paymasters, were organised into units along military lines and for the past ten days they have been conducting a campaign of uninhibited violence. Their leaders played with great skill on the fears and doubts of millions of decent, ordinary people, putting themselves forward as the defenders of law and order. Behind this cover, said the Prime Minister, they did not hesitate to resort to kidnapping, hi-jacking, violent assault and murder. That some of their victims were men of doubtful reputation or worse, in no way excuses their criminal activity. Murder is murder.'

At this point the studio announcer cut in. 'Nigel,' he said, 'can I break in there for a moment. Can you hear me.'

The reporter adjusted the thin cable attached to the earpiece he was wearing, and cupped a hand round the instrument. 'Yes, Gordon. I hear you.'

'Did the Prime Minister name any names? The people behind the Commando, the men who are in active command?'

'No. He asked the House not to press him on that point and said he'd make a fuller statement when investigations were completed. What he did say was that the organisation had supporters in the police, the Civil Service, even the security services and the Army. But he also stressed that they were comparatively few in number, that the vast majority were unaffected and loyal. And he did say something else which was rather interesting.'

'What was that?'

'He said it was quite possible that some of these people saw themselves as genuine patriots, that they supported the campaign because they believed that the country was drifting to disaster, and that only the most desperate measures could save us. We should take serious note of this, he said. We should look to ourselves and to our institutions. Something was seriously wrong if fundamentally good people felt that they had no choice but to act outside the law. Nevertheless, they had allowed themselves to be led down a dangerous path, and there was no doubt that they had been used by men with more sinister motives.'

The girl appeared again with some more sheets of paper. The reporter glanced at the notes quickly, and then began to read them to the camera, his voice rising with excitement.

'The Prime Minister has finished – the Leader of the Opposition is now on his feet. It seems the Prime Minister kept the most sensational part of his statement to the end. He told the House the police had proof of a plan by the Churchill Commando to rob the Government of its majority by kidnapping six M.P.s and holding them captive until after the motion of no-confidence had been put to the vote. He described it as a monstrous plot to destroy the authority of Parliament and to plunge the country into a state of chaos from which the conspirators hoped to profit.'

'But this attempt never took place?' said the studio man.

'No. Apparently the police got word of it and put their men in the house where the M.P.s meet each Wednesday for lunch. Someone must have tipped off the Commando because they didn't show up.'

'We must leave you now. We'll come back to you as soon as possible.'

'Just one quick point,' said the reporter quickly. 'The motion of no-confidence has been withdrawn. The Leader of the Opposition has announced that in the circumstances it would be wrong to press it.'

'Thank you, Nigel.' The camera moved into a close-up of the man in the studio. 'Exciting and startling news from Westminster. We're going to stay with this story, and as a result our normal programmes will either be cancelled or shown later. We'll keep you in touch with the debate. In the meantime, we have with us in the studio a group of prominent men and women.' The view changed to a wider angle, taking in a group of eight people ranged on either side of the speaker. 'I want to ask them their views on this crisis, what they feel should be done – '

Drage leaned across to switch off the set, but the General checked him.

'Wait.'

'There's no time, sir – '

'Wait.'

The General was staring at the screen, a little smile of irony on his face. A familiar, puckish face came into full-shot on the screen, and the interviewer said: 'First, may I call on you, Lord Leggatt? You're an industrialist and what is sometimes called a Press Baron. Would I be right in saying that your newspapers have expressed a certain – shall I say – sympathy for what has been called the Churchill Movement?'

'We are not here to talk about my papers,' Leggatt said curtly. 'I give my editors complete editorial freedom, and I am not responsible for what they write. If you want my personal view – '

'Please.'

'Very well. I have just listened to your report of the Prime Minister's statement and I think I agree with every word he said – which is a rare occurrence. It is monstrous that armed gunmen should set themselves up as some kind of super-vigilante organisation and subject this country to a campaign of terror. I never thought that I would live to see the day – '

This time it was the General who switched off, and the

smile on his face had deepened. 'I always find it fascinating to see the rats swim for the shore. The ship must be sinking.'

'It never stood much chance of keeping afloat, sir,' said Barr.

'I didn't convince you, Major, did I?'

'I'm a merc, a hired gunman. You heard what the man said. If I'm paid, I'm convinced.'

'You sell yourself short, Major. You take refuge in your professionalism, you use it as a shield. But it isn't enough, is it? It's cold comfort, it doesn't warm the heart. Find yourself a cause, Major. There are plenty of good ones left, despite what the cynics say. Find something – or someone – you can believe in.' He held out a hand.

'I'm not going anywhere just yet,' Barr said. 'How about you?' He ignored the hand.

'I have a job to finish,' answered the General. He looked at Drage, who seemed to be near to tears. 'Drage. Thank you. You know what to do. There isn't much time.' He turned back to Barr. 'A means of escape has been organised, Major. Drage will take you along. You'll find your friends there.'

'I'm not leaving,' said Drage.

'I give you one minute,' said the General. 'That is an order.'

Drage hesitated, drew himself up as though to give a full salute, but checked his arm and contented himself with a little click of the heels. He seemed afraid to speak. As he reached the door, he stopped and looked back at Barr.

'Don't wait for me,' said Barr. 'I resigned five minutes ago. I'm not under orders. Good luck.'

The General said nothing, and Drage went out, closing the door quietly.

'What's this job you mentioned, sir?' said Barr. 'The sooner we get it done and move on, the better.'

'Just as soon as I've changed into uniform,' said the General.

4

There were times when Police Sergeant Frensham thought that he was back in Northern Ireland. He had served over there with the Green Howards some years before and he had never in his wildest dreams imagined that he would see similar sights on the streets of London: but it seemed that it was all happening again, history was repeating itself.

At the end of the street, a few yards away, a bulldozer was just completing the demolition of a huge barricade, wheeling, turning, charging, while a shower of bricks and stones clanged and clattered against the driver's protective shield. From this side a crowd of sullen whites watched and waited. All around there was the evidence of the night's destruction, a litter of stones, broken pavements, smashed windows, the smouldering ashes of fires, men and women with bandaged heads and limbs.

From time to time the little group of policemen tried to move the white people away, to get them back into the houses, but they always drifted back, and in the end the police more or less gave it up. They were tired, leg-weary and sore. I could lie down in the gutter, thought Frensham, and sleep like a baby.

Why the hell didn't they leave the barricade? The police were outnumbered, they couldn't hold this lot if they started fighting again – which they will do for certain sure as soon as it's dark. What chance will we stand then? Why don't they send us reinforcements? Better still, why don't they bring in some troops from Ulster, they know how to handle this sort of thing, they've got the gear, they're the experts.

As if in response to his thoughts, a car drove into the street, bumped forward over the littered roadway, and pulled up alongside him. One of the rear doors opened and a tall, distinguished man in army uniform stepped out. Frensham recognised him immediately and tiredness forgotten, his fingers went to his helmet in a crisp salute. He'd served under the General in Northern Ireland, if any man could clear up this bloody mess he was the one. Thank God they'd had the sense to call him in!

'Good to see you, General,' he said his eyes shining.

'Thank you, sergeant.' The General was looking down the narrow street towards the bulldozer.

'Can I help you, sir?'

'No, it's all right, sergeant.' He turned to his companion. 'You'd better wait here by the car.'

'No way,' said Barr and to emphasise the point he gave the car door a push. It closed with an emphatic click.

The two men walked towards the crumbling remains of the barricade, watched by the astonished crowd of whites. The General held his head up, looking forward, his face set. When they reached the corner, he turned to Barr.

'Wait here, please. This is something I have to do on my own.' It was a plea, not an order. Their eyes met and Barr nodded.

The General stepped across the rubble into the black area. A crowd of black and brown faces looked on, surprised and bewildered by the sudden appearance of this man who walked with such calm authority. He moved towards them, smiling a little, but they backed off. He held out a hand to one of the older men who took it uncertainly.

'I've come to help you – to explain,' said the General. His eyes seemed to fascinate and hold them, as they had done with so many other men, so that even some of the young men dropped the stones they were holding, as though ashamed.

A small coloured girl, no more than three years old, pretty as a picture, ran to the General, and he picked her up in his arms. She laughed and waved, delighted with her new eminence. He hoisted her on to one shoulder and began to walk down the centre of the narrow road. The crowd, which was growing rapidly, kept to the sides, still uncertain, still watchful. The whites started to move in now, curious to see what was happening.

The General stopped after about sixty yards and lowered the little girl to the ground. A woman ran out of the crowd and snatched her up. The General looked from one side to the other.

'I've come to talk to you,' he said. 'This – all this – is wrong. Wrong for all of us. I didn't want it like this. Nothing can be achieved by prejudice. I say this to you – ' he turned to the whites who were now crowding in behind him – 'and I say it to you. Surely we have enough to hate – without hating each other? Surely we have enough to fight? Our country needs all the strength – '

'It's your country, man, not ours!'

The voice came from the back of the crowd and a young brown-skinned man in sweatshirt and jeans pushed his way through. He stood facing the General, hands on hips, the sun glinting on the medallion at his throat. He swivelled on the balls of his feet, his eyes moving round the crowd.

'Don't you know who this is? This is the General, the world-famous General, the man who wants to lead us all to salvation. Well, we don't want none of your white salvation, General! We've had a gutful!'

A white woman pointed at the General and screamed, 'He's the one who started it. He started it! It was his men who came down and started it!'

The crowd began to murmur, and soon the murmurs became shouts, so that the General's voice was drowned in a rising wave of sound. He stood quite still while they circled round him, black and white together, spitting out years of hatred and bitterness at the common enemy, the figure of authority, the man in a uniform. They kept a space between, so that he held the centre, like the hub of a spokeless wheel.

He was silent now, it was useless to try and speak above the noise. Yet still he made no attempt to retreat, and he smiled at the mob as though he was seeing the faces of his friends.

The first brick caught him full in the mouth. He staggered back, but recovered and stood upright again. He made no attempt to shield himself, and he seemed almost indestructible as the heavy rocks and stones hailed down upon him.

Before the police could reach him, the crowd seethed in and the General went down. White and black scrambled to get at him.

Barr drew Onslow's pistol and fired it into the air, and it was as if someone had put a cord round the throat of the mob. The shouting stopped and they moved back, pace by pace, opening up a space around the General.

A coloured woman ran out of one of the houses and crouched over the fallen figure. She put a hand to the General's heart and when she drew it back, blood dripped from her fingers. She looked up as though praying, her lips moving. Tears splashed on to her face and suddenly she found her voice.

'Trash!' she screamed. 'Trash, trash! You ain't people, you ain't fit to be people – you're trash, murdering trash!' The mob backed away, silent now; some were fearful and some were ashamed, and a few didn't care.

A white woman came forward with a blanket. Barr took it from her and covered the General. Frensham helped him carry the body into the front room of one of the houses.

They laid him on the carpet before the fireplace. Barr went on his knees and pulled the blanket back. The face was almost unrecognisable, the skull smashed, the body bleeding from stab wounds. Only the eyes seemed to be untouched; clear and bright, they stared up at Barr out of the torn and bloody flesh. He closed them and replaced the blanket.

Later, as they carried the General into an ambulance Barr slipped quietly away.